BATTLE
FOR THE
NETHER

MARK CHEVERTON

BATTLE FOR THE NETHER

A GAMEKNIGHT999 ADVENTURE

SIMON AND SCHUSTER

First published in Great Britain in 2014
by Simon & Schuster UK Ltd
A CBS company
Originally published in the USA in 2014 by Sky Pony Press

10 9 8 7 6 5 4 3 2 1

Simon & Schuster UK Ltd
1st Floor, 222 Gray's Inn Road
London WC1X 8HB

A CIP catalogue record for this book is available from the British Library

Battle for the Nether is an original work of fan fiction that is not
associated with Minecraft or MojangAB. It is not sanctioned nor has
it been approved by the makers of Minecraft.

PB ISBN: 978-1-4711-5843-8
Ebook ISBN: 978-1-4711-2500-3

Printed and bound by CPI Group (UK) Ltd, Croydon, CR0 4YY

www.simonandschuster.co.uk

ACKNOWLEDGMENTS

As always, I would like to thank my family: Geraldine, with her ever-present optimism and glass-half-full view of the world, Jack, who reminds me to face my fears and pursue my dreams, and Holly, my inspiration, my rock, and the one that brightens my life. I'd also like to thank the many readers who have reached out to me and given me encouraging messages of support, without which I would have succumbed to discouragement and doubt, and likely not finished this book. I hope you all enjoy it.

CHAPTER 1

GAMEKNIGHT999

He sped down some kind of track, a set of metal rails stretching out into the darkness. The rhythmic clatter of the wheels beat at a constant pace—chu-chunk, chu-chunk, chu-chunk—that echoed throughout the tunnel, reflecting back like a percussive symphony. Looking about, he could see short grey sides and a boxy interior to the vehicle in which he rode, the appearance and the clatter of the wheels telling him that he was in a minecart. The cramped space made him feel like a giant in the small iron cart, but the blur of the cold stone walls speeding past gave him a feeling of being small and insignificant.

Gameknight999 was scared.

Uncertainty and fear filled his mind. He didn't know where he was, what he was doing in the minecart, or even where he was going. All he knew was that he was heading somewhere—fast.

Just then, the tunnel wall opened, and he could see a huge cavern—no, it was a giant crevasse that opened up to the blue sky. He could see zombies, spiders, and creepers on the sheer walls, leaping from one position to the next, the clumsiest of them falling to their deaths. Looking down, Gameknight saw the floor of the crevasse filled with monsters from the Overworld, all milling about as if looking for something to devour... or someone. Many of them looked up at him, and their ravenous, burning eyes chilled his soul. They wanted to destroy him for no reason other than that he was alive. Shuddering, Gameknight was glad when the crevasse passed by, the tunnel wall once again filled with solid stone.

Looking back along the track, Gameknight could see the metal runners disappearing into the distance, the wooden cross braces a blur of brown streaks. But then he noticed that the cart was decelerating, the clickity-clack of the wheels slowing their drumming until the minecart gradually came to a halt in the middle of a tunnel. Feeling that he was expected to get out, Gameknight stepped out of the cart, his body shivering with fear. Looking around, he could still see the minecart tracks stretching out to infinity, the iron rails standing out against the gray stone. But then they started to fade, becoming fuzzy and out of focus somehow, the straight rails losing their definition until they dissolved into nothing. At the same time, the rocky walls that hugged close to the tracks seemed to fade as well, turning from hard granite to a swirling gray mist. The cold, wet fog enveloped him, its clammy presence wrapping around him like a heavy, damp cloth. Something about the blurring cloud of obscurity frightened him, like it was hiding something dangerous and threatening.

And then the mournful wails started.

It was a sorrowful moaning that seemed to suck all hope from him, a moaning that sounded doomed and sad at the same time, but also hateful and angry at those living things that still possessed any faith in a good life. It was aimed at the creatures of light who still clung to the thought that being alive was a good thing, and not just a lesson in torment and despair; it was aimed at him.

The wailing was from a zombie...lots of them. Gameknight started to shake, the morose wails stabbing at him with icicles of fear.

And then green claws reached out to him from the darkness, the terrible moaning filling the air as razor-sharp nails sliced just inches from him. Overwhelmed with panic, Gameknight999 stood frozen in place as the decaying zombie approached, slowly materializing through the fog, the putrid stink of its decomposing flesh assaulting his senses and adding to his fright. Looking down, he realized that he had an iron sword in his hands, his arms and chest also covered with iron. He was wearing armor and had a weapon; he could fight back. Struggling to draw a morsel of courage, Gameknight willed his arm to swing the sword and strike down the beast, but fear ruled his mind. Memories of clawed zombie hands and fanged spiders striking out at him filled his mind—the pain of that moment when he'd detonated the TNT on the last server still haunting his dreams. That last Minecraft world had been saved because of his selfless, heroic act—probably his first ever. But the cost had been his spirit and courage, and that had left his mind in a constant state of panic. Monsters terrified him, the great Gameknight999; how was that possible?

Stepping away from the zombie, he turned to run. He knew this was only a dream, but the terror and panic still felt real. As he turned, he found himself facing a tangle of furry black legs, each tipped with a dark, curved, wicked-looking claw: giant spiders, at least half a dozen of them. They were pressed together, forming an impenetrable wall of hatred and spite.

"I can't fight that many," Gameknight said to nobody.

He shuddered.

Just then, a rattling noise trickled through the darkness, the sound of loosely fitted bones clattering together. He knew exactly what those sounds meant—skeletons. The pale white figures slowly emerged out of the swirling fog, closing off any avenue of escape to the right. Each of the boney monsters held a bow at the ready, arrow already notched and drawn, the barbed projectiles pointing directly at him.

Gameknight started to shake.

How was he going to fight all of these monsters? He wasn't brave anymore, his courage having been blown apart by all that TNT—no, torn to shreds by all those claws and fangs on the last server. He was just a hollow shell, a husk filled with dread.

Turning to his left, he slowly shuffled away from the three groups, hoping to escape without having to fight, but as he moved, a high-pitched chuckle filled the air. It was a maniacal kind of sound, like laughter focused on another's misery, like glee being felt while another creature suffered. It was a terrible sound that echoed throughout his soul, causing needles of panic to pierce the last vestiges of control he had over his own mind. And then the source of the chuckling came forward out of the darkness. It was a shadowy creature, the color of dried blood, a dark, dark red, with long, lanky arms hanging down, nearly reaching the ground, and skinny legs supporting an equally dark torso.

It was Erebus, the King of the Endermen from the last Minecraft server—the server that Gameknight had saved. This beast was his personal nightmare, the most violent and evil creature that he could imagine.

Turning, he faced the monster. As always, its eyes were burning bright white with a hatred for all living things. Its desire to destroy emanated like its own personal force field of malice. Gameknight took a step back. The creature was partially transparent, as if not completely there. The monsters behind the enderman were visible through its translucent body.

"So, User-that-is-not-a-user, I see that we meet again," Erebus cackled in a high, screechy voice.

Chills ran down Gameknight's arms.

"This is just a dream; it's not real," he said to himself over and over.

Erebus laughed a spine-tingling laugh, making him become momentarily solid, then faded back to partial transparency.

"It is indeed a dream," Erebus screeched, his voice reminding Gameknight of the sound of glass grinding against glass; it made his teeth hurt. "But that does not mean this is not real, fool. You still know nothing about Minecraft and the server planes on which it exists." He laughed again. "Your ignorance will cause your downfall."

"No, you aren't real," Gameknight said, pleaded. "You can't be. I...killed you on the last server...You can't be real."

"You keep telling yourself that, User-that-is-not-a-user, and when I find you on this next server, I'll remind you of how unreal I am...when I destroy you."

Erebus cackled again, the laughter resonating within his mind like a hammer to a crystal vase, his will to live nearly shattered.

"I... w-will... fi-fight you, like on the last server," Gameknight stammered, his words unconvincing.

"Ha... what a laugh," Erebus screeched in his high-pitched, piercing voice. "I can see the cowardice within you like a malignant tumor. All of your bravery was apparently left behind on the last server. You are an empty husk, a hollow casket waiting for a cold body.

You will be mine soon enough."

The enderman stepped forward menacingly, the transparency of its body not diminishing its threat in the least. Gameknight looked down quickly, not wanting to provoke the creature with a direct gaze. The dark monster towered over him, seeming to get taller and taller as he approached, until Gameknight felt like a tiny gnat standing before a giant.

"I can see defeat in you, User-that-is-not-a-user. I have already won; your cowardice guarantees the outcome of our battle." Erebus paused, then tilted his head down so that his glowing, malice-filled eyes were glaring straight down at Gameknight999. "You may have defeated me on the last server, but I still made it to this server plane. And when I destroy this world, I'll reach the Source, and that too will feel my wrath until all living things cry out for mercy that will never come. Await my arrival and despair."

With a flick of his wrist, Erebus signaled the monsters around him to advance. Decaying green-clawed hands reached out toward him, tearing at his flesh, while a hundred arrows pierced his body. Poisonous spider fangs then darted into the fray until his body was consumed with pain. Slowly, the world dissolved into darkness, with the eyes of the enderman being the last thing visible, their expression filled with overwhelming, unbridled hate.

Then, finally, the cold, black emptiness of his subconscious embraced him as the dream faded. But the feeling of pain and dread still filled Gameknight's soul.

CHAPTER 2

A NEW WORLD

Reality gradually formed around him, the blocky confines of their hastily prepared cave coming slowly into focus. Torches lit the interior of their hidey-hole, the flickering glow showing walls of rock and dirt, with his companion, Crafter, sitting opposite him. Crafter was a young boy with shoulder-length blond hair and bright blue eyes, but the odd thing about him was the look of knowledge behind those blue eyes. They showed a wisdom forged through years of living as his village's crafter on the previous Minecraft server; the one that they had saved with terrific blasts of TNT.

Every village had a crafter—a village elder who was responsible for identifying the things that Minecraft needed. These items were then built by an army of villagers, or non-player characters (NPCs), who populated all of the servers. The NPCs worked deep underground crafting their wares, then distributed their work throughout the digital world of Minecraft using a complex rail network, with minecarts delivering the items as needed. Their purpose was to populate the land with items for the users to find: a chest here, a weapon there...It was the job of the village crafter to keep the mechanism of Minecraft working. Gameknight's friend, Crafter, had been the oldest village crafter on his server—maybe even the oldest NPC on all of the servers across the Minecraft universe.

But in this world composed of textured blocks,

all was not as it appeared. Gameknight was a long-time user, playing the game every chance he had, but he had assumed—like every other user—that this world was just a game, electronic lines of code being executed within some computer's memory chips. Now he knew the startling truth, a fact that shocked him to his very core—the creatures in the game and the NPCs were alive! They had hopes and fears, dreams for their children, and felt moments of happiness and joy, as well as despair at the loss of a loved one. Gameknight had learned this digital truth after he had accidently activated his father's latest invention, the digitizing ray. It had blasted him with a burning white ray of light that scanned every facet of his being and then pulled him into the program running on the control computer, which in that instant had been Minecraft. Gameknight had been transported into the digital realm, and now he was fighting, not just for his own survival, but for the survival of all living creatures, both physical and digital.

A great war had been waging across the servers of Minecraft, with the zombies, spiders, and creepers trying to destroy all of the villagers to take their life force—their experience points (XP). With enough XP, a creature could be transported to the next server, moving higher and higher up the planes of digital existence until it reached the Source. The Prophecy, known by all creatures in Minecraft, foretold that the destruction of the Source would usher in the Gateway of Light, which would then transport all of the monsters into the physical world, where they would be able to destroy all living things. Gameknight had inadvertently created that bridge while the Source was still intact by activating his father's digitizer, and now his own world could very well be destroyed. And Gameknight999, the User-that-is-not-a-user—as he was named in the

Prophecy—was the only person who could close that Gateway.

After killing Erebus, the King of the Endermen, and successfully stopping the monster horde on the last server, both Crafter and Gameknight had been propelled to this next server plane, one level closer to the Source. He'd thought that they were now safe, but his dream gave him second thoughts. He could feel that the war for Minecraft still raged here on this server, his dream about Erebus proved this. Should he tell Crafter about Erebus speaking to him, threatening him and this server, or had it been just a silly dream, a silly-but-terrifying dream?

"Are you OK?" Crafter asked, his blond hair matted and tangled after sleeping on the hard ground all night.

It still felt strange seeing him as a young boy. On the last server, Crafter had been a gray-haired old man, but after transitioning to this new server, he'd respawned into the form of the young boy before him.

Sometimes Minecraft does what it wants, whether you like it or not, he thought.

"Yeah, I'm OK, just didn't sleep very well," he said truthfully.

Standing up, Gameknight pulled out his shovel and faced the dirt wall. Looking down at the shovel, he realized how lucky it had been that they'd come across these tools in that empty village, though he still wondered where everyone had gone. It had been half destroyed, with many of the buildings burned to the ground.

What had destroyed that village...and where had everyone gone?

Gameknight was still puzzled by this. A crafter would never have abandoned his own village... unless he had been... he didn't want to think about it. Shaking his head, he pushed the disturbing thoughts to the back of his mind and turned to face his friend.

"Is it morning?" he asked his companion.

"Yes," Crafter answered with a nod. "We can dig our way out."

It was always important to know whether it was day or night in Minecraft. Zombies, giant spiders, slimes, creepers, and the terrifying endermen came out after sunset, hunting the unwary. The best way to survive was to have a home to hide in, or to dig a hole and seal yourself in for the night. That's what they'd been doing for the past few weeks: traveling by day looking for villagers, and hiding in caves at night.

They needed to find villagers so that they could form an army to defeat whatever was threatening this server. The Last Battle for Minecraft was drawing near and the only thing standing between the monsters and all the electronic lives on all the servers was Crafter and Gameknight999...and that was not going to be enough. They needed villagers... lots of them.

So far they'd come across three NPC villages, all of them abandoned and partly destroyed. None of the villagers remained. The silence within the collection of buildings had been deafening. Gameknight could imagine the terrible battle that had driven them from their homes...or worse. *Could it have been Erebus?* If it had been the King of the Endermen, then Gameknight would have somehow sensed him here in this land. No, this was the work of something else. Maybe it was some new creature that was worse than that dark red nightmare.

Pulling his mind back to the here and now, Gameknight drove his shovel into the wall of dirt. He quickly loosened the blocks, making them fall to the ground. The brown cubes hovered momentarily, then somehow moved into his inventory; he still wasn't sure how that worked. Pushing his stone tool hard, he quickly made an opening in the wall, allowing golden shafts of sunlight to stream into their little burrow.

Stepping out into the open, he quickly put away his shovel and drew his wooden sword, scanning the area for threats. A small group of cows grazed lazily nearby, their gentle moos filling the air. Gameknight walked toward the cows as Crafter stepped out of their hidey-hole. They would need food soon; their supply of bread and melons was steadily shrinking, and cows were a good source of sustenance. But he didn't want to attack the cows for food, not unless he had to. Turning, he looked at his companion. He wished Crafter could do it for him, but the young boy had his arms linked across his chest like all villagers did, their hands hidden within sleeves, unable to use a tool or weapon. Until they found some wood to make a crafting bench, Gameknight could not release Crafter's arms. That meant that he had to do all the killing, something he was not ready for...at least not yet.

Shaking his head, he stepped away from the cow and turned back to his friend.

"Let's wait for another day before we start killing animals," he suggested.

Crafter nodded; their hunger was still manageable... but not for much longer.

"Then let's get moving," the young boy said, turning to face the distant mountain range. The landscape before them revealed gently rolling hills covered with grass, with the occasional splash of yellow, red, or blue flowers dotting the scene. "I think I can feel something in that direction, toward the mountains. The sounds of Minecraft's mechanism, the music of Minecraft as we call it, seems to be calling me in that direction."

"That's what you've been saying for days now."

"I know, but something still feels strange about this world. Something is out of balance, somehow. The dissonance in the music of Minecraft is somewhere in that direction."

"OK, lead on."

Crafter headed toward the looming mountains at a quick pace, humming a playful tune as he walked. Gameknight trailed behind, his head swiveling to the left and right, looking for threats. They were in a grassy plains biome with no trees in sight. The only threat would likely be the occasional giant spider or creeper, but with the terrain so flat, they'd see those monsters from far off; their danger level was minimal. But he was still afraid. The battle that saved the last server had been horrific, and had drained every ounce of courage from the User-that-is-not-a-user. The memory of all those claws and teeth tearing at him, the overwhelming pain and sheer panic still haunted his every waking moment, and apparently now his dreams as well.

"I wish we had some trees for wood," Gameknight muttered softly.

"My great-aunt once told me of a time when she found a land that had no trees at all. She said there were only giant mushrooms instead," Crafter said. Gameknight could tell this was going to be another one of Crafter's stories and rolled his eyes. The old NPC in the young body loved telling stories. "She and her friend decided to go out looking for adventure. They sailed off in a boat, to see what was on the other side of the great sea."

"That doesn't seem like a very smart thing to do."

"Probably not, but she was known for doing dumb things that always seemed to lead to great discoveries. Well anyway, they took this boat and sailed away from their village. They sailed for days and days, through stormy nights and blazing hot days, until finally they came upon a new land. My great-aunt—her name was Milker, but I used to call her Milky—anyway, she told me that this land was covered with gigantic mushrooms. They were huge red things with white spots on the side. She thought that maybe it was some kind of testing area that the Creator was using, experimenting with some kind of new server update."

"The Creator...you mean Notch?"

"Yes, of course, Notch, the creator of Minecraft," Crafter said, as if it was obvious.

He stopped walking for a minute to survey their surroundings, scanning the area for danger. They were alone with nothing but cows and pigs nearby. Satisfied that all was well, the duo continued.

"Anyway, she said that it was an incredible land, but she was glad to get home again."

"Did she get in trouble for going on that adventure?" Gameknight asked.

"Of course. I was told that she was always getting into trouble for trying new things like that."

"Wasn't she afraid of doing these new, crazy things?" he asked, feeling his own fear coil about him like a venomous serpent.

"It's funny you say that, Gameknight, because long ago, when Milky was the oldest person I knew, she told me something that I'll never forget. She said, 'Remember, boy, things that are new only seem scary because they aren't old yet. After you finally do the new thing, then the fear it held over you will fade away like the morning mist, because *the new* will have become *the old*. Focus on what it will be like *after* you do this thing, and *the new* will become *the old* in the blink of an eye.' She died the next day. That was the last thing she ever said to me."

Crafter stopped walking again for a moment, and then slowly raised one hand up into the air. Gameknight was shocked; *his hands...were separated!* Before the

User-that-was-not-a-user could speak, Crafter held his hand up higher, his fingers spread wide, then slowly clenched his hand into a fist, squeezing it tight. He bowed his head slightly, then brought his hand down, his arms linking again across his chest.

"Your arms..."

"The salute for the dead," Crafter explained. "It is the only thing NPCs can do with their arms...paying tribute to those loved ones we've lost over the years."

Gameknight looked at his friend and could see the sadness in his eyes as he thought about his Milky. Crafter then looked up at him and gave his trademark life-affirming smile, and continued walking. Starting a melodious tune, the young NPC began to hum, the music raising their spirits. In lockstep, they continued across the grassy plain, eyes scanning the horizon for what they desperately needed: A village with NPCs.

They began to run, and as they did Gameknight could feel the square sun slowly creep away from the horizon and move high up into the sky. Its illumination made his skin feel warm and alive as it bathed the landscape with a cheerful glow. He loved the morning, mainly because it was far from the night. The thought of that boxy sun gradually kissing the horizon at sunset gave him brief stabs of fear that covered his arms with goose bumps.

This is ridiculous, he thought to himself. *It isn't even dusk yet, and I'm already afraid of the coming sunset.* He shook his head, trying to dislodge his irrational panic.

"Are you alright, Gameknight?" his young companion asked.

"Yeah, just thinking," he lied.

"Seems like more than just thinking," Crafter said. "It's important that we work as a team on this server, for I'm sure we will encounter perils that will make the last server look like a child's playground." He paused and turned to look at his friend as they ran. "You have something you need to tell me?"

Gameknight hesitated. He wanted to tell Crafter about his worries, hoping that sharing them would unburden him of all this fear, but he knew it would do nothing except make him look pathetic and weak.

How would telling him about my fears do any good?

Instead, he just sighed.

"Nope, just thinking about my parents and sister," he said truthfully. "I hope they're alright; I mean, gonna be alright...you know?"

"You mean you hope we can stop this war and keep the monsters from flowing into your world."

"Exactly."

"Well, User-that-is-not-a-user, I think it's safe to say that we all hope that. For if the monsters get to the physical world, it would mean that the lives on all the Minecraft servers—across all the planes of existence— would have been destroyed. I'm guessing nobody wants that," Crafter said almost playfully.

Gameknight smiled.

"Except Erebus," he added softly.

"What?" Crafter asked, his bright blue eyes seeing into the very depths of Gameknight's soul.

"Ah...nothing."

Turning quickly away from his friend so that those intense blue eyes would not see the lie on his face, Gameknight looked forward and continued to run. They were starting to climb a gentle hill, and having to jump up every few blocks or so as they made their way up a grassy mound. Gameknight drew his sword, unable to see over the crest, while unknown threats prowled just past the summit, lurking in his imagination.

When they reached the top of the hill, he stopped for a moment to catch his breath. Turning, he scanned the terrain, looking for anything that might help them: a tree, a village, users...anything. But there was nothing. The land was bare, with the exception of the cattle, pigs, and sheep that lazed about, grazing on the grass that was abundant in this biome. And then two specks crested a distant hill to the north.

"You see that?" he asked, pointing toward the specks with his wooden sword.

Crafter turned and looked.

"I can't be certain what they are from this distance," the young boy said. "But my guess is that it's either two villagers or two users. I'm not sure which."

"We don't care which. They'd be a welcome addition to our group, no matter who they are."

"What are you thinking?" Crafter asked.

"I'm thinking we need help and we need information. We could keep running all over this biome and never find a village. Maybe they know where one is. I say let's go talk to them."

"OK, let's go."

The pair turned and headed toward the two specks on the horizon. As they ran across the rolling hills, they lost sight of the two visitors frequently, only seeing them when both groups were at the top of a hill. This made Gameknight nervous. He wanted to get a good look at the two before they were too close, but it didn't seem like that was going to happen.

Were they trying to avoid being seen? Gameknight thought as feelings of uncertainty spread through his mind, slowly changing to fear.

Glancing at Crafter, he wondered what his old friend was thinking, but kept his own fears to himself. He was probably worrying about nothing—just two villagers out looking for game to feed their village.

As they crested the next hill, he stopped, pulling on Crafter's arm for him to stop as well.

"What is it?" the old NPC asked, his young eyes still looking in the direction they had been running.

"I have a funny feeling about this, Crafter. Let's wait here and see what we can see."

The pair stood motionless and waited, watching the hill the visitors should soon be reaching. But then, two large black bodies suddenly sprinted over a closer hill, and in an instant his blood turned to ice; spiders, two of them.

"You see 'em?" Gameknight asked.

"Yes, and I'm sure they see us," Crafter answered, his voice filled with tension. "We need to run...NOW!"

The pair sprinted back down the hill they'd just climbed. When they reached the bottom, Gameknight turned to the right and followed the gentle ravine, keeping out of sight.

"What are you doing?" Crafter asked. "We need to run away from them, not sideways."

"No, we need to go where they won't be expecting us, and that's off this way. Now come on."

Crafter grunted and followed, sprinting as fast as his little legs would carry him. Weaving his way along the shallow ravine, Gameknight led his friend away from the spiders, staying out of sight for as long as possible. As they ran, they glanced over their shoulders for the fuzzy black monsters that would eventually appear behind them. Staying hidden like this would likely confuse them for a while, but once they were spotted, the race would be on. After a few minutes, the ravine ended and they had to climb another hill. When they reached the peak, Gameknight looked over his shoulder.

Oh no!

The spiders were heading straight toward them, and had closed the distance. Now the monsters were maybe 70 blocks behind them and getting closer.

Spiders were faster than people in Minecraft, and eventually the two creatures would catch them.

"RUN!" Gameknight shouted as he started to sprint.

Using all his strength, he tore off across the plains, running directly away from the two monsters. Glancing behind, he could see the two monstrosities heading straight for them, their multiple eyes glowing bright. Excited clicking sounds could be heard as the spiders closed the distance, their toothy maws gnashing together in anticipation.

"You doing OK?" Gameknight asked his companion.

"Yeah, just not sure how long I can keep this up."

Glancing to the spiders again, Gameknight could see that they were now only 50 blocks away. Sunlight reflected off one of their claws, making it sparkle in the distance. It brought back memories of his dream—all of those spider claws reaching out to him out of the mist. He shuddered and ran on.

Cresting a small hill, they started to descend into a narrow valley, and at the bottom of that valley was what they desperately needed—a tree.

"Crafter, the tree."

"I see it," the young NPC replied. "What do you want to do?"

"We have to release your hands or else we have no chance of fighting off these two monsters. Get ready."

When they reached the tree, Gameknight pulled out his pick and started tearing into the wooden trunk. With four hits, a chunk of the tree burst, a block of wood going into his inventory. Four more hits and another block appeared. Dropping his pick, he instantly started to craft, changing the blocks of wood into wooden planks, then forming a crafting bench. Placing the crafting bench on the ground, he looked up at the hill; there were no spiders...yet, but he could feel them coming, gnawing away at his courage.

He motioned for Crafter to come near, and the NPC approached the bench. His arms were still linked across his chest, his hands hidden in opposite sleeves. That was how all the villagers were designed, except for when they were building things—crafting, as it was called in Minecraft. Only a village crafter had free hands, and here on this server, Crafter had no village; he was just another NPC.

When he was close enough to the crafting bench, his arms suddenly separated, and he started to craft, his hands a blur of creativity and purpose. While he was crafting, Gameknight hammered away at the bench, smashing away at it with his pickaxe. The square bench shattered under the assault, splinters flying in all directions, but Crafter's hands remained free. It was something they'd learned on the last server; break the crafting bench while an NPC was crafting, and their hands would remain separated and able to do things, like grip the handle of a sword. It had been the secret that enabled Gameknight and Crafter to defeat the mobs on the last server, and he was sure it would be critical in this world as well.

"Quick, give me the wood," Crafter said as he started to craft.

Gameknight tossed his friend some wood, then glanced up to the hill; he could feel the spiders getting closer. His skin started to itch as more images of curved claws tearing into his body flashed through his mind.

I have to get out of here, he thought. I've gotta go.

"I'm going to make a sword," Crafter said. "I'll be ready in just a minute, then I can..."

Crafter paused for a moment as he watched Gameknight run back up the hill.

"Gameknight, where are you going? Are you running to meet the spid—"

Crafter   stopped   speaking   as   the

User-that-is-not-a-user glanced over his shoulder at his friend, fear and panic ruling his mind. The memory of all those spiders attacking him on the last server, their black curved claws slashing at him, bright fangs reaching out for his flesh...it was as if it were happening all over again. And now there were two more coming to finish the job.

I've gotta get out of here...they're coming...they're coming.

Gameknight ran up the hill and stopped. He could see the spiders coming fast, now only maybe 20 blocks away. Taking off to the left, he sprinted away from the deadly spiders. He wanted to glance back at his friend, but shame and guilt kept him looking straight ahead.

I'm so afraid; I won't be any help to him. I'll just be in the way and probably make things worse. The words sounded hollow within Gameknight's mind, within his soul, but he continued to run.

As he sprinted, he could still hear the deadly clicking sound from behind. Turning his head as he ran, he saw both spiders following him and closing fast. They were only 10 blocks behind him now. He could see their multiple angry eyes glowing bright.

Fear shot through his veins like bolts of lightning, lighting up every nerve.

They're both chasing me...oh no! he thought. *At least Crafter will be safe...maybe.*

Glancing over his shoulder, he could see their sharp mandibles snapping together in anticipation of their next meal...him. The realization that he'd have to turn and fight soon made him shake with fear.

Sprinting as fast as he could, Gameknight snatched another glance over his shoulder. He could see that the spiders were running side-by-side. If he turned to fight, he'd have to battle them both simultaneously. He couldn't survive that. So instead, he bolted off to the left, letting the spiders close the distance but also forcing them in a single file line, one behind the other. Turning around, he drew his sword in a fluid motion and, holding it out in front of him, waited for the first spider to close the distance.

When it was within reach, he stopped and let the spider's momentum bring it near. He slashed with his wooden sword. Two quick hits resonated through his blade, the spider flashing red. Running backward again, he dodged a black curved claw. It whistled past his ear...that was close. Swinging again, he struck at its forward leg, then lunged for its head. He landed a strong blow, and the creature flashed red again. But this time, it followed with a leaping attack. Pain erupted along Gameknight's side as the spider's claw found flesh. Reaching to his side with his free hand, he found no blood, just a torn shirt. That's how it was in Minecraft—no blood and guts, just damage to your health points (HP).

Shaking his head in an attempt to drive away the echoes of pain, he continued to run backward, slashing at the spider at every opportunity. The creature landed more devastating blows...more flashes of pain...more HP gone.

He was losing this battle.

The spider lunged again. This time, Gameknight leaped straight up into the air, causing the arachnid's attack to miss. He landed directly on top of the beast. Hacking downward with his sword, he killed the monster just as the second spider reached out and struck him in the back. The first creature disappeared with a pop, leaving behind a bit of spider web and three glowing balls of experience points (XP). The balls of XP flowed into his inventory as he turned to face the second enemy. He knew he didn't have enough HP to fight this last spider, but if he were to die here, then at least he'd die fighting rather than acting like a coward.

"Come on you eight-legged beast...you wanna dance...come on and get some," he yelled.

Just as the creature was about to attack, a battle cry filled the air.

"FOR MINECRAFT!"

It was Crafter.

The spider flashed red, then flashed red again and again as Crafter attacked it from the rear. The creature turned to face the small NPC, but as it turned, Gameknight moved in and attacked, landing decisive blow after blow. It turned back to face the User-that-is-not-a-user. Crafter attacked, then Gameknight, then Crafter, until the monster's HP expired and the fuzzy beast disappeared, leaving behind more spider web and spheres of glowing XP.

"You did it," Crafter exclaimed. "That was a brilliant idea, leading them away so that I could finish crafting a sword. You were very brave."

Brave, what a joke, Gameknight thought to himself. *I'm just a coward, a hollow shell...I'm nothing. He thinks I'm a hero, but I'm not. How am I supposed to save this server...or save Minecraft when I'm not even brave enough to face two spiders...I'm pathetic.*

The young NPC patted him on the shoulder, his wise old eyes filled with respect.

"THE USER-THAT-IS-NOT-A-USER IS HERE!" Crafter screamed as loud as he could. "YOU HEAR THAT, MONSTERS?"

The NPC's words flowed out across the landscape, the gentle rolling hills letting them travel unabated, but then an echo returned from the right.

"You hear that?" Crafter asked. "An echo. What could have made it?"

"Let's see."

The duo ran up the next small hill to find the source

of the echo, and were grateful at what they found. It was their salvation—a village, the thing they'd been searching for these past few weeks. But this village had the look of death about it: homes blown apart by creeper explosions, doors shattered by zombie fists. It was just like those other three villages they had come upon; an empty, shattered village. Huge craters dotted the landscape, places where creepers had detonated themselves, their explosive ends taking with them as many innocent souls as possible. Arrows could be seen lodged in the few walls that still stood, many also embedded in the ground, as if sprouted from tiny seeds. Skeleton archers had taken their vengeance on the living inhabitants. None of them could have survived this onslaught. It was a terrible scene to behold, but worse than the destruction was the sound—or the lack of it; there was nothing. Complete silence. There wasn't a living soul within this village. Gameknight's heart sank, his glimmer of excitement replaced with panic and fear.

"It's begun for sure...the war," he said solemnly.

Crafter sighed. "It appears so," the young NPC said.

Holding his sword tightly with his blocky hand, Gameknight led the way down toward the village.

CHAPTER 3

SURVIVORS

They approached the village slowly. Destruction was everywhere: Buildings had been blown apart, doors were shattered, and homes were burned to the ground. The village was completely devastated. Dark tendrils of smoke curled into the air across the village from fires still burning. Gameknight could feel the heat from darkened patches of ground where homes had once stood, the charred earth looking somehow sick and diseased. He stopped and looked at his friend.

"This must have just happened," Gameknight said, his voice shaking with fear. "Look, some of the places are still smoking."

Crafter just grunted a response as his blue eyes surveyed the damage.

"I don't have a good feeling about this," the young NPC said. He looked around the devastated village and sighed. "We have to find some help or we'll fail here."

"We won't fail," Gameknight said, trying to sound confident, though the fear in his voice betrayed him. "Remember, we saved the people on the last server. We should be able to save them on this server too."

"We didn't save them, Gameknight, not yet. We only delayed things." Crafter walked around a crater in the ground, the center of the hole smoldering with heat. "I can feel that the Source is just past this server plane. If we don't stop them here, then everyone will be at risk, even my friends and family back in my village."

And mine as well, Gameknight thought.

"We have to stop the monsters here, on this server, or all is lost," Crafter said. "It's my responsibility."

"It's *our* responsibility," Gameknight said, trying to ease the tension in his friend.

He could see creases of worry etched in Crafter's face; his unibrow furled and strained, and began to worry for his friend.

Would the weight of this responsibility be too much for Crafter? Gameknight thought, *as it is for me. No, Crafter is strong and confident. He's like an adult even though he looks like a kid on this server. He can take the pressure. He can do it...but can I?*

Sighing, Gameknight gripped his sword firmly, and continued walking, peering into shadows and darkened buildings with trepidation, the jaws of fear snapping at him from within. Shaking slightly, he moved to one home that was partially destroyed and collected some of the wood and stone blocks that floated on the ground, then quickly made a new crafting bench and more stone tools.

Sighing with relief, he handed his friend a stone sword, as well as other stone tools: a pickaxe, a shovel, an axe...Now they were a real duo.

"How does that feel?" he asked.

"Better," Crafter replied as he swung the stone sword through the air. "I seem to feel better these days when I have a strong sword in my hand...unfortunately."

Gameknight tossed his own wooden sword to the ground and pulled out the new stone sword he'd just made. Looking about the village, he scanned the area with a keen eye. He could almost hear the screams of terror from the inhabitants as their village was ravaged; the feelings of panic and fear for loved ones still echoed through the cluster of destroyed buildings. Gameknight could somehow sense those feelings of terror, the hopeless despair that had flooded across this village. But there was something strange about the destruction. Not all of the buildings were destroyed. In fact, some of them remained completely untouched. Crafter pointed out some of these pristine buildings, gesturing with his new sword.

Gameknight would have been curious about this if he wasn't so scared.

"Come, follow me," Crafter commanded. "Watch our backs."

He swallowed, fear nibbling at his senses, then followed the small boy as his eyes darted over his shoulder, looking for threats.

They moved quickly through the village, starting from the outer buildings then gradually moving inward, toward the center. The wooden homes at the edge of the village were completely destroyed, some of them just large craters in the ground, with cubes of wood, stone, and dirt floating where the buildings had once stood. When they circled around the other side of the town, they were shocked at what they found.

"Look at this, Crafter. The homes on this side of the village are completely untouched," Gameknight said, curiosity replacing fear for a moment as he peered into windows and open doors.

"It's as if the monsters never even came to this side," Crafter said softly, more to himself than to his companion. "Why would they do that?"

"Maybe there were chased away?"

"No," Crafter answered. "There is no sign of battle, just creeper explosions and zombie-shredded doors... and only on one side of the village...why?"

Crafter went into a few of the homes while Gameknight stayed outside, on guard, searching for anything that would help, especially food. They investigated building after building as they moved through the village, and found nothing but empty dwellings. Crafter was getting more worried with every deserted home.

"Where do you think the villagers went?" he asked, his own fear subsiding a bit.

"I don't think they were killed," Crafter yelled from the back room of another deserted house. "They must have gone somewhere...but where?"

Gameknight thought back to his first trip to Crafter's village after he'd been pulled into the game. The village has been filled with NPCs...with life...and at the time with monsters as well. That battle had been the first of many; his first test under fire. And the next day, the Mayor had taken him to see Crafter deep underground in the...

"I know...underground, in the crafting chamber."

"Of course, the crafting chamber," Crafter said as he stepped out of the doorway and into the sunlight.

Every village had a large chamber built deep underground, where all the crafting for Minecraft was done, hidden from users and monsters. Connected to the crafting chamber would be a complex rail network on which minecarts moved, ferrying the crafted goods throughout the digital world. This would be the only safe place for the villagers.

Heading toward the center of the village, they passed from the pristine, untouched section to the devastated part of the village again. The remnants of walls stood, still smoldering, marking the outlines of homes, burn marks slashed across the wood.

What could have burned these walls? Gameknight thought. *Creepers don't burn things... they just blow them apart.*

This question nagged at the User-that-is-not-a-user. It seemed important, but was lost within the cloud of fear that filled his mind. Smoke bellowed from a few still-burning homes; their interiors consumed by flame. The heat from these fiery wrecks hammered at the duo as they passed, causing small, square beads of sweat to form on their faces. The acrid smoke from the burning structures bit at the back of Gameknight's throat, making him cough as he moved through the village. It cast a gray, hazy pall across the village, coloring everything with a dull and dirty hue.

At the center of every village, there always stood a tall stone tower that loomed high above the rooftops of the other buildings, with a watchman usually stationed at the top; he was a lookout for monsters. In the distance, they could still see this tower standing tall, but as they neared it, Gameknight could see pieces of the stone sentinel were missing. Sprinting past more torn-up and smoking buildings, he and Crafter streaked toward the structure. They jumped over piles of rubble and around craters, their eyes cast upward, focused on the remains of the tall building that was still standing vigil.

When they reached it, they were shocked at what they found. A huge chunk of the building was completely gone, the base and side torn away as if some gigantic beast had taken a bite out of the tower and left a huge, gaping wound in its side.

They approached carefully, with Crafter leading the way, Gameknight following close behind. Heading first for the smaller room adjacent to the tower, they peeked around the remains of a wall. The entrance to the room had been completely blown away, the side of the structure obviously the victim of a creeper explosion. They must have been commanded to blow open this structure so that the mobs could get inside.

As the duo jumped over the shattered wall, they found that the room was partially destroyed, with one wall almost gone. The far wall was still solid, and the wooden door leading to the next room remained intact, but stood open. Sorting through the debris, they picked up pieces of wood and stone to add to their inventory. As he collected block after block of wood, Gameknight was surprised to find a golden sword, or a butter sword as some called them in the Minecraft community, buried amidst the rubble. Its keen edge sparkled in the bright sunlight, the golden blade shimmering with an iridescent blue glow. It had some kind of enchantment on it; magical power was locked within the blade.

"Crafter, come look at this," he said.

The young NPC came quickly to his side and looked

down at the shining weapon. It bobbed gently above the broken floor, the blade almost glowing as shafts of sunlight streamed in through the gaping hole in the wall and reflected off its edge.

"You think a user left this here?" Gameknight asked.

"I doubt it. We haven't seen a user on this server yet."

"Then how did it get here?"

Gameknight reached out and picked up the enchanted golden weapon, putting his stone sword back into his inventory. The new sword gave off a subtle whistle as he swung it through the air, its razor-sharp edge slicing with keen efficiency. He wondered how many lives this sword had taken, how many families it had destroyed, how many hopes and dreams it had extinguished. Gameknight shuddered at the thought and hoped that the user who had crafted this weapon had been a kind soul—not like he had been, a griefer. In the past, he had played Minecraft like a cyber bully, using his expertise and library of hacks and cheats to get weapons and items to make him much more powerful than the other users. He'd then used those items to take advantage of those around him, killing them for their inventory or maybe just for fun. He had played the game at the expense of others, rather than with them, and had learned the painful consequences of those actions on the last server. Although it had taken him awhile, Gameknight had learned the true meaning of sacrifice with his and Crafter's death; he finally knew what it meant to selflessly do something for someone else. Pulling his eyes from the shining blade, he looked at Crafter.

"I'm not sure how it got here," the NPC counseled. "But we should keep it in case it proves useful."

Gameknight nodded.

"Come on, let's check the other side of the tower," Crafter said as he stepped through the open door that led to the tower room, stone sword held out before him. Gameknight followed close behind with his golden sword held at the ready, anxiety pulsing through his veins.

Though they already knew the tower had been damaged, the two friends were still shocked at what they saw. The base of the tower had been blown open, the ladders that led upward to the higher floors now laying on the ground. The ceiling was completely destroyed, leaving the roof of the tower now visible from the ground floor, with patches of blue sky showing through small holes. Gameknight knew from the last server that the tower room also covered the long vertical tunnel that led to the crafting chamber, deep underground. Usually hidden under the cobblestone floor of the building, it was now clearly visible, the floor completely blown away. A gaping hole marked the location of the tunnel. It looked like a festering wound in the flesh of Minecraft. Hastily constructed steps had been carved into the side of the hole until the blocky stairway met the ladder that descended into the depths.

"Come, we must go down and see if everyone is alright!" Crafter shouted as he ran forward, taking the steps two at a time.

"But we don't know what's down there," Gameknight cautioned as he took a step backward, the serpent of fear slowly coiling around the last vestige of his courage, ready to strike.

Crafter stopped and turned to look at his friend.

"There might be people down there that need our help."

"Or a monster horde," Gameknight replied.

"We have to help those in need, and can't delay.

Now come on."

Gameknight stayed still, his gaze slowly lowering to the ground, fear ruling his mind.

"What happened to my friend? You still have your name floating above your head, but no silvery thread connecting you to the server. You are part of our world and part of the physical world, the one in the Prophecy. You are the User-that-is-not-a-user, savior of the last server, and soon the savior of this server. But you cannot save us if you don't start, if you don't try. Come, there will be people in need, people who need to know that the User-that-is-not-a-user has finally arrived. It is time for you to be what you were meant to be."

Gameknight's head sank lower, cowardly shame coursing through his body.

"I...ah..."

"I don't understand what's going on," Crafter snapped. "But I'm going down there with or without you." Turning, he ran down the steps, then climbed onto the ladder and started descending down the vertical shaft that led deep underground.

What am I doing? Gameknight thought. *I can't just let him go by himself...but...*

He was so afraid.

Looking around, he noticed that he was now completely alone, and the sun was heading toward the horizon. Night was coming soon. As he watched Crafter's sandy blond hair disappear into the dark tunnel, Gameknight felt, for the first time since meeting Crafter, totally alone. Glancing around the half-destroyed village, he imagined monsters rising from the destruction to attack him. Could he protect himself until Crafter returned? would he return? Then images of a zombie horde waiting deep underground now haunted his imagination, their dark claws reaching out for his friend. He had to help him—he had to be at Crafter's side in case there was danger.

I won't let you go down there alone!

Gripping his sword tightly, he moved forward, one uncertain step after the next. With a sigh, he finally plunged into the pit, following his friend into the darkness.

Running down the steps, he quickly found the ladder and started to descend. All of the torches that normally dotted this vertical shaft had been removed, the darkness hiding imagined monsters and creatures that reached out and fed his ever-present fear. Moving his hands, one after another, he quickly made his way down the ladder, establishing a rhythm that kept him going in spite of the fear that nibbled at the edges of his mind.

Suddenly, a light flared far below him. It was a torch lighting the end of the ladder; it was Crafter. Accelerating his pace, Gameknight shot down the dark tunnel attempting to catch up with his friend. In a few minutes he reached the bottom of the ladder, glad to have solid ground under his feet again. But he could tell that he was not alone.

"You decided to come," a voice said from the darkness.

"Yeah, I wanted to come and help," Gameknight lied.

"I knew the User-that-is-not-a-user couldn't resist the chance to help those in need, to help Minecraft," Crafter said as he stepped out of the shadows and into the torchlight.

"Well, come on. Let's find your villagers and figure out what happened here. Lead on."

Crafter nodded, then drew his sword and headed down the horizontal tunnel that was connected to the vertical one they had just descended. Darkness filled the passageway, with more fictional beasts reaching out at Gameknight from his imagination. He followed close behind Crafter, his eyes trying to penetrate the shadows, to no avail. He clutched his sword so tightly that his fingers hurt, but for some reason the pain seemed to push back the shadowy beasts that hid within his mind. His fear was held in check...for the moment.

They traversed the tunnel quickly, sprinting the last thirty blocks when they saw the end lit with torches. As they entered the next illuminated chamber, Gameknight eased the grip on his sword and moved the blade to his left hand, flexing the right to get blood flowing again through his fingers. The chamber was identical to the one in which he'd first met Crafter. It was a large, round room with no real features—no furniture and no decorations, just stone walls dotted with torches. But the far end of this chamber was bathed in darkness, the torches there gone. He could remember passing through a similar chamber for the first time in the last server, and being surprised at what he had seen. Would it be the same thing here? Would he see a cavern filled with NPCs crafting the items that Minecraft needed?

Or would the room be filled with a mob of Minecraft monsters, ready to tear him apart?

Fear raged through him, filling him with dread, but he knew he had to continue. He couldn't turn around without losing the respect of his friend—his only friend—so he moved one foot in front of the other as he followed Crafter through the chamber.

Moving slowly, the duo reached the other end of the chamber, swords held tight. Where there had once stood an iron door and thick cobblestone wall, there was now only rubble. The wall and iron doors had been completely destroyed, and the remnants of their destruction floated on the ground. Gameknight could see that the stone walls were charred as if they had been subjected to some terrible heat.

"Creepers?" Crafter asked, the word sounding as if it were poison on his tongue.

"I don't think so. Why would they have come down here? Besides, they wouldn't leave any burn marks...it had to be something different...something from the..." He shuddered, not wanting to say the word.

Stepping through the rubble, Crafter charged ahead, entering the crafting chamber with the reluctant Gameknight on his heels. They were both greeted with cries from villagers on the chamber floor.

"They're coming back!"

"Quick, hide."

"Run!"

"To the Minecarts, quickly!"

"WAIT!" Crafter shouted as he entered the chamber, his voice echoing off the stone walls.

All eyes moved up to the chamber entrance and were shocked to see an NPC with a sword—something that was unheard of. But then their eyes fell on Gameknight999. The villagers could see his name floating above his head, crisp white letters standing out against the gray stone walls.

"A user?" someone shouted.

But then their eyes carefully studied the space above Gameknight's head.

Users were always connected to their server through the server thread, a thin, silvery line that stretched upward from their heads, reaching up all the way into the sky, piercing any material in the way. Only NPCs could see the threads, which was how they distinguished users from other NPCs, but Gameknight had no server thread. He was disconnected, yet his username still floated over his head. He was a user, but at the same time, he was not a user.

"User-that-is-not-a-user," another voice said.

"User-that-is-not-a-user," yet another voice whispered.

"User-that-is-not-a-user."

"User-that-is-not-a-user."

The words rippled through the chamber as villager after villager realized who he was. The Prophecy that all NPCs learned during childhood foretold the arrival of the User-that-is-not-a-user, signaling the time of the Last Battle—the battle for the survival of Minecraft. It would be a time when the monsters of Minecraft would try to destroy all servers on all the planes of existence until they reached the Source, where all Minecraft code originated. Gameknight's presence here made two things abundantly clear for the NPCs: The Last Battle had finally arrived, and the User-that-is-not-a-user was there to save them.

With this realization, a cheer erupted throughout the chamber. First it started as a single person yelling out, then the lone voice started an avalanche of jubilation which spread across the crafting chamber, making the walls reverberate and the ground shake.

Moving down the sloping path, Crafter walked to the chamber floor, and Gameknight followed close behind. They could see the charred remains of crafting benches as they approached, along with craters in the floor where explosions had torn into the cavern. As they descended the pathway, Gameknight could feel all eyes glued to him, the NPCs' expectations that he would save them pounding away at his soul like a mighty sledgehammer. When they reached the end of the path, Crafter jumped up onto a crafting bench and addressed the crowd.

"Quiet down, quiet down," he shouted over the din. "Tell us what happened here."

The crowd ignored the young boy glaring down

at them and instead focused their attention on Gameknight, all of them talking at once, uncertainty and excitement filling the air.

Crafter shouted again, but was still ignored. All of the villagers continued talking, murmuring to each other.

Jumping down, Crafter ran to Gameknight and yelled into his ear.

"Jump up onto the crafting bench and get them to quiet down, then find out what happened here!"

Gameknight nodded and jumped up onto the crafting bench. Instantly, the crowd grew quiet, the villagers' eyes all looking up expectantly at their hero, their savior.

"What happened here?"

"The mobs," someone yelled from the back of the chamber. "They came out of the east at sunset."

"You mean zombies, spiders, creepers, endermen, and slimes?" Crafter asked. "The monsters of the Overworld?"

"Yes," someone answered.

"But more," another person also yelled.

"More?" Gameknight asked. "What do you mean?"

Silence filled the chamber at his question, the painful memories being replayed in the minds of the NPCs before him. Many of them turned their gaze toward the golden sword that was still in his hand, a look of fear painted across their blocky faces, their unibrows furled with dread.

"Nether creatures," someone said in a low voice, as if afraid that saying the word might summon the creatures into existence.

"What?" Gameknight asked.

"Nether creatures," the voice said, loud enough for all to hear.

Gameknight stepped off the crafting bench and

moved to the villager that had spoken. She was an older woman with chocolate brown hair and bright green eyes. Her smock was a light green that complemented her eyes, and had a dark gray stripe running down the middle; her clothing betraying her occupation as a farmer.

"What do you mean?" he asked in a reassuring voice, Crafter now at his side.

"It wasn't just the mobs of the Overworld," Farmer said in a cautious tone (NPCs were named based on their job). "There were Nether beasts here: blazes, zombie-pigmen, and..."

"And what?" Crafter asked, his voice shaking slightly.

"Ghastssss," she said, her voice trailing off like the hiss of a snake.

Gameknight gasped in shock—no, in terror.

The Nether was a land that existed in a parallel dimension, accessible only through teleportation portals. It was a dangerous place to visit, with burning sands, lava lakes, and waterfalls of molten rock. It was a terrible land of smoke and flame, and the ghasts ruled there. They were like huge, floating gasbags with gigantic cubic bodies and nine long tentacles dangling beneath them. With a childlike face and terrible, hateful eyes, they looked like vile, floating jellyfish. They roamed the Nether in complete safety, because the terrible fireballs that they could throw would eat through a user's HP in seconds, killing them. If you stayed motionless for too long in the Nether, you tended to end up barbequed, unless you had strong armor and potions to protect you from fire, both of which were difficult to get. But to know that these creatures had come here, to the Overworld, was terrible news.

One step below the ghasts were the blazes. A blaze was an elemental creature made of fire and blaze rods.

Looking like floating, fiery apparitions, the blazes' bodies were composed of long yellow rods that rotated through their midsections; these were the blaze rods, the source of their fiery power. No flesh connected the rods together—no arms, no legs. Their flesh was flame. Bright yellow fire licked up around the blaze rods, giving the impression of a bodily form, with smoke and ash billowing up from the burning creatures. They were terrifying to behold. These creatures could also throw fireballs, but they always stayed close to the ground, so they could be killed...if you had strong enough armor to survive their barrage of flames. Blazes were creatures you trifled with only if you had to. They were powerful fighters, and hated everything living, with a thirst for death and destruction that could only be rivaled by the ghasts.

At the bottom of the Nether hierarchy were zombie-pigmen. They looked and sounded like the zombies of the Overworld, but part of their bodies had a pinkish hue, as if they were part pig. This healthy side was in stark contrast to the zombie side, their exposed skull and ribs looking diseased and decayed. They were half-alive, half-dead monsters that hated the living and wanted to exact their vengeance on the NPCs and users of the Overworld.

In the Nether, these creatures were armed with golden swords and sometimes armored. They were relatively harmless, as long as they weren't attacked. If one was attacked, then all of the zombie-pigmen in the area would come to the aid of their brother and attack their assailant until he was killed; the relentless attack was nearly impossible to survive. Users that ventured into the Nether quickly learned to avoid these monsters, careful to give them a wide berth since accidently bumping into them could be misconstrued as an attack, and draw a violent response from all.

Gameknight looked at the shimmering, golden sword in his hand, then shot Crafter a glance. The NPC nodded in understanding. This blade had come from one of the zombie-pigmen; it was a weapon of the Nether, a weapon of hatred and destruction. He wanted to throw the sword as far away as he could, but knew that it was stronger than his stone sword—sharper and more deadly—and in Minecraft, the person with the best weapons and armor tended to win, and tended to live. Putting the sword back in his inventory, he put a reassuring hand on the woman's shoulder, trying to comfort her. The fear slowly faded from her face.

"Please, tell us what happened here," Crafter said.

The woman turned her head and looked to a gray-haired NPC behind her. "Planter, you tell," she said with a trembling voice. "I cannot bear the memory, could not speak the words. The horror of the event is still too fresh. You must tell them."

"Very well, Farmer, I will tell them," the gray-haired Planter said with a scratchy but calm voice that was filled with wisdom and age. "Everyone come close and listen, as I will not repeat this gruesome account twice."

Planter shuddered as Gameknight and Crafter drew near, the rest of the NPCs doing the same, the tight cluster of bodies pressing against each other. Then Planter began his terrible, horrific tale.

CHAPTER 4
THE ATTACK

T hey came out of the east, just at sunset," Planter
said, his scratchy, gravelly voice filling the
chamber. "We don't know how they made a portal
to get out of the Nether. Maybe it was from some users
on the server, who knows? We haven't seen any users
for a while, and were glad to have all the griefers gone,
but sad that there weren't any friendly users about.

"Anyway, the first wave came at sunset—a
collection of monsters from the Overworld. The
creepers and zombies entered the village directed by
a couple of blazes, the fiery monsters giving silent
orders to the other creatures to get into every building.
They began on one side of the village and just started
blowing things up. Zombies smashed in doors while
the creepers detonated themselves, destroying walls,
giving the mobs access to those inside."

"Were the occupants of these homes killed?" Crafter
asked, his attention focused with laser precision on
Planter's tale.

"That's the strange thing...they didn't kill anyone.
They just pushed everyone out of their homes and
herded them toward the center of the village."

"You mean that they—" Gameknight began to ask,
but was interrupted.

"Let me finish the tale," Planter said with a sorrowful
voice, his eyes moist with grief. "This is painful to
recount. You can ask your questions after."

Gameknight and Crafter nodded and allowed the
old NPC to finish.

"So the mobs crashed into the village, creepers blowing open homes and zombies crashing through doorways. At first I thought it was thunder, the explosions echoing across the land. I had just come back from planting the fields to the north, and was at the well at the village center when the explosions started. I looked up at the sky, but it was clear—no clouds. How could there be thunder without clouds? And then the zombies started hammering on doors. We all know that sound…right?"

Planter looked around the cavern at the sea of nodding faces, eyes filled with despair at the memory of those lost to the mobs, then continued.

"They started breaking into homes. Those villagers too close to a wall where a creeper exploded were…" The old NPC paused for a moment as a small, blocky tear trickled down his pale cheek. Wiping it away, he went on with the terrible tale, his voice sounding a bit more gravelly as emotions crashed over him. "They didn't attack anyone if they came out of their homes right away. But those that stayed inside were attacked by the zombies and infected so that they became one of them…villager-zombies. Most of the children…the children…"

"What about the children?" Crafter asked, but Planter was too overcome with emotion to speak.

"Most of the children were too afraid to come out," said Farmer, her voice choked with sadness, but also having a cold, violent edge. "The zombies fell on them and either killed them or infected them." She paused for a moment as she become overcome with sadness, but then her face took on an angry look as her unibrow became creased with rage. "Do you have any idea what it's like to see your own child become one of…one of them, a zombie?"

Crafter remained silent. No answer was needed,

because his sorrowful eyes said it all.

Coughing and clearing his throat, Planter continued.

"Thank you, Farmer. Yes, our children were taken from us...made into *them*." He paused again to compose himself. "They drove us like cattle to the center of town; anyone complaining or hesitating was killed instantly. Then the blazes and zombie-pigmen arrived, their golden swords flashing out to silence any remarks with sudden and fatal certainty. The blazes went to the other side of town with some zombies and a few hostages. They put the hostages in front of the windows and then banged on the doors. When the villagers opened the door, the blazes streaked in like bolts of lightning and drove the people out of their homes with balls of fire. If they were too slow, they were...they..."

Planter stopped again as uncontrollable sobs washed over him. Moving off to a corner, he sat down on a stone, lowered his head and wept, unable to continue. One of the NPCs raised a hand slowly into the air, fingers held wide, then clenched them into a fist, the knuckles turning white as he squeezed his hand with sorrow and rage. Finally, he lowered his hand. Gameknight and Crafter looked at the old NPC and wanted to comfort him, but knew there was nothing they could do. Instead, they gave the old man sympathetic looks and turned back to Farmer.

She stepped forward, her bright green eyes boring straight into Gameknight and Crafter as she stood before them, her sadness reflected within those pupils. She brushed her brown hair out of her face so that she could see Crafter and Gameknight clearly, then spoke.

"The monsters drove us all to the center of town and just kept us there, near the tower. And then the ghasts came. They surrounded us, hovering maybe six blocks in the air. Their childlike faces were filled with anger and hatred, and their dangling tentacles twitched about as if they wanted to reach out and grab anything within reach. A few villagers decided to make a break for it, running off toward the forest to the north...They never even made it out of the village. The ghasts just followed them lazily, waiting until they were out of sight from the rest of us, then blasted them with balls of fire. We could hear their screams as they were consumed, and then there was silence."

She had to stop to take a breath. Her breathing had become strained during the telling, as if she had also been running with the villagers to escape the nightmare. Pausing, she took a minute to catch her breath, looking at the sea of faces around her, hoping someone else would step up and continue the tale from where she had left off. But everyone she looked at moved their gaze to the ground rather than look back at her. Sighing, she kept going, her green eyes cold, as if they were in a battle to purge all emotion from her soul; they were losing.

"Once they were convinced that they had us all under control, they separated us, moving maybe twenty of us off to the side. One of the wither-skeletons said that they would have the honor of working for the King of the Nether. A group of blazes then surrounded that group and led them off, probably back to their portal. Once they were gone, the creepers blew up the tower entrance and opened the tunnel. It was like they knew it was there, somehow. After they tore up the floor, the blazes shot fireballs at the hole, carving steps into the walls so that the mobs could go into the tunnel. A group of zombies went in first, then they forced us into the tunnel, one at a time. A few refused. The ghasts blasted them with fireballs and—"

"Builder, my beloved husband," one of the villagers

moaned—a young, blond-haired woman, who had tears streaming down her face and her arm raising in salute, fist clenched tight.

"Yes, Builder was killed," Farmer said, moving to the NPC and leaning against her—the only way an NPC could console another. Others came forward and also leaned against the woman, though they knew nothing would help.

"And Picker..."

"And Carver..."

"And Tailor..."

The litany of the dead flowed from the crowd in a cathartic torrent of emotion, the names of those lost forever chiseled into the memory of the village.

Planter stood and moved back to Gameknight and Crafter. He turned to look at everyone in the cavern, getting their attention, then raised his hand into the air, fingers spread wide. A few followed his lead, also raising their hands into the air, but most of the NPCs were too overcome with grief to notice. The cavern filled with sobs of despair. Looking around the room, Gameknight could see that the villagers' eyes were filled not only with sorrow, but also with an overwhelming rage toward the mobs that had committed this atrocity.

Slowly, Planter lowered his hand and turned back to Crafter and Gameknight.

"The monsters drove us down here into the crafting chamber like we were cattle," he spat. "Many of us thought they were going to bury us in and let us starve, but instead they came and took him."

Planter paused, again overcome by emotion.

"Who?" Gameknight asked in a soft, shaking voice. "Who did they take?"

"After they drove us all down here, they herded us into the corner of the chamber," another NPC explained. Gameknight could tell by the color of his smock that he was the blacksmith. "Then they demanded that we turn him over to them."

"Turn who over?" he asked again, this time a little louder.

Smithy stepped forward so that he could see Crafter and Gameknight directly, without having to look around other blocky heads. "They demanded that we turn over our village crafter," he said.

"Your crafter?" Crafter asked. "Why would they want him?"

"Runner asked that same question," Smithy replied as he brushed a lock of his salt-and-pepper gray hair out of his face. "The blazes killed him, blasted him with balls of fire. Oh...his screams...I can still hear them. He was in such agony, but the worst part was listening to the sadness in his voice. He cried out to his wife and children, telling them goodbye. I had to hold his son back so that he wouldn't embrace his father and catch fire as well."

Smithy raised a hand in the air and then clenched his fist, squeezing so tightly that Gameknight could hear his fingers crack, the knuckles turning white. His arm started to shake as he squeezed his hand tighter and tighter before he lowered it and continued.

"Thankfully, Runner didn't suffer very long; his torment only lasted a minute or so. Then the biggest ghast I've ever seen...I don't remember his name..."

"Malacoda," Planter said, his voice filled with rage. "He said his name was Malacoda. He referred to himself as the King of the Nether."

"Right," Smithy said, "Malacoda. He was pale white, like parched bone left too long out in the sun, with a large cube-like body and all of his tentacles hanging down waiting to grab something...or someone. Malacoda demanded that we turn over our crafter or more villagers would be killed. None of us moved. We just stood there, silent, afraid to refuse, knowing it would mean certain death, but we couldn't give up our crafter."

A square tear rolled down Smithy's blocky face. Turning away, he cast his eyes to the ground.

"So he gave himself up," Planter said, his voice now filled with pride. "Crafter just walked right up and gave himself up to this ghast king. He probably saved all our lives. They would have…"

He stopped speaking as teary rivulets continued their journey down his cheeks, but he fought for control over his emotions. He then looked around at the others in the chamber. Most of his fellow villagers also had wet cheeks. After another moment of silence, Planter looked back to Gameknight and Crafter.

"Our Crafter saved all of our lives by sacrificing himself. He was a great NPC, and the greatest crafter a village could ever ask for." He looked about the room again, making eye contact with every survivor, then continued. "We will remember him for the rest of our lives."

He raised his hand high above his head again with fingers spread wide, and held it there for a minute, his hand shaking slightly. This time Gameknight saw that others were also raising their hands, fingers stretched. Then they all formed a fist, held high as the salute to the dead, the movement spreading contagiously through the chamber until a sea of fists were growing above the field of blocky heads, each being squeezed with all its might. It was an awesome display of respect and love, coupled with an overwhelming anger and rage toward their attackers. Gameknight felt a tear start to trickle from his eye, the emotion infecting him as well. Quickly wiping his eye with his sleeve, he also raised his hand in salute, clenching his fist and squeezing it tight until his knuckles hurt.

Finally, the villagers lowered their arms and brought their attention back to Gameknight and his companion. An awkward silence filled the room with no one wanting to be the first to speak, but then the User-that-is-not-a-user stepped forward.

"I don't understand why this ghast king, Malacoda, would want to take your crafter. In our last server, the mobs wanted to kill everyone and take their XP, but they left all of you alive...I don't understand."

"Nor do we," Planter replied. "We expected that they would kill us all, but once they had our crafter, they led him away and just went back up the tunnel to the surface. We've been here since, afraid to go back up in case they were still here."

"Well, they're not here anymore," Crafter explained. "They've left, but something strange is definitely going on here."

"Have you and the User-that-is-not-a-user come to save us?" a young voice asked from the crowd. It was a small girl, maybe the same height and age as Crafter— one of the few children in the chamber. "Has the Last Battle finally found us?"

"I'm not sure, little one," Crafter answered. "It did come to my server, and the User-that-is-not-a-user and I were able to defeat the mobs and save our world, but I fear that the battle still rages here, and we are very near to the Source. These monsters must be stopped on this server plane, or I fear the Source may be in grave danger."

"If the Source is destroyed, then all of us will die. Isn't that so?" the young NPC asked.

"That is correct, child," Crafter answered. "In my last world, I was a crafter like the brave NPC you just described, but when I respawned here, I came in this form." Crafter gestured to his small body. "But we know that the battle for Minecraft has not ended. The

User-that-is-not-a-user and I are here to continue the fight, until we stop all these monsters."

"A crafter...a crafter...a crafter..."

The words rippled throughout the chamber, the people looking at each other excitedly; their need for a new crafter was great. Only a living, breathing crafter can transfer his powers to a new NPC, passing on the responsibility from one generation to the next. But a village without a crafter could not survive in Minecraft; they would become the Lost—NPCs without a community. Each village must have a crafter to keep the machinery of the digital world functioning. Without one, the Lost would have to abandon their homes and strike out in random directions, hoping to survive the journey and find a new village; most would do neither. Stepping forward, Planter leaned up against Crafter's shoulder and looked the young NPC in the eyes. Farmer then stood and leaned against Planter's shoulder. In an almost instantaneous ripple, all of the villagers leaned toward Crafter, with those nearest actually leaning against him, the others leaning on those in front of them, until a complicated pattern of bodies had formed a giant starburst, all of them leaning directly toward Crafter.

"We ask that you, companion of the User-that-is-not-a-user, be our crafter," Planter recited from memory, his words drawn out slowly, reverently. "We humbly ask that you look after our village, our people, and Minecraft, and in return, we will serve you so that we may serve Minecraft." His words reverberated throughout the chamber like hopeful thunder.

All eyes were focused on Crafter, anticipation in every pair, furled unibrows creased with concern and excitement. Gameknight saw Crafter swallow, a worried look on his face. He knew Crafter was considering the consequences of his decision. If he accepted, then he would have the heavy responsibility of helping this village rebuild, but if he refused, then these people would be doomed to leave this village and search the land for another. Those without a crafter were referred to as the Lost. If these people became Lost, then few of them would survive long enough to find a new home; there were just too many monsters spread out across the surface of Minecraft.

Turning, Crafter glanced up at his friend, looking for a sign from the User-that-is-not-a-user. Gameknight just gave his friend a warm smile and a subtle nod. Crafter then turned back to the crowd.

"Though I will never be able to fill the shoes of your last crafter...I agree."

A great cheer resonated within the crafting chamber, followed by a burst of light that seemed to come from Crafter himself. Gameknight had to raise his hand to his eyes to shield them from the glare. The brilliant illumination receded almost instantly, leaving behind the same young boy, but instead of a green smock, he was now clothed in the apparel of his station: a black smock, with a wide gray stripe running down the middle from neck to hem; he was a village crafter again.

The villagers in the chamber all jumped up and down in jubilation, though the pain of their loss was still vivid in their minds. Their village had been saved. They were a community again; their families, or what was left of them, could continue here in their homeland.

"What are your instructions?" Planter asked Crafter, the question hushing the crowd.

Crafter put away his sword, which he just realized he'd had out all this time, and paced back and forth, gazing past the arms and legs of the full-grown villagers, each wanting to lightly touch or brush the new crafter as he passed, the physical contact strengthening their newly established connection. Gameknight stood back and just watched, grateful that the attention had shifted away from him. His eyes followed his old friend's young frame as he marched back and forth, mind deep in thought.

And then suddenly, Crafter stopped and looked up at the crowd.

"The first thing we do is release all of your hands."

"What?" came from many of the villagers.

"We can't release our hands," Planter complained. "Only crafters have their arms separated, and a village can have only one crafter. I don't understand.

"The User-that-is-not-a-user can do this. He did it on my server—released the hands of all my people, and put a sword in each."

A shocked silence spread through the chamber.

"A sword...?"

"Yes, a sword," Crafter replied. "We fought the mobs, all of us, and we turned back the tide. We're going to do the same thing here."

Murmurs of surprise rippled through the crowd. Villagers fighting the monsters of Minecraft...it was unheard of.

"I know what you're thinking...how can this be true? Well, we did it. We fought off the monster horde and saved our server, and we're going to do it here as well. We won't—no, we *can't* let the monsters reach the Source. If they do, all will be lost. It's our job to stop them, and as my friend, Gameknight999, said to the last Enderman king: 'The line is drawn here. THEY CAN GO NO FURTHER!'"

A cheer burst forth from the NPCs, filling the chamber with the thunder of hope. Crafter moved to Gameknight and stood next to his friend, drawing his sword and holding it up high. The User-that-is-not-a-user did the same.

"The Prophecy says that when the User-that-is-not-a-user appears, the time of the Last Battle is near. Make no mistake about it. The Last Battle is upon us, and we must resist these monsters with every ounce of strength we have, with our very lives if necessary." Crafter motioned for Gameknight to pull out his crafting bench, then motioned for Planter to come forward.

"Planter, craft me a stone sword."

Planter looked back at Crafter, confused, but then acquiesced, his arms suddenly separating as he started to craft the stone sword, blocky hands a blur. Crafter looked at Gameknight and nodded. With a sudden swiftness, the User-that-is-not-a-user pulled out his pickaxe and shattered the crafting bench with three quick blows, a shower of splinters flying into the air and leaving the crafting bench as a small, floating cube, hovering just over the ground. Planter gasped when he looked down at his own hands, now permanently separated, a stone sword held tightly in his right. Slowly raising the sword high over his head, Planter drew a gasp from the rest of the NPCs in the chamber.

"Planter is no longer just a planter," Crafter said in slow, drawn-out words, his voice shouting loud to fill the chamber. "He is now a fighter, a warrior for Minecraft, as you all will be. Today, at this moment, in this chamber, we start the war to save the Source. Today, we push back against the mobs and say NO MORE. Today, we save Minecraft!" He reached out and slowly pulled down Planter's arm, getting him to put away his sword, then continued.

"Now let me tell you what we're going to do," the young NPC started to explain, his old blue eyes sparkling with hope. "First, we're going to call all NPCs to us. You will spread across the land and bring every NPC you find to me. We will deny

Malacoda any more lives to destroy, then we will..."

All the NPCs leaned forward as they listened to the plans from their new crafter. But as Gameknight listened, he could feel waves of uncertainty and fear fill his soul. This was dangerous...very dangerous.

What if it doesn't work, Gameknight thought. *What if I'm not strong enough...or brave enough...or...*

All the *what-ifs* played through his mind as he listened to Crafter's plan, giving strength to the serpent of fear that coiled about his soul.

CHAPTER 5

MALACODA

Malacoda floated over the sea of lava, the heat from the molten stone bringing a sense of security and safety and home. He was a ghast, one of the many creatures that prowled the underworld. He was different, however, because he claimed to be king, the ruler of the Nether on this Minecraft server—and soon on all servers.

Moving lazily above the molten sea, he looked down at his tentacles, which were dragging through the thick magma. He could see that they almost glowed as his pale limbs reflected the light from the boiling sea. He had a large, cube-like body that was gigantic—larger than any other creature in Minecraft, with the exception of the Ender Dragon. His face had a baby-like appearance to it; almost peaceful and calm... except for the eyes, however. They glowed blood red, always seeming to be filled with rage and hatred at those of the Overworld. Blotchy stains on his skin stood out in the orange illumination, looking dark and menacing. His entire body was covered with these gray blotches. They could be likened to the spots on a cheetah, but these patches somehow lacked any sort of natural beauty. Instead, they looked like ugly scars, put there to accentuate this creature's hateful and evil nature. The most prominent of these scars were located beneath the ghast's eyes, giving him the misleading look of having a constant flow of sad tears. Malacoda hated these tear-like scars, but they were something that all ghasts wore, a sign of shame that few dared to point out lest they be consumed by fire.

Looking about his kingdom, Malacoda admired his surroundings. The burning sands, lava waterfalls, rivers of molten stone, soul sand, and netherrack all seemed beautiful to him. Off to the right stood his fortress, a dark citadel that covered most of the Nether in that direction. Its looming towers and tall, raised walkways stretched across the landscape like some kind of giant, prehistoric beast. This was the home of his massive army; his Nether fortress. It had gigantic rooms, covered with spawners that produced monster after monster to grow his massive horde. With high balconies and tall walkways, the monstrous citadel looked as if it were watching the terrain, guarding Malacoda's dominion.

This was his land, his realm to rule, and his word was law. Soon that would be the case across all servers, and then eventually the Source itself, the digital spring from which all computer code flowed to keep the server planes functioning. He would destroy this Source, and at that time, as the Prophecy predicted, he would rule all of Minecraft. Then, and only then, would he be able to take his army of monsters across the Gateway of Light and into the physical world, extending his rule to encompass all living things. Shuddering with excitement, Malacoda imagined the destruction he would bring to the fools in the physical world. Those arrogant users thought *they* ruled Minecraft. Well, he'd educate them soon enough, but first, he had to get to the Source and rid these digital worlds of all the NPCs—the living segments of code that infested the server planes. They would be purified soon enough, though. His plan was proceeding just as he had foreseen.

In the distance, he saw a group of zombie-pigmen approaching. These creatures were related to their cousins in the Overworld, despite the fact that their coloring was not the putrid, decaying green of normal zombies. The zombie-pigmen were like a combination of a zombie and a pig, with splashes of pink across their mottled bodies and exposed bones jutting out here and there. It was some kind of sick joke by the Creator, Notch, to make these creatures half-alive and half-dead. It made them hate those of the Overworld, the NPCs and users, even more.

Today, he could see that his zombie-pigmen were escorting their latest captive, a crafter from the Overworld. Malacoda had personally led the attack on that village, destroying any that stood in his way until he had this crafter, the key to his plans. Gliding effortlessly across the lava sea, he approached the shore, which was composed of rust-colored netherrack blocks—the most common material in the Nether. Smoke and ash clouded the air, making the approaching party difficult to see at times. As the haze momentarily cleared, Malacoda watched them slowly drawing nearer, the party having crossed onto a patch of soul sand, which was slowing their progress. The gray soul sand had this effect on anyone who crossed its grainy surface, effectively reducing any progress to a mere crawl.

Malacoda became impatient while waiting for the stupid monsters to approach.

What idiots, crossing soul sand instead of going around it, he thought.

He approached the party just as they cleared the soul sand, his tentacles twitching with agitation.

"So we meet again," Malacoda boomed, his voice resonating within his huge cube-like body. When he spoke, his eyes became wide and angry, taking in all that was before him.

"What is it you want of me, ghast?" the crafter spat.

"Why, nothing, other than your Minecraft-given skills," Malacoda said with his most sincere voice, an eerie, toothy smile on his face.

Seeing this terrible smile, the crafter took a step back and bumped into one of his guards. A grunt came from the zombie-pigman, the sharp point of its golden sword pushing the NPC forward again.

"I want you to craft something for me. That is all. After you and your little friends are done, I will release you."

"Why should I believe a ghast? You killed my people and destroyed part of my village. None of us will craft for you," the crafter said, the tone of his voice resonating as if imparting some kind of universal truth. He paused, then continued, glaring up at the beast. "You and your kind down here are abominations to life, a stain on everything that is creative and good and alive in Minecraft. You are a programming mistake!" He then took a step closer to the floating monster. "You really expect me to do anything for you? I saw you attack NPCs—innocent people—SOME OF THEM CHILDREN! What makes you think I will do *anything* for you?"

The crafter realized he had been screaming, a fact that brought the zombie-pigmen a step closer, their stinking flesh assaulting his senses.

Malacoda floated closer as well, so that the crafter had to look straight up into his childlike eyes, which were now blazing as if aflame, blood red with rage.

"You will do as I say, when I say, because you are a fool and have no choice," the ghast king said with complete confidence, dangling tentacles twitching aggressively. The childlike face then softened as he looked at the zombies. "Take him to the others."

One of the foul creatures grunted, then placed a rotting, clawed hand on the crafter's shoulder, pulling him backward and shoving him off in another direction. Another zombie-pigman moved in front of the NPC, leading the way toward the massive Nether fortress that dominated the area, the great lava sea fading away to the right. The lead zombie turned to make sure that his captive was coming. Then it motioned to the other monsters. The remaining creatures surrounded their charge, moving in close and effectively closing off any possibility of escape or suicide.

They moved quickly across the netherrack, heading directly for the menacing Nether fortress that loomed in the distance. Shining cubes of glowstone illuminated the land here and there, many of them stuck high overhead, embedded in the rocky ceiling. The glowing cubes added splashes of light as they glowed a bright yellow from within crevasses and off walls.

Glancing up at the ceiling that covered the entire land, the crafter saw bats flitting about in the distance while others hung from upside down perches. Many of the bats darted about in all directions at once, their beady little eyes watching, always watching.

He was ushered across the smoky landscape, the prodding needle-sharp tip of a sword poking him in the back to keep him moving. The zombie-pigmen were driving him toward the massive fortress that loomed before him. It was the biggest structure he'd ever seen, and made him tremble and shake with trepidation. After about fifteen minutes, the forced march ended up at the gigantic entrance to the massive citadel. It was built out of dark nether brick, the blocks a dark red just barely a shade above black. Torches dotted the exterior of the massive structure, their purpose not to illuminate, but to decorate and make the building look more threatening.

The crafter was grateful to enter the massive building. As he walked up the long, steep staircase, the oppressive heat from the nearby sea of lava diminished a bit. But now, instead of feeling like he was standing in the center of a flame, with blaring heat and brilliant light trying to burn away the last layers of his hope, he felt like he was trapped in the sooty remains of a blast furnace, the darkness chasing away his last bit of courage. Resignation washed over him as he realized that this was his fate. A feeling of overwhelming failure and despair settled down on the crafter like a leaden funeral shroud. He could still hear the creeper explosions in his memory, the sounds of his village being destroyed. He hadn't been able to protect them, his villagers; he'd failed.

Moving forward in a numb, dreamlike state, he walked behind his captors. Every now and then, the sharp point of a golden sword poked him in the back to keep him walking. The monsters led him down the main passageway, where the wall-mounted torches cast warm circles of light that tried to push away the darkness; they didn't do a very good job. Blazes stood guard at points of intersection with other passages. These fiery creatures, composed of flame and ash, cast more light on the dark corridor, making the torches seem dim by comparison. The zombie-pigmen pushed him this way and that as they took him through many different passages, plunging deeper and deeper into the Nether fortress. As they followed the featureless corridors, the crafter's sense of hopelessness grew until he felt like an empty husk of himself, a shell that once held life and now only held shadows and a desire for death.

Eventually, they reached their goal; a large room built in the center of the fortress. The crafter was shocked at its size. It must have been at least a hundred blocks across, and easily that many high. Many balconies had been placed on the inner walls, overlooking the interior of the gigantic chamber. Yellow circles of light illuminated each balcony, and together they looked like evil eyes dotting the towering walls, all looking down on the new captive. The crafter could see blazes and zombie-pigmen standing in the lower balconies while the occasional ghast floated above, moving across the opening. He could feel all of their violent eyes burning down on him, seeking his destruction.

Shaking with fear, he pulled his eyes from the balconies and peered through the smoky air at what was just emerging through the haze. At the center of the massive chamber stood a large structure that had numerous small windows on its sides, each covered with iron bars. It was a prison. Faint illumination filled the inside of the cell, and he could see shadowy figures moving about within. The creatures stayed near the back of the cell, away from the windows, making them difficult to identify, so that they seemed all the more terrifying. An iron door stood open on one side, a couple of blazes standing nearby with balls of flaming death ready to rain down upon anyone trying to escape. The new crafter was brought forward and shoved into the cell by one of the zombie-pigmen, the sharp point of its sword digging into his back. He took a few uncertain steps forward, and the door clanged shut behind him, reverberating like thunder as he glanced around the dimly lit cell. The room slowly darkened a little as the blazes moved on about their business.

Only one glowstone lit the room; it was recessed into the center of the floor, and cast strange shadows in the corners.

Is there something in here with me? he wondered. A wave a panic crashed over him. *What type of monster have they put me in with?*

Squinting his eyes, he peered into the darkness, trying not to move and attract the attention of whatever foul beast was there. And then he heard it—a shuffling of something across the ground, and the scraping of bodies, many of them, brushing against each other. He could see movement in the shadows, and realized that something was coming toward him, stepping out of the darkness. Looking about the room, he sought a place to hide. There was nothing, just bare walls.

"Oh well," he said aloud. "I welcome death. Come forward, beast, and do your business. Kill me and make it quick."

"Kill you?" said a voice from the darkness.

Another crafter stepped out of the shadows, then another, and another, all of them garbed the same. They each wore black smocks that reached from neck to ankle, with a wide gray stripe running down the center.

"What's this?" the new crafter asked those already here. "What's going on here?"

"We don't know," answered one of them. "But rest assured, friend, you are not alone here."

"I can see that."

In total, there were seven crafters already in the prison. The haggard NPCs came forward and patted the newcomer on the shoulders, hoping to bring a little comfort to their fellow prisoner, and maybe push away some of the uncertainty, some of the fear. He sighed, comforted by the support of his peers. Looking around the room again, he smiled and stood up a little taller, his despair fading away just a bit.

"We are now eight," one of the crafters said, the sense of command in his voice marking him as their leader. He was a tall NPC, with short brown hair and an ugly, fresh scar across one cheek. He stepped forward into the light, and a limp could be seen, his left leg dragging ever so slightly. Glancing at everyone in the room, the tall crafter smiled. "This is enough for us to now try our plan."

"Your plan?" asked the newest crafter. "What plan?"

The leader turned and faced him, his steel-gray eyes filled with confidence.

"We need to find out what's going on...what Malacoda is planning," the leader said in a soft voice. "One of us needs to escape and look around."

"Escape...how?" asked the latest prisoner.

"There are now eight of us. We can create a tool just by using our innate crafting abilities. Something only crafters can do."

"I never knew this," the newest crafter said.

"It is something few know," the leader explained as he took a step closer to the glowstone that illuminated the room. "A bug in the Minecraft code. It has gone unnoticed for many CPU cycles, and now it is time to take advantage of it. Everyone, move close together and link arms. Good. Now close your eyes and focus on crafting a pickaxe. Imagine yourselves placing the three blocks of stone and the two wooden sticks together, forming the tool."

The newest crafter scrunched his eyes and focused on the image of his crafting bench, the empty slots slowly getting filled with materials: stone across the three top slots and sticks down the center. Forcing all of his crafting knowledge into the image, he tried to project it before him, using every fiber of his being to will the shape into existence. It felt ridiculous at first, like he was pretending to craft, just wishing it into existence, but then something strange happened; he could *feel* the other crafters, though "feel" was not the right word. Somehow, their crafting powers had linked, their proximity to each other adding to the connection. Opening his eyes, he looked about the room and found seven pair of eyes also looking around in surprise. All of the crafters could sense the connection, and were shocked at how it *felt*; their crafting power had magnified and was growing. The tall leader wore a satisfied smile.

Slowly, a buzzing cloud of purple started to form at the center of the circle, growing in size as they concentrated harder and harder. It looked to the new crafter like the purple particles that always seemed to accompany endermen when they teleported from one location to another. The cloud started to grow, shooting shafts of purple haze up to the ceiling as if they were trying to kiss the sky. As the particles expanded, they also thickened, coalescing into a definite form on the ground. Then suddenly there was a pop, and something came through the plum-colored portal. The sound shocked the crafters and made a few of them step back, breaking the circle and severing the link. As the particles cleared, they could see something sitting on the ground; it was now substantial and solid—a pickaxe.

"We did it!" someone exclaimed.

"Shhh," the leader said, casting a furtive glance to the cell door.

Quickly moving forward, one of the other crafters grabbed the pickaxe and put it in his inventory, hiding it from view.

"Excellent, friends," the leader said in a whisper. "We have accomplished something that has never been done before. We teleported something to us from somewhere else in Minecraft."

"You mean we didn't craft it?" asked the newest crafter.

"No," the leader said "We cannot create something from nothing, but we were able to bring something to us from somewhere else. This is a great thing, and possibly a powerful weapon to use against our enemies."

"Maybe if we can bring something to us, we can also send something away, out of the Nether."

"Hmmm," the leader considered. "Possibly, but I don't think it works that way."

"This has never been done before," the newest said. "So you don't know. Maybe it can be done, you know, send one of us back to the Overworld."

"Hmmm..."

"Forget about that right now," one of the other crafters interjected. "We need to get one of us out of this cell and figure out what the ghast king is doing."

"That's right," the leader agreed. "Only one can go. More than one would be easily detected. Who shall it be?"

All of the crafters looked at one another, trying to decide who would go. The newest crafter noticed that all the others looked a bit haggard and worn, like bits of cloth wrung out a few too many times, their strength seeming to be at their limits, threadbare and ready to break.

"I should go," he said, a ripple of fear flowing across him. "Who knows when the last time was that any of you have eaten? You're all weak and tired; I can see it. Your health is nearly consumed. I'm the newest here, and have been exposed to this insufferable heat for the least amount of time. I should go."

Silence filled the room as all eyes settled on him. Fear rippled through his soul.

"I know how this will likely end," he said to the leader. "But we have to know what's going on."

"No, I won't ask you to risk your life for this," the leader said. "I'll go."

The newest crafter looked at the leader with a critical eye. He could see he was wavering on his feet, his body shaking slightly while his life force was on the verge of evaporating into oblivion. The leader was already near death.

"I'm the only one who has any hope of success," the newest crafter stated. "I'm going, and that's the end of it. As soon as I know what Malacoda is doing, I'll get back here, and we'll figure out what we need to do." He paused, jaw clenched and back rigid with determination, waiting to hear the others' objections; there were none. "Then it's decided. Give me the pick."

One of the other crafters tossed him the pick, then stepped back. The newest crafter took the tool and moved to the wall. Another crafter moved to the iron door and peered out of the small window, looking for guards.

"It's clear. Go now."

The crafter swung the pickaxe, breaking two blocks of nether brick with only a few swings. Putting the tool into his inventory, he stepped out of the cell, replacing the blocks so as to leave no trace of his escape. Then he sprinted for the shadows, adrenaline pushing him blindly forward in spite of his fear.

CHAPTER 6

ESCAPE

The gigantic room was cloaked in darkness, the ever-present haze of smoke and ash that drifted through the air burning the crafter's throat when he breathed. Moving silently with his back against the outer wall of the prison cell, he slid his way to the edge of the structure and peered around the corner. No monsters were near. Malacoda was so confident in the crafters' hopelessness that he hadn't even bothered to post any guards. Looking upward, his eyes followed the tall, looming walls. He could see the glow of blazes floating on balconies higher up, but they were too far away to see him in the darkness. Moving as quietly as possible, the crafter sprinted across the chamber to the nearest passageway and looked around the corner; it too was empty. Turning, he looked back at the prison cell. He could see the other crafters standing right up against the windows, their terrified faces peeking through the bars, but now their eyes were filled with hope.

Taking the passageway, he hurried through the dark nether-brick corridor, pausing at intersections to listen for pursuit. No alarm had been sounded...yet. Peering around corners, he streaked down the tunnel, looking for a way to get outside. Torches dotted the passageway walls, but they were spaced far apart, their circles of illumination not touching. Taking a sinewy path, the crafter was able to weave his way around the patches of light and stay in the shadows, hoping all the while that this would help him avoid any watchful eyes.

Suddenly, sorrowful moans filled the air; zombie-pigmen were coming! Moving quickly to the edge of an intersecting corridor, the crafter peered quickly around the corner. A group of monsters were coming: three zombies and one blaze. Pulling his head back abruptly, he looked for a place to hide. This passageway had no doors and no alcoves; just long straight tunnels of nether brick. He could now hear the mechanical breathing of the blaze, its strained wheezing adding a harsh dissonance to the melody of moaning wails.

What do I do, what do I do? he thought. *I can't just stand here. I have to hide.*

Casting more glances about the corridor, he still couldn't see a place to hide. Panic flooded his mind as he imagined the monsters rounding the corners and finding him just standing there. But then he noticed a large shadowy space between two torches. Moving quickly, he scurried into the darkness. The sound of his feet echoed off the hard stone walls and hammered away at his courage.

I hope they didn't hear that.

Diving to the ground, he laid down flat, his body stretched out and pressed against the wall on one side. Just as his head reached the ground, the zombies and blaze moved into the intersection.

If they come toward me, I'll be seen. Then I'll be dead.

The crafter held his breath and waited. The zombie-pigmen stopped in the middle of the intersection. Moving forward, the blaze looked down the corridors, deciding which way to go. Floating on its rotating blaze rods, the creature of flame started to move toward the crafter, the corridor growing slightly brighter—but then a zombie said something in its guttural, moaning voice. The blaze stopped and turned, glaring at the half-rotting monster.

"What did you say?" the blaze wheezed.

"This way. I think we go this way," the zombie grumbled, his shining sword pointing down a different corridor.

The other zombies nodded.

The blaze took a long, strained, mechanical breath and glared at the zombie, then floated away from the crafter.

"You should have said so earlier," it spat as it flicked the decaying creature with a small needle of flame.

The blaze moved past the monster and headed down the new corridor. Slowly, the zombie-pigmen followed, the glow of light from the blaze receding into the darkness.

The crafter's lungs started to burn. He hadn't realized that he had been holding his breath the entire time. When he breathed in again, the air tasted sweet, despite the smoke and ash; his body was starved for oxygen. Standing up slowly, he crept back to the intersection and looked around the corner. No monsters were in sight. Sighing, he let the overwhelming sense of panic flow from his body as he relaxed just a little.

That was close, he thought to himself.

Continuing his trek, he kept going in the same direction he had previously decided upon, looking for some kind of exit or window.

Fear ravaged his mind as he sprinted, making it difficult to think. He was not afraid of being killed— that was a fact that he'd come to accept since being brought down here to this terrible place. No, the burden that made coherent thought nearly impossible was the responsibility now heaped upon his shoulders. He had to find out what was going on down here, what the ghast king was doing. This task was critical, and the crafter could feel that all of Minecraft depended on him. His failure might mean the destruction of everything he loved and held dear.

He sprinted down the corridor for maybe another two hundred blocks, then slowed. He could see a glow suddenly start to light the passage ahead, a mechanical breathing sound filling the air. With the strained wheezing came the crackling sound of something burning, the smell of smoke getting stronger and stronger. In an instant, the crafter knew what it was... blazes, lots of them.

They were coming straight toward him.

Looking around, he saw nowhere to hide, just a long corridor stretching out before him and behind, an intersection ahead in the distance. And then the smell of something rotten and putrid wafted to him from behind, the sorrowful moans of creatures with no love for living things adding to the crackling sounds ahead; zombie-pigmen were surely behind him.

He was trapped.

His only hope of hiding lay in the intersection ahead. Sprinting with all his strength, he streaked forward. Disregarding the circles of torchlight, he shot through the patches of illumination. Their flickering glare stabbed at his eyes, which by now had become accustomed to the darkness. Ignoring his surroundings, the sounds of zombies getting louder behind him, and the glow of the blazes ahead, he simply charged forward with all his might, his focus on the intersection ahead.

Can I get there before the blazes do?

He thought about his fellow crafters back in the cell, the look of hope on their faces. Then the faces of his villagers floated into his mind: old Planter, and Farmer, and Digger, and Runner...poor Runner. The faces of friends and children looked down on him from his memory, all of them relying on him to find out what

Malacoda was doing down here.

I must make it to that intersection. I can't fail my village again!

Pushing aside the sense of panic and fear, he sprinted. As he ran, he could feel a wave of heat surging down the passage, heralding the oncoming blazes. The smell of smoke and ash was getting stronger, making it difficult to breathe. Using the last bits of his strength, he shot forward and turned the corner just as the glow of the blazes filled the corridor. Looking down this new passage for a place to hide, he saw a set of steps that led up to a balcony. Running up the steps, he leaped up onto the balcony and hid around the corner, his feet shuffling on the ash-covered ledge that overlooked the Nether. Pressing his back against the wall, he moved as far out onto the ledge as possible, hoping to disappear in the shadows. Bright yellow light lit the corridor as one of the blazes moved into the passage he had just left, its mechanical breathing filling his ears. It sounded as if it were right next to him, the smell of smoke making him want to cough, though doing so would mean his death. Swallowing the urge to clear his throat, he stayed completely still and waited.

He could hear the blaze get closer, its wheezing, mechanical breathing getting louder, but it did not ascend the steps to the balcony. Satisfied that all was as it should be, it moved back to the main corridor, then drifted away quickly to catch up with its kind. Letting out a soft cough, the crafter sighed and relaxed a bit. He was safe—for now.

Turning to look out over the Nether, he could see monsters everywhere; there were zombie-pigmen, blazes, magma cubes, skeletons, and of course, the ever-terrifying ghasts. A gigantic lava sea stretched out before him, its far shore not even visible. The lava bubbled and oozed, casting orange light all throughout the massive subterranean chamber. He was shocked by the immensity of the boiling sea. It seemed to stretch out, forever; the opposite shore lost in the ever-present haze.

And then, through the haze of smoke and ash that seemed to permeate everything in the Nether, he noticed an island of stone sitting in the middle of the huge sea of fire. A narrow bridge of rock stretched from the shore to the island; the grayish stones almost glowing with heat. He could see the rocky bridge stretch across the rusty netherrack to a massive opening in the fortress. A gigantic set of stairs spilled down from the dark opening of the citadel, reaching to the stone causeway below.

Numerous monsters were traversing the bridge and moving onto the massive island. Peering through the haze, he could see that the island was ringed with glowing blue cubes, maybe ten of them, with two places that still seemed incomplete, each standing out in stark contrast to the gray stone and nearby molten orange rock. The blue cubes sat atop blocks of obsidian, the dark blocks with their purple flecks of teleportation magic easily visible against the gray of the stone island. They looked almost translucent, as if they were made of glacial ice, even though the crafter knew that this couldn't be true. Ice could never exist in this fiery domain. They had to be made of something else, something strong enough to resist the intense heat. But what, and why did they need these blocks?

Just then, a group of zombie-pigmen emerged from an opening beneath him with a collection of prisoners: a crafter and six villagers. They drove the group of doomed souls toward the bridge, then pushed them single file across the pathway until they were all on the massive island. The NPCs walked with their heads down, shoulders slumped. They had the look of defeat about them, coupled with a sense of unbridled panic and fear. One of them walked with a limp, his left leg dragging on the ground ever so slightly. He had short dark hair that looked even darker in the orange light of the Nether. He was clothed in the black smock of a crafter.

It was the one from the prison cell!

As the NPCs walked, their eyes darted about at the collection of monsters nearby: the many blazes floating overhead, the armored skeletons (called wither skeletons) ringing the group, and of course, the ever-present ghasts floating high above the ground. There was no chance of escape for these poor villagers.

Slowly, Malacoda slid into view, drifting in on unfelt winds, his tentacles writhing like a nest of snakes. His disturbingly childlike countenance looked down on the villagers with a malicious, knowing smile that brought a chill to all—a strange feeling in this land of heat and flame. The crafter was separated from the group and pushed to an empty spot in the ring of blue blocks, a zombie-pigman's golden sword poking the man in the back without remorse, trying to hurry him, though the limp kept him at his pace. Once he was finally in place atop one of the obsidian blocks, a crafting bench and diamond blocks were tossed in front of the NPC.

"Now, crafter, it is time for you to craft," Malacoda said in a booming voice that seemed to fill the Nether, the sounds reaching the fortress.

"I won't craft anything for you, ghast," the crafter spat back.

The King of the Nether flicked a tentacle toward one of the villagers. In an instant, balls of fire streaked from the many blazes floating above the island and struck the villager, destroying him in an instant, the body of the NPC disappearing with a pop and leaving the few remnants of his inventory on the ground.

Malacoda floated down so that he was nearly face to face with the crafter.

"Now, let me ask you again," the ghast king continued. "You know what I want you to craft. Now do it, or more will die because of your disobedience."

"You're just going to kill us anyway!"

Another tentacle flicked. Zombie-pigmen advanced on one of the prisoners, pushing her backward with razor-sharp swords, driving her closer and closer to the edge of the island. Suddenly, one of the decaying beasts stepped forward and swung his mighty sword at the villager, pushing her back into the lava. She thrashed for a few seconds, then sank quickly, mercilessly, popping into non-existence as her health, her HP, was quickly extinguished.

Another villager had been killed.

"Must I ask you again, NPC?" Malacoda inquired, his eyes now starting to burn red with rage, his pupils looking as if lit with fire from within. "I have more of your pitiful villagers to kill, not just this rabble here." The ghast pointed up to his massive fortress, at the hundreds of NPCs that were slaving away. They were building extensions to his already gigantic castle of dark nether brick, expanding it to house his growing army. "I will kill a hundred of your precious NPCs to convince you of my resolve. You will, in the end, do as I command. NOW DO IT!!!"

The crafter looked up at the doomed souls working on the fortress, then down at his own villagers. The remaining four looked terrified beyond reason, and their eyes all sought him for hope...for mercy. All they wanted to do was live. They didn't care what the ghast wanted. The crafter looked into the eyes of each and could see the overwhelming sense of panic, their faces silently begging for life. Sighing, he acquiesced.

"Fine, I'll do what you ask, ghast," the crafter said

in a resignation.

Carefully picking up the crafting bench, he placed it on top of the obsidian block in front of him, then picked up the blocks of diamond. His hands became a fluid blur as they moved quickly across the bench. Pouring all of his crafting ability into the materials, he drove his very life force into the creation, cementing his magical Minecraft power into the object. The crafting bench started to give off a strange icy glow, a sapphire radiance shading those around him, driving the ever-present fiery red from their faces and making them look alive again, as if everything was OK. As the crafter built this new item for the ghast king, he flashed red, his HP diminishing. Waves of pain streaked across his face as his unibrow furled with agony. Square beads of sweat started to drip from his short brown hair. They fell to the hot ground, where they instantly turned to steam.

Another flash of red.

The crafting bench started to glow a soft blue.

More red...the crafter was losing more HP.

The bench started to glow brighter. The crafter poured the last bit of himself into the creation, his body cringing with every flash of red. Then a sound started to fill the air. They were his wails of pain. The crafter was now screaming as he expended the last threads of his life, infusing all that he was into the blocky object. And then a pop sounded as he disappeared, yet another victim of Malacoda's lethal plan.

What remained in his wake looked like a diamond crafting bench, with an intricate series of lines etched into each blocky face, its cobalt blue glow lighting the stones nearby. Smiling, Malacoda looked down at his newest addition and then nodded, flicking a curled tentacle toward the remaining villagers. Fireballs from the blazes overhead rained down on them, killing them all where they stood, their bodies disappearing in an instant as their remaining HP was extinguished.

Malacoda laughed, then drifted away.

The crafter on the balcony was surprised at what he'd just seen. He was not shocked by the needless death of the NPCs or the death of the crafter. No, he was amazed by what the crafter had created: a diamond crafting bench. There could be only one reason why the ghast king would need such a thing, and the very thought left his skin prickling with needles of fear. He had to get back to the others and tell them...The Lost Prophecy was true! Everyone had thought it just a myth, but he could see that it was true...and this was a great threat to Minecraft. He had to tell everyone, warn all NPCs in Minecraft somehow, or they were all lost. Standing, he started to head back down the stairs to the long passageway, but he hadn't noticed that it was now filled with light. A company of blazes stood at the bottom of the stairs, their fiery bodies blocking his escape.

His stomach dropped; he was trapped.

As he readied himself for their balls of flame, a sound filtered into his ears from behind. It was like the sound of a purring cat, coupled with the cries of some terribly sad child, like a baby torn from his mother's arms. The sound was overwhelmingly sad and terrifying at the same time. Turning around slowly, he saw that he stood face to face with Malacoda, the King of the Nether, his ironically childlike face filled with venomous hatred.

Oh no!

"What have we here?" Malacoda asked.

"Ahhh...ahhh..."

"Good answer," the ghast king said sarcastically.

"You can't do this," the crafter said in a desperate, shaking voice. "We will stop you—somehow."

"Stop me...ha ha ha," the ghast boomed. "You idiot crafters have done nothing but help me. I will have my victory here, then take my army to the Source and see it destroyed. When my dominance is complete and all of you insignificant NPCs are dead, I will take the Gateway of Light and consume the physical world. I will rule everything, and all living creatures will fear the name Malacoda."

The crafter swallowed as waves of terror rippled through him.

"We will stop you...*He* will stop you."

"HE?" Malacoda snapped as he hovered closer to the doomed crafter. "He is nothing but an insignificant bug that you NPCs cling to for salvation. I will have my victory and the User-that-is-not-a-user will bow to me for mercy...and then I will destroy him."

The ghast king slowly moved away from the crafter, his face softening a little, as if he were going to let him go.

"Say hello to him when you meet him," Malacoda said, his voice dripping with sarcasm.

And in the next instant, the crafter was enveloped in flame, fireball after fireball raining down upon the NPC.

Surprisingly, there was no pain. The crafter's mind was instead consumed with thoughts of his village and faces flashing through his mind: Carver, Planter, Runner, Builder, Farmer...his people, his responsibility. They had relied on him to keep them safe, and he had failed. Overwhelming grief swept over him as his health plummeted, but the emotion had not been evoked by his imminent death. Instead, he grieved over what Malacoda was trying to do. If the King of the Nether was successful, then...then... everything in Minecraft—everywhere—would be destroyed. The thought filled him with despair. The

Prophecy was actually unfolding; the Final Battle was here, and by the looks of it, Malacoda had a huge head start. Their only hope—no, their sole salvation—was the User-that-is-not-a-user.

Gathering the last bit of his life force, the crafter filled his mind with a single thought and tried to extend it, to hammer it ruthlessly into the very fabric of Minecraft, in hopes of reaching their savior. With his last breath, he screamed a cry of defiance and hope, reaching out to the User-that-is-not-a-user.

"USER-THAT-IS-NOT-A-USER, THE LOST PROPHECY IS—"

And then the darkness took him; the only evidence that he'd ever existed was a stone pickaxe on the ground.

CHAPTER 7

SHADOWS OF LIFE

Gameknight and Crafter emerged from the dark tunnel into a torch-lit crafting chamber. It hadn't been a long journey—only about twenty minutes or so in Minecraft time—but the small minecart had forced the two of them to crowd together and keep their heads low. It felt good to stand and stretch their legs again.

"I can't believe we didn't think of using the minecart network when we found that first abandoned village," Crafter said.

"Yeah, I know," Gameknight replied. "Maybe we had a lot on our minds."

They had used the vast network of tunnels that

wove throughout Minecraft to leave Crafter's new village in hopes of finding other NPCs who would help take up their cause. All of the villagers had been sent out to gather forces and prepare the Minecraft army for the battle that was about to crash upon their shoreline, and this minecart network was a critical tool in gathering forces. Thankfully, the monsters of the Overworld knew nothing about it. Gameknight and Crafter had chosen a random tunnel, and as expected, the rail line had led to another village; but by the smell of smoke and ash that instantly assaulted their senses, it was clear that they were too late.

"It looks like Malacoda has already been here," Crafter said, his young voice still sounding aged and wise to him.

The cavern was empty. Giant craters were gouged in the floor and walls. These sections had probably been destroyed by creepers...or fireballs...or...? A faint haze filled the chamber, and acrid smoke bit the back of their throats. Looking at the ground, Gameknight could see a fine coating of gray ash covering everything. It puffed up into small clouds as he walked across the floor. In one section, he could see smoky black soot on the walls, likely remnants from fireballs that had been thrown by ghasts or blazes. He had seen this before—charred remains of buildings and structures—but this sight was still something different altogether. The charred stain covered a section of the wall, but he could clearly see the outline of a body in the sooty patch; it was a clean section shaped like a person in the middle of the blackened stone. Someone had been standing there and had been blasted by fire, his body and life protecting the wall from being completely scorched.

It was horrible.

"You see that?" Crafter asked, gesturing to the wall.

Gameknight grunted and nodded, fear tickling the

edges of his mind. He couldn't bring himself to look at the sooty remains without imaging the terror that must have pulsed through that poor NPC's mind as his life ebbed away.

"This is terrible," Crafter said in a low, morose voice. "If only we'd gotten here in time to help."

"Yeah, I wish we could have been here to help," Gameknight lied. He hoped his deceit didn't show on his face, but he had no desire to face Malacoda and the monsters of the Nether.

The Nether was a place of fire and smoke. He had been there many times when this had been just a game to him, trolling many a player down there in that underground world, back when he'd been a griefer. He had loved taunting the zombie-pigmen and blazes, his arsenal of hacks and cheats keeping him safe. Now, he had no desire to go there. Just the thought of it made him shiver with fear.

But how had those monsters gotten here?

The Nether was a subterranean world that was carved out of solid rock, but not the normal material that made up the Overworld, the land in which the two friends now stood. No, the Nether was chiseled into a world of netherrack and soul sand—materials that didn't even exist in the Overworld. You could never reach the Nether by tunneling; a portal had to be used to move from the world of light to that world of smoke and flame. It was an alternate dimension that existed within Minecraft. Nobody really knew where the Nether was, nor understood what it meant to be in another dimension. Maybe only Minecraft's creator, Notch, understood what his twisted and self-aware computer code had created...or maybe even he didn't. Some theorized that the Source code had taken on a life of its own, and had created the Nether, as well as other dimensions, just because it could, its digital awareness stretching out and testing its capabilities. Gameknight had never understood how this could be true, and had read numerous debates on the Internet. But right now, he really didn't care. Right now, his every waking moment was consumed with fear and uncertainty. His very nightmares seemed to lurk within every shadow.

Glancing about the chamber, he scanned the cavern for threats, his butter sword (designated as such by the YouTuber who refused to say the word "gold") held at the ready. He had to admit that it kind of looked like butter in this light, although the magical shimmer to it reminded him of its true purpose...to take life.

"We should look around," Crafter suggested. "See if anyone is hiding and afraid to come out."

"You sure?" he asked, not wanting to look into those shadows. "Maybe we should just take a minecart to the next village and skip this one."

"Don't be silly. We have to see if there are any survivors and make sure that they are safe...maybe bring them with us. My great-great-grandfather used to tell me, 'The only thing worse than being alone is being forgotten.' We can't forget those who might still be here."

"Well...I guess..." Gameknight replied, his voice tinged with fear.

"It will be alright," Crafter answered, then jumped off the minecart rails and headed up the steps to the cavern entrance, small clouds of ash following each small footstep. "Come on, let's go up to the surface. We can split up and search the village twice as fast, then head out if it's not too late."

"OK," Gameknight999 replied reluctantly. He followed the young boy up the steps and into the tunnel that led to the tall cobblestone tower above.

Streaking through the rocky passageway, the pair headed toward the long vertical tunnel that stretched up to the tall cobblestone tower above. As they ran, they had to traverse multiple craters that had been blasted into the passage, some of them still warm. Gameknight could sense all of the hatred and malice that had smashed into this community coming from those smoldering holes; the echo of wicked malevolence was still strong. The monsters that had attacked this village had wanted to do nothing but kill and destroy. It made him cringe.

Finally, they reached the ladder that led to the surface. Crafter shot up instantly, without hesitation. Gameknight, however, grasped the rungs and stood still for a moment. He could feel the danger awaiting their arrival at the top of this ladder and was afraid, but knew he had to follow. That was his friend above him, and he could not let him go alone. Sighing, he started to climb.

They climbed as fast as they could. He could hear Crafter up ahead of him, though his small frame was lost in the darkness. Their hands and feet beat a steady rhythm on the ladder as they climbed, almost instantly falling in step and striking the ladder at the same time. The darkness around him seemed to be filled with shadowy forms. Imaginary clawed hands reached out at him, slashing away at his courage as he climbed. The higher they went, the closer they were to danger, and the more scared he became.

There were monsters up there, somewhere, I can feel them, he thought.

Well, he *thought* he could feel them. But maybe it was just the cowardice that seemed to be growing within him like a thorny weed...or maybe it was something else.

Suddenly, a sound echoed through the tunnel; it was a faint sound that seemed to come from very far away, but was still clearly audible. And soon it became clear that it was a strained voice, belonging to a speaker who was likely in terrible pain and also terribly sad. A sense of overwhelming despair and defeat resonated within the echoing words.

"*USER-THAT-IS-NOT-A-USER,   THE   LOST PROPHECY IS—*"

Gameknight stopped climbing. Chills crawled down his spine as goose bumps spread over his skin. Shivering, he felt terribly cold and alone, the sorrow in that voice bringing a tear to his eye.

"You hear that?" he shouted to his companion.

"What?"

"I said did you hear that voice?"

Crafter stopped climbing, then came back down a few rungs so that he was directly over him. "What are you talking about?"

"I heard someone yell out my name," Gameknight said quietly, his own voice sounding uncertain.

Crafter paused for a moment before answering, then spoke with a slow, calm voice.

"You probably imagined hearing this voice. It has been a long and trying day and you're tired...we both are. Let's just keep going."

Gameknight could hear the worry in Crafter's voice, as well as the disbelief, but he knew what he'd heard. Someone had been calling out to him. The despair in that sad person's voice still echoed within his mind. He was sure that person had died, and his last words had been sent out to the User-that-is-not-a-user. For some reason, that NPC thought Gameknight999 could help, that he was the answer to the problems that plagued Minecraft.

What a joke! I'm not the answer; I'm just a kid, a kid that was afraid of everything. What can I do? Nothing!

"Are you coming?" Crafter asked from higher up on the ladder.

Sighing, Gameknight999 continued his climb.

When the pair reached the top of the ladder, they found a similar scene; the entrance to the tunnel had been blown apart at the surface, evidence of Malacoda's rage. But instead of the remains of the castle-like tower surrounding the tunnel, they were shocked to find nothing. The entire tower had been destroyed, erased from the face of Minecraft.

Stepping through the rubble, the duo moved to the edge of the crater. Gameknight could see that it was late afternoon, with only a scant few hours until sunset. He shivered. Nighttime was monster time.

"We don't have much time," he said. "Let's get this search done."

"Fine," Crafter replied, his small form casting a shadow that was barely half the length of Gameknight's. "You search to the west, and I'll search to the east. We'll meet right back here at sunset."

Before Gameknight could object, his friend was gone. Sighing, he drew his sword and gripped it tight, then headed out.

Most of the homes on the west side were now little more than rubble, giving the impression that a mighty tornado of hatred had touched down here. Sections of the village were completely missing, with floating cubes of wood and cobblestone marking where homes had once stood. Looking at the destruction, Gameknight felt sad. He could imagine the terror the NPCs must have felt as the monsters moved through their village. They were helpless inhabitants of this community, unable to fight back or do anything other than hide. And from what he had heard in the last village, hiding could get you killed.

Sprinting past the completely obliterated sections, he moved to a part of the village that was only partially destroyed. Some homes still stood, though the scars of violence were clearly visible. Smoking roofs and shattered doorways marked each structure, some of them more damaged than others. Walking amidst the destruction, Gameknight saw more charred walls where the outlines of people clearly stood out as a testament to the many lives extinguished by the monsters of the Nether, by Malacoda. He shuddered and turned away. The thought of the terrible fiery event that had left these gruesome works of art on the walls made his stomach heave. There was too much death and destruction in this digital world.

"Minecraft was supposed to be fun," he said aloud to no one, hoping his voice would push back the specter of fear that stalked his soul.

He thought he heard something, and instantly stopped to listen. It sounded like the shuffling of feet... or was it just his imagination?

"Anyone here?" he yelled.

Silence.

He moved through the half-broken homes, sifting through the remains, looking for chests or tools or anything else that could be helpful. Moving to the next building, Gameknight saw another sooty shadow of life, this one burned into the ground near what must have been the front door—though now it was little more than a charred threshold. Blocks of cobblestone floated on the ground near what had once been a wall, bobbing up and down as if riding on some invisible ocean swells. Giving the blackened stains a wide berth, he stepped cautiously into the house and peered into the shadows. He half expected some kind of nightmare to jump out and devour him.

"Hello. Is anyone there?"

More silence.

Moving out of the house, Gameknight walked past three completely devastated structures, their walls and roofs burned away, with only the remnants of their foundations hinting at their past existence. He wished he had Shawny, his only friend, here...well, his only friend except for Crafter. In the past, Gameknight had been a griefer, a cyber bully who would go onto other people's servers and do as much damage as possible before getting kicked off. He used to think it was fun, destroying other people's creations for his own enjoyment, but that only lasted until he had been pulled into Minecraft for real. Now, he saw firsthand the consequences of that sort of destructive and anti-social behavior. Because of his griefing, he basically had no friends in Minecraft except for Shawny—a fact that had nearly caused his destruction on the last server. If Shawny hadn't brought all those users to help him fight against the monsters of the Overworld, then that server would have been destroyed, extinguishing the lives of all the NPCs who called it home. And in those last moments on that server, when their defeat had seemed imminent, Gameknight had finally come to understand the meaning of sacrifice, and what it meant to help other people just for the sake of helping them. It had felt good knowing that he was probably helping to save lives he didn't even know, Minecraft NPCs he'd never met; it had filled him with an overwhelming sense of courage and purpose.

He wished he had that courage now.

Moving to the next house, Gameknight shook with fear as he peered into the blasted remains. The scarred exterior of this structure, with its signs of fire and explosions painted on the walls, showed the effects of Malacoda's angry brush. Sticking his head slowly over a broken wall, he peered into the room. There was a chest in the corner sitting in a pile of rubble, the wall behind it completely collapsed. The street was visible through the missing wall. The brown dirt road was starting to fade to a rosy red as the sun neared the horizon.

He had to hurry.

Jumping over the shattered wall, he moved into the broken home. On one wall was a sign with the words 'BLACKBLADE48429 WAS HERE' written in tall letters; it was obviously something left there by some user. Next to it was another sign, the edges slightly charred. It said 'PHASER_98' and 'KING_CREEPKILLER.' Below that was another sign with the names 'WORMICAN' and 'MONKEYPA...' the bottom edge of the sign too badly burned to read. There had been users on this server at one time...but where had they all gone?

Gameknight sighed. He wished he had some of these users with him right now.

I wonder how old that sign is? he thought to himself.

Shuffle...shuffle...shuffle.

What was that?

A tickle of fear slithered down his spine.

Was that something moving outside?

Casting his gaze back to the exploded doorway, Gameknight peered into the shadows. Nothing... probably just his imagination again. Focusing back on the interior of the battered home, he moved to the chest and opened it. A bow...there was a bow...and arrows, two stacks of arrows. This was something he could definitely use. Taking the bow and arrows, he put them into his inventory, removing stacks of cobblestone to make room. As he turned and closed the chest, he heard the shuffling sound again, like many feet moving all at once.

"Who's there?" he yelled, his voice cracking with fear. "Crafter, is that you?"

Thunderous silence.

Moving slowly to the shattered wall, Gameknight peered into the street outside. The shadows from the surviving buildings stretched across the ground, trying to reach the other side of the street before darkness overtook them. He had to hurry. Moving out into the street, he glanced around, looking for threats.

"Is anyone here?" he said, this time not so loudly.

More silence—not even a pig oinking or a cow mooing. There was not a single sound anywhere. It was as if every living thing had been removed from this village. He shivered and started to head back to Crafter when he heard the shuffling noise again; it was definitely the scuffling of many feet across a hard ground. Spinning around, he looked behind him... nothing, only the empty street staring back at him. Turning to head back, Gameknight was suddenly face to face with a creeper, its mottled black and green face starting to glow white as the monster readied itself to detonate. This close, the creeper would certainly kill him. All he had to do was strike out at the beast to stop the detonation process, but fear paralyzed him, fear and panic. He couldn't move. The hissing of the creeper became louder as it got closer to detonating.

And then suddenly an arrow streaked out of the darkness and hit the creeper in the head. This wound stopped the creeper, making it turn to look for the source of the arrow. Another arrow shot out of the shadows and struck the creeper, this time in its chest.

"MOVE!" a voice yelled from the darkness.

The command was enough to shock Gameknight into motion. Drawing his enchanted sword, he hacked at the creeper before it could respond. He could feel his sword collide with the creature's flesh, biting into its mottled skin. The creeper started to hiss and glow again as it tried to explode, but Gameknight was giving it no quarter. He swung his golden sword, smashing its side. More arrows shot out of the darkness, piercing it again, and the detonation process was interrupted. The creeper flashed red again and again as Gameknight999's blows landed home. And then the creature disappeared, its HP completely consumed by the joint attack, a small pile of gunpowder on the ground where it had stood.

That was close.

Gameknight started to shake at the thought of how close he'd come to death.

Why did I freeze? he thought. *Why didn't I attack the creeper as soon as I'd seen it? Why didn't I...*

"Are you crazy or something?" a woman's voice said from the darkness. "That was a creeper. You don't just stand there...you move...you kill...or you get killed."

She emerged from the long shadows that were starting to kiss the other side of the street, the rosy glow of sunset slowly fading to black. She was young—not quite an adult, but not a child either. Something in between. Bright red hair flowed down across her shoulders, the tangle of curls glowing in the light of sunset, framing her face with a scarlet halo. In her hand was a bow, an arrow notched and ready to fire, the barbed end pointed at him.

"Who are you? What are you doing here?" she demanded. "Are you a user...maybe a griefer?" She drew back the arrow and aimed it at his chest.

"Aaaaah...I'm Gameknight999, and we're just here to help," he stammered.

"As you can see, you're a little late, and not very much help either."

"You mind aiming that thing somewhere else?" he said, pointing at the arrow with his sword.

"How about you put that sword away first?" she snapped. "I don't trust anything that carries a gold sword. That's the sword of a Nether monster, probably a zombie-pigman. How is it *you* have it? Are you some kind of new Nether creature?" She took a step forward, moving farther out of the shadows and drawing the arrow back a little farther.

"Don't be ridiculous," said a young voice from down the street.

It was Crafter.

"This is Gameknight999, the User-that-is-not-a-user, and we're here to look for survivors."

"Well, you found one, though I don't need your help," she said, turning to look at Crafter as he approached. Her face showed surprise when she saw the young boy in the traditional garb of a village crafter. "Who are you?"

"I'm Crafter, as you can see," he said, holding his arms out wide to show his black and gray smock, the sigil of his station. "But right now, we need to get somewhere safe. It's getting dark. Come, I found a secure place to hide through the night."

Feeling safer in the presence of Crafter, Gameknight put away his sword.

"Hide? Who wants to hide?" the woman asked as she slowly lowered her bow, her menacing glare still on the User-that-is-not-a-user.

"What?" Gameknight asked.

The woman glared at him in silence; her trust had not been completely won.

Suddenly, a terrible moaning filled the air. Shivers trickled down Gameknight's spine as a group of zombies stepped out into the street, the burning sun completely set. Their cold black eyes spotted him instantly and shuffled toward him, arms extended. The light from the torches reflected off their razor-sharp nails, making them appear to glow for just an instant. Crafter moved to his friend's side.

"Gameknight, I count eight of them...too many. What do you want to do?"

Glancing around, he saw a narrow alleyway that

ran between the backs of some homes, the walls along the alley still intact. Remembering the spiders he'd led along the valley, he spoke quickly.

"We'll lead them down that alleyway," the User-that-is-not-a-user said, pointing with his golden sword. "You, Hunter, find a good vantage point to fire from down in the alley and get ready, we'll bring them to you."

"I don't run from monsters," she said as she notched an arrow.

"Just do as the User-that-is-not-a-user says," Crafter snapped. "And stop being a fool."

"Come on," Gameknight said, his mind in a blur.

He and Crafter ran into the narrow alleyway and waited while Hunter sprinted down to the end, looking for a good vantage point. The sounds of the zombies grew louder as they approached, their sorrowful wails chiseling away at Gameknight's courage.

Hold your ground, he said to himself. *I won't abandon Crafter again.*

Soon, the putrid smell of the decaying creatures began to fill the air; they were getting close. He wanted to hold his breath, hoping to keep the rotten smell out of his mouth, but knew he had to keep breathing.

And then their sad moans echoed down the alleyway as the group of monsters rounded the corner. They stood there for a moment, eyeing the surroundings. Gameknight could see their cold, dead eyes scanning the confining cobblestone walls with concern. On the last server, these beasts would have instantly charged, but these creatures were the best of the best, the smartest and strongest, and had made their way up through the server planes to this server. These zombies were not fools; they'd need some prodding.

"Hey filthy zombies, why don't you come down here

and say hello," Gameknight taunted. "What's wrong, are you afraid of two helpless NPCs?"

The zombies stirred a little.

"You see, Crafter," he said in a loud voice, "I always told you zombies were not just stupid, but cowards as well."

The zombies now looked visibly agitated, but the one at the front did not budge. Its black eyes were fixed on Gameknight, a look of vile hatred on its face, but it stood fast. He had to get them into this narrow alleyway to neutralize their numerical advantage. That way, they'd only have to fight two at a time, while at the same time leading them down to alley to Hunter. Trying to release this flood of anger, he took a few steps forward and glared into the cold, dead eyes. Pulling a block of cobblestone from his inventory, he threw it at the beast.

"Come on, let's dance."

The block struck the decaying creature on the side of the head with a thump. This made the monster wail a blood-curdling scream that brought a chill to Gameknight.

The monsters surged forward. Gameknight jumped backward as the lead zombie swiped at him, its razor-sharp nails whistling through the air, just missing his head. Memories of Erebus and his monster horde flashed through his mind. He could almost see all of those terrible creatures slashing and tearing at him on the last server. Panic and fear flooded through him, overwhelming his brain. In his mental haze, everything began to feel like a dream, as if he were watching it from somewhere else.

And then something flashed across his vision, something sharp and vicious. His body jumped back without thought, then moved forward and struck at the zombie, his sword slashing with practiced precision.

The monster screamed and charged forward, the others following its lead. He and Crafter stepped back as the monsters crowded into the alleyway, the narrow confines only allowing two to stand abreast. Gameknight moved without thought, his mind filled with panic but his sword arm filled with rage. Stepping further back, he and Crafter drew the monsters forward, slashing at the two zombies at the front. Crafter said something, but Gameknight could not understand. All that reached his ears were the wails of the zombies, their sad, angry moans filling the air.

Suddenly, something streaked through the air and passed right between Gameknight and Crafter; it was an arrow. It struck the lead zombie, and was followed by another and another until the zombie disappeared. More arrows shot into the monsters as they advanced. Between shots, Crafter lunged at the beasts, attacking then retreating. Gameknight tried to help, but all he could do was just slowly back down the alley, letting the dream play itself out.

Crafter screamed next to him as zombie claws found his shoulder. This snapped Gameknight out of the dream. Jumping forward, he slashed his golden sword toward the zombie while Crafter retreated, his body moving on autopilot even though his mind was still consumed by fear. He now became a whirlwind of death. Moving like the Gameknight of old, he spun from one target as he lunged at the other. Chopping at an outstretched green arm, then slashing under a clawed attack, he focused his rage on these creatures.

I HATE BEING SO AFRAID, he screamed within his mind as he killed another zombie.

Continuing their attacks, he and Crafter slowly back down the alleyway as Hunter's missiles plunged into the monsters. Between the three of them, there was soon only one zombie remaining. With its health nearly depleted, it stopped its attacks and stepped back. Looking straight at Gameknight, it spoke in a guttural, animal-like voice.

"You can't stop us. Malacoda will cleanse all the servers of the infestations that are NPCs when he destroys the Source." The monster then trained its black eyes on Crafter. "All the King of the Nether needs is your kind to complete his task, then he will lead us to victory. Your days are numbered."

"What do you mean he needs my kind?" Crafter asked. "Tell me, if you are so confident."

The zombie smiled an eerie, rotting smile then opened his mouth to speak, but just then an arrow streaked over Crafter's shoulder and struck the zombie in the chest. With its HP consumed, it disappeared, leaving behind a piece of its rotten zombie flesh and three balls of XP. Crafter looked at Gameknight as the glowing balls streaked to the duo.

"What do you think he meant?" Crafter asked. "All he needs is my kind...you think the zombie meant he needs NPCs?"

Gameknight shrugged his shoulders. Footsteps sounded behind them, making them spin and get ready for more fighting. But it was Hunter. She had a huge smile on her face, her wild red hair streaming behind her as she ran.

"That was fun," she said.

"Fun?" Gameknight snapped. "That wasn't fun, that was terrifying. You don't know what it's like to kill something face to face, with their claws and fangs tearing into your body. You have the luxury of killing from a distance like it's some kind of a game. Next time, we'll switch, and you stand here with a sword while I shoot the arrows from 30 blocks away."

"As if you could," she snapped.

"That's enough," Crafter said in a commanding

voice. "Right now, we need someplace safe to rest and heal, and I've found just the place."

He then turned and ran off down the street, Gameknight and this new stranger obediently in tow.

Is she friend or foe?

Something about this woman was very unsettling; an angry and violent shadow seemed to envelop her, even more than the darkness that was now claiming the village. Gameknight shuddered and tried to push back his anxiety, but wasn't very successful, as the icy fingers of dread still clung onto him.

CHAPTER 8

HUNTER

Crafter led the party back to the center of the village, where the tall cobblestone tower had once stood. The homes near the tower were also heavily damaged, with the charred shadows of life burned into the walls nearby. Gameknight looked away as soon as he saw what they were, the shadowy remains filling him with a sense of sadness and unease. He'd be glad to get inside as soon as possible.

Turning down a side street, Crafter took them to a small wood and stone house that had a porch extending out from the side. Gameknight instantly recognized the structure; it was a blacksmith's home. He could see the line of furnaces on the stone porch, with a crafting bench and chest standing nearby.

"Quickly, let's get inside," Crafter said as he mounted the steps, pushing open the door.

They filed through the doorway, Gameknight

closing it once they were all inside. Torches lit the interior, filling it with a soft yellow glow. A table sat in one corner of the room, with two wooden seats up against the wall. Windows had been placed evenly on the walls of the home, but one of them was missing. He moved to the missing window and filled the space with a block of dirt, making it impossible for a skeleton's arrow to find someone inside. At the other side of the room was a dark stairway that led up to the second level. The woman pulled out her bow and ran upstairs, an arrow notched and ready to fire. Crafter followed, his stone sword drawn.

"Come on, let's make sure everything is safe," Crafter said to his friend.

Gameknight sighed, then drew his golden sword, its shimmering razor-sharp edge staining the walls with an iridescent blue glow. Reluctantly, he followed the pair up the stairs to the second story. There was nothing there—just another torch-lit room. Two beds sat in the corner, each covered with the typical red blanket, the pillows a crisp, clean white. Glass windows adorned each wall, giving a spectacular view of the village; it had likely been an excellent and terrible vantage point from which to watch the horrors that had befallen this village.

"This was Blacky's house," the woman said. "Our village blacksmith. He used to make the best arrows and armor, until they..."

Slowly she raised her hand, fingers spread wide, then clenched it into a fist high over her head. A tear trickled down her face as she squeezed her hand, an angry scowl etched on her face as her arm shook with strain. She then looked down and lowered her hand. When she raised her face again, Gameknight could see a cold, violent look in her eyes. It was as if she was going to make the entire universe pay for what had happened to her village.

"Come, let us sit down and introduce ourselves," Crafter said, gesturing to the beds. "We should be safe here tonight."

Crafter sat on one of the beds and motioned for the others to sit opposite him. Gameknight put away his sword and sat across from Crafter, making room for the woman to sit next to him. They could hear the sounds of night just outside the walls of Blacky's home. Monsters were emerging from the nearby forest to prowl through the village. The moaning of zombies and the clattering sounds of skeleton bones filled the air. Gameknight saw the woman move to the window and look out into the night as if she longed to be out there with the monsters instead of safely hidden within this building...strange.

Backing away from the window, she took a step into the torchlight. Her hair surprised him. He faintly remembered something about it, but the battle with the creeper and zombies had driven it from his mind. Now he could see it clearly. Her hair was vibrant red, long and wiry, with tight curls on each strand like clusters of stretched-out springs. Her dark brown eyes glared straight into him as she stood there, looking at the duo. Her gaze was filled with a peculiar sadness that was both sorrowful and hateful at the same time.

Sighing, she put her bow back into her inventory. As soon as the bow disappeared, her arm linked across her chest, hands tucked up into sleeves. Casting a cautious glance at Gameknight, she moved to his side and sat.

"My name is Hunter, and this was my village."

"It is good to meet you, Hunter, even though it's under sad circumstances," Crafter said. "You have already met Gameknight999 here. He is the User-that-is-not-a-user, the one mentioned in the Prophecy."

Her unibrow rose with curiosity as she looked at Gameknight, her deep brown eyes boring straight into him.

"So he is the one who will save us all?" she asked Crafter. "Then I guess we're in a whole lot of trouble." She turned to face Gameknight. "Nice job with that creeper back there," she said sarcastically.

He frowned.

"First things first," Crafter said. "Gameknight, let's free her hands."

"What are you talking about?" Hunter asked.

"You'll see," Crafter replied.

Gameknight pulled a crafting bench from his inventory, then placed it on the ground. Pulling out his pickaxe, he stood in front of the block and glared at the newcomer.

"As quickly as you can, craft something," Crafter said.

"Like what?" she asked.

"It doesn't matter," Gameknight999 replied. "Just craft anything...you'll see."

Hunter grunted, then stood and moved toward the crafting bench. As soon as she was in front of the brown striped block, her hands separated again as they started to move, making some kind of wooden tool. In an instant, Gameknight swung his pickaxe down onto the crafting bench, shattering it to pieces with three quick blows. In the shower of splintered wood, Hunter stared down at her hands in wonder, her eyes wide with amazement.

"How did you...?"

"We'll explain in a minute," Crafter answered, a wry smile on his face. "First, tell us what happened here. What attacked to your village?

"You can't tell? They destroyed my village—killed men, women, and children while they had everyone herded into the crafting chamber." Her voice was filled with rage. "You saw the scorch marks outside. The blazes just launched fireball after fireball at the people, my friends, if they didn't move fast enough."

She paused to take a breath, the horror of those memories playing back within her mind, her body shaking ever so slightly. The moan of a zombie floated through the air, making her glance at the window with a venomous glare. Then she continued.

"At first they didn't even say anything, just blasted away at us. Then the creepers came and started blowing open the walls to homes so that they could herd the people out into the center of town, near the tower. They used people as...as..."

She had to stop speaking for a moment, but not because she was on the verge of tears. Rather, her rage was barely held in check. Gameknight could see her hands clenched into tight fists, ready to strike out at any monster within reach. He moved to the other bed and sat down next to Crafter.

She continued. "They used people as target practice, attacking them with fireballs if the others didn't come out of their homes. I saw them blast away at some kids. The blazes and ghasts were just shooting fireball after fireball at them, for no reason at all. The zombie-pigmen kept the village surrounded so that nobody could escape. A few tried, but they didn't get very far.

"I had been coming back from hunting when they fell on the village. A couple of zombie-pigmen saw me come out of the forest and came after me, but they didn't realize I was a hunter. I ran back to the forest, then took 'em down with my bow. They didn't die right away, though...I wouldn't let 'em. The zombies followed me through the forest with my arrows sticking out of their bodies. Those rotting creatures didn't have enough sense to go back to the village where it was safe; that's what these monsters do, chase their prey until it's over, one way or another. Well, I wouldn't let it be over. I wanted those two zombies to suffer as long as possible."

She stopped again to take a breath. Some locks of her fiery hair had fallen onto her face, and she pushed them back over an ear with an annoyed look, as if they did it on purpose. Glancing down at her newly freed hands, she continued.

"After I killed them, I went to the edge of the forest, but I could see that there were too many monsters in the village for me to return. Stitcher...my little sister...I knew I couldn't help her, so I waited it out until they left with their prize: one lone survivor. I was too far away to tell who it was, but I could tell that they had what they'd come for. I'm pretty sure everyone else is dead."

"Why do you say that?" Gameknight asked.

She gave him an angry glare, as if his question had been responsible for the whole tragedy.

"Because they left before sunrise," she snapped. "If there had been anyone else alive, the monsters would have stayed and hunted for them."

"What did you do after the monsters left?" Crafter asked, his young voice strained with emotion.

"I hunted in the forest for a time, looking for something to do, somewhere to be, then found a cave. It was filled with a handful of zombies and spiders. I focused my rage on them and made them pay for what their cousins did to my village. They didn't die quickly—no, they were not worthy of a quick death, so I played with them and made them suffer." She turned her head and looked up at the ceiling, her mind lost in the memories. Her voice lowered, almost to a whisper, and there was a hint of sadness to it. "I thought it would make me feel better somehow, making those creatures suffer, but it only made me thirst for more revenge." Her gaze came back to Crafter and Gameknight, her voice louder again and filled with venom. "I thought I would live in that cave and just stay away from every living thing, but knew that I had to come back and see what happened to my village and my family."

"And then you ran into us?" Crafter said.

"Right."

"And you didn't see the monsters take any villagers away?" the young boy asked.

She shook her head as the sounds of moaning filtered into the house, with the clicking of spiders adding percussion to the zombies' vocal performance. Hunter turned and glanced longingly at the window before addressing Crafter.

"When I came back from hunting, the monsters were already here...why?"

"In the last village we were in they took prisoners," Crafter said.

"So what's his deal?" she asked, gesturing to Gameknight. "Is he really the one from the Prophecy?"

"You see his name over his head?" Crafter asked.

She grunted and nodded.

"Only users have their names over their heads, But as you know all users are connected to the server with the server thread that we can see shooting straight up into the air. As you can see, he has no server thread connecting him to the CPUs."

She grunted again.

"He *is* the one," Crafter said confidently—a little too confidently for Gameknight's taste. "He saved the last server, my server. I'm sure he'll save this one as well, right Gameknight?"

This time it was Gameknight's turn to grunt.

Hunter scowled, then stood and moved back to the window. The clattering sounds of skeleton bones now filled the air. Her bow suddenly materialized in her left hand, an arrow in her right. Gameknight wasn't sure she'd known that she'd pulled them out. The sounds of monsters had drawn her to the window, and now it looked as if all she wanted to do was go out there, into the night, and kill. Recovering herself, she looked at Crafter and Gameknight. A scowl was etched on her face, her eyes filled with a cold, dead light, like a creature that no longer had any emotions…except for hatred and spite. Gameknight stood and got ready to draw his sword, unsure what her next move was going to be.

"So what now?" she asked.

"We're gathering NPCs to fight the monsters," Gameknight said. "We're going to stop them on this server and not let them get to the Source."

"The Source…" she said in a dreamlike voice.

The Source was where all the Minecraft computer code came from, where updates, bug fixes, and processing power flowed from to keep all the Minecraft worlds functioning. If the Source was destroyed, then all of Minecraft would be destroyed.

"Are you going to stop the mobs like you did with that creeper?" she asked in an accusatory tone.

"That creeper surprised me, that's all!" Gameknight snapped.

"Sure it did."

He grunted, then moved to the opposite side of the room to look out another window. The village was lit with pale moonlight, a silvery illumination that made things look ethereal and dreamlike… except for the monsters. They looked like nightmares. He could see the occasional zombie or skeleton walking through the streets, looking for something to kill. A few creepers lurked on the outskirts of the village, but not very many. It was as if the monsters knew that this village was used up, and most had already gone off somewhere else.

"Why did you return, Hunter, if you thought everyone had been killed?" Crafter asked.

"I had to see if any of my family had survived," she said in a quiet, dejected voice. "My mother and father had been working down in the crafting chamber. And my sister, Stitcher, had been...had been..."

She stood there silently, a pained look on her face.

"I'm sure she's alright," Gameknight said. Crafter nodded his blond head.

"What do you two know about it?" she snapped. "She might be dead."

"Or she might not," Crafter replied. "The monsters came here for your crafter, not your sister. They didn't care about the villagers—only your crafter."

"How do you know this?"

"Because we've seen it in many other villages," Gameknight replied. "We aren't sure why they're doing it, but the ghast king in the Nether, Malacoda, is responsible for all this destruction."

"Yes, Gameknight's right," Crafter added. "Malacoda is methodically collecting all the crafters he can get his hands on, for some scheme as well as taking a few prisoners back to the Nether"

"Malacoda," she grumbled, looking down at the ground for a moment. She eyed Crafter again. "You mean Stitcher could be alive...they could all be alive?"

Crafter stood and put a small, reassuring hand on her shoulder. "Yes, and we'll help you to find them if you come with us."

She stood there for a moment and considered the offer, then turned and looked outside at the random collection of monsters on the street below, her fingers stroking the feathers of an arrow almost lovingly. Then she addressed Crafter.

"Fine. I'll go with you, but in the morning, not now."

"That's fine," Crafter interjected. "We need to rest as well. In the morning, then."

"I'll stand the first watch," she said.

She then turned and headed down the stairs. Gameknight heard the stairs creak under her weight, then listened as the front door swung open and closed abruptly. Stepping to the window, he could see her move with the grace of a predatory cat, flitting from shadow to shadow, an arrow notched in her bow, ready, waiting.

"A sad story," Crafter said, shaking his head.

"A strange girl."

"Sorrow can change anyone, but come, let's get some rest."

Gameknight moved to the other bed and lay down, his body suddenly feeling very weary, and in the next instant sleep overtook him.

CHAPTER 9
DREAMS

T he haze from his restless dreams lifted slowly from Gameknight's mind. His arm was slightly numb, with pins and needles prickling his nerves as blood flow gradually returned to it. Sitting up, he stretched his aching back, sore from being hunched over for so long. His cheek felt hot and a little numb, like how it usually felt after he had fallen asleep at his desk in history class. Reaching out, he stretched his arms wide, then rubbed his cheek, the feeling slowly flowing back to the side of his face.

It was dark and cold. He felt as if he were underground somewhere, and an icy, damp feeling chilled him to the bone. Stretching out his right hand without thinking, he reached forward, not sure why. His hand bumped into something hard, its sharp edges scratching his fingertips. Grabbing for the switch that he'd flipped a thousand times, he turned on the desk lamp, spilling light into the room. Looking at the lamp, he could see that it was made out of old jet engine parts, all of them welded together in a complicated spiral pattern that looked like a mechanical tornado; it was a creation his father had called the CFM56-lamp—he still had no idea what that meant.

The desk lamp...his father's desk lamp...he was back at home!!!

He had made it out of Minecraft...somehow.

Looking down at his hands, Gameknight could see his fingers—round fingers, not square ones. Extending his arms, he saw the subtle curved shape to his wrists and forearms. He wasn't a blocky Minecraft character anymore; he was human!

Glancing about the basement, he saw the licorice 3D-printer and the ketchup bottle opener and the glasses-iPod thing and the machine-gun marshmallow launcher...and...the digitizer, which was pointing directly at him. He was back in his basement again. He was home! Sound trickled down the stairway from above. It was a bouncy song from some kid's show... his sister.

Gameknight smiled.

He was back. Grinning, he thought about his adventure in Minecraft, thought about the terrors and the nightmares, and shook ever so slightly. The thoughts of zombie claws reaching out at him and creepers hissing nearby...and Erebus...were all still fresh in his memory. He shook again, this time a little harder...

Erebus—the nightmare of nightmares. Looking around the basement, he could see strange shadows cast upon the concrete walls; they were long, jagged shadows formed by the many tall contraptions that populated the room. Some of the shadows looked like monstrous hands reaching out from the darkness to ensnare some poor unfortunate soul. Peering into these shadows, places where the weak lighting couldn't quite reach, he felt like he was momentarily back in Minecraft, looking for zombies in the shadowy crevasses and dark corners of an underground cavern.

"This is ridiculous," he said aloud, to no one.

Pushing away these lurking fears, Gameknight turned back around and faced his computer monitor. An image from Minecraft was displayed on the screen, but nothing was moving. It showed the original location where he had spawned. There was a tall waterfall raining down from a high overhang, the water cascading down into an underground cavern. He could see torches around the opening to his hidey-hole and a tall tower of dirt atop the outcropping, torches decorating its peak. And at the center of this image stood his character, his Minecraft moniker, Gameknight999, floating above the iron-clad character in tall white letters. Reaching out, he placed his hand gently on the mouse and gave it the smallest of nudges.

Suddenly, a buzzing noise started to fill the air behind him, like the sound of many angry hornets approaching from afar. The buzzing became louder and louder in the time it took him to turn in his chair to see what it was. The digitizer, it was glowing yellow. At first, it was just a faint glow, but then it grew in intensity as the buzzing sound became angrier and angrier. It was turning on and getting ready to reach out with its burning hand of light to draw him back in again.

"I don't want to go back," he moaned to the empty

basement.

The buzzing grew louder, and the yellow glow was now like the sun.

"No...NO!"

Just as a white beam of light shot out of the end of the digitizer, he launched himself out of his chair and away from the desk, rolling across the dusty concrete floor. Crawling away from the buzzing, fiery sphere of illumination, he glanced over his shoulder. He expected to see the blazing shaft of light lancing into the desk, either cutting it apart like a high-powered laser or enveloping it in its luminous grasp and drawing it into Minecraft. But instead, the beam of light had formed a glowing circular patch of light that just floated in the air. The center of the circle then shifted in color, from a glaring white to a brilliant yellow and then to dark blue, the shading oscillating from one to the next in seconds. Gradually, the color settled to a consistent, deep lavender, something he recognized, though he couldn't recall where from. Dark purple particles started to decorate the edges of the circle, flying out of the patch of light, dancing about for an instant, and then falling back in as if drawn by some invisible current.

This thing looked like...like...oh no!

Just then, something emerged from the purple circle. Two long, straight things extended out from the purple surface, each tipped with five sharp black claws. The things were a mottled green, as if they were made of decayed matter. A rotten, stinking aroma wafted into the air and filled the basement, making Gameknight gag. He knew that terrible smell.

Oh no...not again!

The two long, straight green things emerged farther, revealing that they were both joined to a blocky shape that was shaded light blue on the top half, dark blue on the bottom. The colors looked tattered and faded, like clothes worn for a century too long. The thing moved forward until a face appeared from the violet circle of light; it was a face with black, cold, and dead eyes that expressed an overwhelming hatred for all living things.

No...no. Gameknight started to whimper as he crawled into the corner of the basement. He drew himself between the wobbly legs of an old table that was covered with twenty years of discarded and forgotten junk, trying to get as far from the monster as he could.

And then the sound hit his ears, a sorrowful moaning from a creature that was grieving for something it could never have yet could almost taste. This was the sound of a monster that thirsted to be alive, but could sense that the promise of life was held just barely out of its reach. This was the voice of a creature that had turned bitter and hateful toward all living things and wanted to inflict its suffering on anyone it came across. This was a zombie...a Minecraft zombie.

The Gateway of Light...they'd found the Gateway of Light!

That meant that the Source must have been destroyed. Crafter...his friend, Crafter...

The zombie slowly stepped out of the circle of purple light, which Gameknight now recognized as a portal from Minecraft. Moving forward, it stretched its arms out, bumping into the licorice 3D-printer and knocking it to the ground, the plywood structure making a sickening crack when it hit. As it moved away from the portal, another zombie emerged, followed by a gigantic spider. The creatures lacked their familiar low resolution blocky appearance as seen on the monitor while playing the game; rather, they had the terribly real, high-resolution appearance Gameknight had come to know while trapped within Minecraft; their blocky shapes covered with realistic and terrifying features. The light from the desk lamp gleamed off the deadly, razor-sharp *fingernails that decorated the zombie's rotting hands, and made him shudder with fear. The shadowy, hooked claws at the end of each spider leg seemed to be glowing with an inner light, their black needle-like tips clicked on the concrete floor as the spider scurried across the room. The arachnid's curved mandibles also reflected the light from the desk lamp, making them gleam with dark intent as they clicked hungrily. Gameknight could see the tiny dark hairs along its legs moving in every direction at once, anger boiling from its numerous red eyes.*

They were here.

The stench of rotten flesh grew stronger as more zombies and spiders flowed from the portal. The clicking of the spiders added a percussive melody to the moaning symphony that was already filling the air, the volume growing louder and louder as more creatures crowded together in the basement. The monsters pressed their bodies up against each other, but seemed afraid of these unfamiliar surrounds, trying to avoid brushing against the many devices that sprouted up out of the clutter. But as their numbers grew, they started to push against the basement chaos, knocking over an old sewing machine that had been gutted for parts, crushing a vacuum cleaner converted into a high-powered bubble maker, upending an old cotton candy machine retooled to shoot Frisbees at high speed...Invention after invention was destroyed by the monsters as they emerged from the portal and moved into the room. And then, as if they were all listening to some silent command, they turned as one and slowly shuffled toward the stairs.

Gameknight wanted to stop them, but he was overwhelmed with fear. He had nothing...no armor...no sword...nothing. What could he do? He was only one person, just a kid.

The stairs creaked as the zombies started to

ascend. He could still hear his sister's cartoon playing upstairs—some musical number likely being performed by a bunch of brightly colored puppets or some other annoying thing.

My sister...MY SISTER!!!

He wanted to yell out and warn her, but he couldn't move. *Run*, he thought to himself, *run...but he was frozen in place. He could only lie there under the collection of useless, discarded things in the basement, being now an appropriate addition himself.*

To his left was an old, forgotten wall mirror with a crack running down its middle. The metal frame was bent and faded, with scratches carved into it here and there. Turning, he could see his own reflection in the silvery surface, his terrified form hiding amidst piles of junk and worthless items. He couldn't bear to look at his image. The appearance of cowardly terror made him feel sick.

I'm pathetic.

Just then, shouting could be heard from upstairs, followed by the crash of bodies against the wall. But the strange thing was that it didn't sound like his sister. The voice had a different sort of sound, not childlike—and not the voice of a startled parent. No, this was the voice of a warrior with a tint of angry violence to its tone. This was not like his parents yelling at him for some transgression; this was someone in a violent rage...a woman's voice, unafraid and with the sound of command and action resonating deeply within it.

Someone was upstairs fighting for her life—no, for all of their lives. He had to do something. He had to help, but his limbs felt as if they were part of the dusty concrete floor, heavy and useless.

More zombies and spiders came out of the portal, followed by creatures of the Nether: blazes, with their flaming bodies lighting the basement with an angry yellow glow, and zombie-pigmen, their golden swords shining bright. Following these creatures were creepers, their multiple green-spotted legs moving in a flurry as they went up the steps. Maybe he could grab one of the creepers and blow up the portal, but that explosion would kill him in a most violent and painful way. Panic flooded through his mind at the thought, images of his body being crushed in the blast, memories of all that terrible pain on the last server pounding away at his courage. No, he wouldn't be able to do that.

Crash...smash...another body slamming into a wall upstairs followed by a faint humming sound, like a single guitar string.

The mobs coming out of the portal didn't seem to care about the noise on the floor above; they just continued their parade out of the Gateway, across the basement, and up the stairs. And then Gameknight's worst fear appeared—endermen. The tall, lanky creatures, with their jet-black skin and long arms and legs, stepped out of the portal, their eyes glowing an angry white. A bitter chill seemed to fill the basement as the black nightmares moved into the room, the walls and floor growing cold. Faceted ice crystals started to spread across the nearby mirror, their frosty fingers mercifully blotting out his reflection.

Turning from the frozen mirror, Gameknight looked back to the portal. More endermen were coming from the purple gateway, the tall creatures having to stoop so as to not hit their heads on the ceiling. This brought the faintest smile to his face, but it was quickly extinguished as one of the monsters moved nearer. Icicles of fear pricked him as the creature turned and surveyed the basement.

Is he looking for me?

The terrifying creature scanned the room, then started to glow as purple particles danced about him.

The dark monster then disappeared, teleporting to some unknown location, likely intent on destruction. Just when he thought the situation couldn't get any worse, a maniacal chuckle came from the portal. It was a vile laugh that brought back memories of past nightmares and turned his blood to ice. A quick glance at the portal caused his stomach to drop so suddenly that he almost gagged. Erebus stepped out of the portal, his dark red skin looking almost black in the dim light of the basement. He still had that translucent look to him, not completely substantial, yet not completely transparent either. The King of the Endermen seemed to be only partially present, but his rage was definitely complete. His eyes were blazing bright red with malice and hatred. He looked about the basement at the collection of stuff and scowled. Swinging his arms with lightning speed, he smashed whatever was nearby, stomping on boxes, and sending books flying. The creature destroyed whatever he could reach, his screechy voice cackling loudly with destructive glee.

Chills ran down Gameknight's spine. He felt ice cold as waves of fear and panic flowed across his body.

Erebus was here, in his house…oh no.

He wanted to run out and attack the monster, but simultaneously, he felt the overwhelming urge to retreat and run away. This creature had to be stopped, but terror ruled his mind and body, courage just the faintest of memories. Cringing, he scooted farther back into the shadows, getting as far from the demon as possible.

Clank…the cracked mirror fell over.

The King of the Endermen stopped and turned his evil head, his burning red eyes peering into the shadows. Moving slowly forward, he picked up a small toolbox and threw it aside. It smashed against the wall, screwdrivers and wrenches raining down across the room.

Gameknight crawled farther back into the shadows and bumped into a wall; he was trapped.

Erebus moved closer, picking up an old chair and tossing it aside as if it weighed nothing, the dusty piece of furniture crashing into a bookcase. He could now only see the monster's feet through the jungle of clutter, his long, dark legs backlit with purple light from the portal. The enderman stepped closer and kicked aside an old trashcan filled with rolls of wrapping paper meant for some party or holiday. A roll of red and green Santa Clauses fell to the ground and unrolled, the jolly old man smiling at him from across the floor. Erebus pushed aside a rusty metal desk on which some of Gameknight999's father's inventions sat. Equipment and experiments clattered to the ground, only to be crushed under the thin, dark legs of the monster.

"Who is it that hides in the shadows?" screeched Erebus. "Is it a little mouse?"

He shoved aside a box of books as if it were nothing, the cardboard box tearing and spilling its contents to the ground. One of the books fell, the cover facing Gameknight. The title on the book was The Crystal Tear—something he'd read a long time ago. The hero on the cover stared back at him with mismatched eyes, daring him to be courageous.

"Maybe it's a long-lost friend," Erebus cackled. "Come out and say hello. No need to be afraid. I won't hurt you...much."

The enderman picked up the table under which Gameknight was hiding and threw it across the room.

"Ahh...it is my friend. We meet again, User-that-is-not-a-user."

Erebus reached down and picked Gameknight up by his shirt, pulling him to his feet. He then lifted him off his feet and held him in the air, Nikes dangling free. Gameknight shook uncontrollably, his every nerve *ignited with burning terror.*

"You had a lot to say to me on the last server. You talked big when you had an army of users at your back," Erebus said, his breath smelling like rotten meat. "You aren't talking so big now, are you?"

Gameknight said nothing, just looked past the blazing red eyes to the portal. More monsters flowed out. There was a constant stream of creatures all heading upstairs, but the commotion from above had gone silent. Sighing, he tore his eyes from the portal and looked back at Erebus.

"What do you want?" Gameknight asked, his voice cracking with fear.

"Why, your death, of course," the monster laughed. "And then I will destroy this world. I had planned to make you watch my victory, witness my troops crushing every living soul in your puny world, but I think I just changed my mind." He paused and glared at Gameknight, his blazing eyes glowing even brighter. "I think I will destroy you first...then destroy this world. How does that sound to you?"

He cackled that spine-tingling laugh, guaranteeing that Gameknight's fear would not abate.

"Now, User-that-is-not-a-user, prepare to die."

Erebus then wrapped his clammy hands around his enemy's throat and started to squeeze. Panic flared within Gameknight999's mind. He was going to die. This was it. Erebus was finally going to kill him, and he was powerless to do anything about it. Despair drowned him as he struggled for breath, trying to hang on for as long as possible. And then the strangest thing happened...the entire basement shook. Erebus' eyes grew wide as he stumbled slightly, loosening his grip and allowing Gameknight to gulp down some air. Thunder then hammered their ears as if a massive hurricane had pulled them into its mighty swirl, but the sound wasn't coming from anywhere outside...it was coming from the portal.

Erebus glanced over his shoulder at the portal as the ground shook again, this time more violently, the thunder getting louder and louder until the enderman had to release his prey and put his hands over his ears.

Gameknight fell to the floor, gasping for breath, his ears aching.

The ground quaked again as if struck by a giant's hammer, throwing them both into the air. The thunderous reverberations made the basement walls crack, patches of concrete falling to the ground. It sounded like the thunder was shouting out his name...GAMEKNIGHT... GAMEKNIGHT...

The User-that-is-not-a-user looked up at the King of the Endermen and tried to scoot away. Erebus looked down at his prey and started to reach down for him, when a massive blow hit the basement, shattering the walls and floor to dust, the collection of discarded inventions instantly turned to rubble. More thunder hammered at their ears, Gameknight's name riding on the wave of sound. Erebus still glared at him, but now, he was floating in the air, as was Gameknight, the basement turned into a cloud of debris. The enderman's black arms reached out to Gameknight999 through the wreckage, trying to wrap his evil hands around the boy one last time. Then everything started to fade away, the remains of the basement slowly becoming transparent and fuzzy. Erebus too started to fade, though his arms still sought out Gameknight999. Even as he faded, his eyes seemed to burn brighter and brighter until the red light from the enderman's pupils filled Gameknight's vision, lighting the darkest recesses of his mind with a blood-red glare.

"You have interfered in my plans for the last time!" Erebus screeched as he faded away. "When we meet *again, it will be your doom..."*

The enderman's words echoed within Gameknight's mind for an instant; then suddenly, everything went dark.

He woke, his mind confused. *Where am I? Where is Erebus? Where is...*

"Gameknight, are you alright?" a voice asked from above.

He realized that he was lying face down on the ground. Rolling over, he looked up and found Crafter and Hunter standing over him, both wearing worried expressions.

"Where am I...where is Er—"

He stopped, not wanting to utter that terrible creature's name.

"You were yelling in your sleep, crying out for help," Crafter said as he reached down and helped him up.

Gameknight stood, feeling embarrassed, then sat on the edge of the bed, his body raked with fatigue as if he had never been asleep in the first place. Looking down at his hands, he could see that they had the familiar blocky shape that he'd come to expect in Minecraft. He hadn't escaped...it had just been a dream. Disappointment washed over him like a crashing wave. Home seemed further away now than ever before.

Well, at least Erebus had also been a dream, he thought silently.

Just then he noticed the pain around his neck. Reaching up, he could feel that the skin around his throat was chaffed and sore, as if scraped by something rough...or as if he'd been choked. Crafter and Hunter hadn't seen him rub his neck, and he swiftly brought his hands down.

"What happened?" he asked as he stood.

"You were screaming," Crafter explained. "I couldn't understand what you were saying, but it sounded like you were terrified, and like something was attacking you."

Crafter moved next to Gameknight and put his small hand on his arm.

"I tried to wake you. I shook you and shook you, but it didn't do any good. I called your name over and over, finally yelling in your ear, but it didn't do any good...so I woke Hunter and asked her to help."

He shifted his gaze from Crafter's bright blue eyes to Hunter's dark brown ones.

"So I gave you a massive shove and knocked you off the bed," she said proudly. "I told this one here," gesturing to Crafter, "that when something needs doing, you do it big. I shoved you with all my might, and you went flying out of the bed. That's when you woke up."

She gave him a self-satisfied smile, as if she'd enjoyed throwing him out of the bed and to the ground.

"What were you dreaming about, Gameknight?" Crafter asked.

He thought about the terrible dream, the monsters flowing out of the portal, the sounds of battle upstairs, and Erebus choking him...and shuddered. Was it a premonition of what would happen in the future or just a silly dream? Reaching up, he unconsciously rubbed his sore neck again, then snapped his hand back down when he realized what he'd just done.

"Ahhh...I don't really remember," he lied.

"Well, whatever," Hunter snapped. "I don't really care about your dreams; I just care about finding my sister. Besides, it's morning. Time to go."

"I agree," Crafter added. "It's time we left this village and found the next one so that we can get some answers and form a plan. Gameknight, are you ready to go?"

Nodding, Gameknight999 stood, his inner being still terrified by the dream...by Erebus. Sighing, he gathered his belongings and followed his two companions out of the house.

"We'll use the minecart network," Crafter said over his shoulder as he headed for the secret tunnel that wasn't very secret anymore.

Gameknight followed Crafter, still lost in the terrible memory of his most recent dream. Had it been real...had Erebus really made it to the physical world? Confused and terrifying thoughts rattled around in his brain as he followed the pair to the crafting chamber, fear seeping into his soul.

CHAPTER 10
THE FACE OF TERROR

The minecart slowed to a stop as it entered the new crafting chamber in the next village. Instantly, their ears were barraged by the screams and shouts of panicking villagers. Crafter and Hunter leapt out of their carts, waiting for the User-that-is-not-a-user, their eyes scanning the room for the threat that had all these people so terrified. Hunter had her bow out, an arrow already notched while Crafter had his sword drawn, a stern look on his young face.

Leaping out of the minecart, Gameknight reluctantly drew his own sword and stood at Crafter's side.

Three villagers stepped forward. They glanced

nervously at the gleaming weapons but when they noticed Crafter's black smock with gray stripe, they seemed to relax. Seeing the trepidation in their eyes, Crafter sheathed his sword and spoke to the frightened villagers.

"What's going on here?"

The three NPCs all started to speak hysterically to the young NPC. Their faces were creased with worry, a look of uncertainty and terror in their eyes.

"Crafter?" he asked again.

The young boy held up a hand to silence the User-that-is-not-a-user for a moment while he listened to the three villagers. When they finally finished, Crafter turned to his friend.

"The village, it's under attack," he said.

Gameknight's fear reared its ugly head as he looked around, but he saw no monsters. Confused, he looked back at his friend.

"Up there!" Hunter snapped, pointing up at the rocky ceiling while she rolled her eyes.

"But it's morning, how could they..."

"They tell me that it's the creatures of the Nether attacking. They must not be as sensitive to daytime as the mobs of the Overworld," Crafter explained. "Apparently they can suffer the sunlight without any ill effects."

Malacoda, Gameknight thought.

"One of the villagers came down and told the village crafter that they'd just seen blazes approaching the village," Crafter explained. "They haven't gotten here yet, but they will be here soon. The destruction of this village is inevitable. We must do something. They need the User-that-is-not-a-user. They need you."

Gameknight looked back at Crafter, a thousand questions tumbling around in his head, doubt filling his soul.

What can I do? I'm terrified.

He didn't want to face a bunch of Nether creatures. He wasn't a hero. He was too scared to be a hero. But then a thought came to him...run away. They could run away, all of them, through the minecart network.

Moving to a nearby crafting table, Gameknight999 jumped up on top of it and yelled for everyone's attention. Crafter leaped up onto the adjacent table as well. The presence of a child clothed in a crafter's robe with a sword in his hand drew everyone's attention. Their panic was momentarily stifled as all eyes shifted to Crafter.

"Listen, everyone, listen," he shouted, holding his sword high up into the air. "The Final Battle is upon us. The legions of the Nether are about to fall upon your village and try to destroy everything you hold dear. But have hope. We have a weapon that they do not expect. We have with us the User-that-is-not-a-user. Listen to what he has to say and be calm."

He turned his head and looked at his friend, and the terrified villagers in the chamber turned their blocky gazes toward Gameknight. Looking up, they could see the glowing letters of his username floating above his head. Their eyes drifted up higher, looking for the server thread that was not there. And in that instant, fear momentarily faded away as they realized that the User-that-is-not-a-user was standing before them.

Swallowing, Gameknight pushed down his fear and spoke to the crowd.

"Here's what you need to do if you want to survive. Half of you start making minecarts—lots of them. The other half of you must start crafting iron swords as fast as you can. You over there—" He pointed to a group of villagers clad in iron armor. "Go up to the surface, and tell everyone to come down here.

Tell everyone to abandon their homes and get down here as fast as they can. They must leave all of their belongings. At this moment, right now, speed means survival. Now GO!"

The villagers just stood there looking at him, clearly confused, but then a battle cry emanated from the entrance of the chamber, a cry filled with so much anger and hatred that it shocked everyone in the cavern. It was Hunter. She had a look of unbridled hatred on her face as she held her bow up into the air.

"When the monsters reach your village, they will kill anyone that gets in their way as they did in my village," she yelled down at the crowd. "I watched them kill my friends and neighbors, then level parts of our village to the ground just for fun. These Nether beasts will destroy until nothing is left to entertain them. I lost my village...my family...because we were not prepared. If you don't want to lose what I lost, then listen to the User-that-is-not-a-user and do what he says."

And then she turned and left the chamber, heading for the tunnels that led to the surface, her bow held in one hand. Gameknight knew what she was leaving to do and hoped she would be safe. Her battle cry could then be heard echoing down the tunnels as she headed to the surface, a tint of violent rage to her voice.

Her actions snapped the villagers into motion. The iron-clad villagers all sprinted up to the cavern entrance, while the crafters started banging out weapons and minecarts.

Someone handed Gameknight some iron armor. He put it on quickly, then pulled out his pick. The cavern quickly filled with the clattering sounds of crafting as fifty NPCs all hammered out swords and minecarts. Moving from one bench to the next, Gameknight shattered their crafting benches, freeing their hands. Each villager looked down at their newly freed hands in wonder, then gazed up into the eyes of the User-that-is-not-a-user and smiled. He released the hands of NPC after NPC. Those that were freed moved to a vacant crafting bench and continued to make swords, the sharp weapons quickly cluttering the floors. Some of the villagers, when they'd expended their raw materials, picked up a sword and stood at Gameknight's side, a grim look of determination on their blocky faces.

Crafter helped the others to create minecarts, pushing the newly crafted vehicles across the rails to be lined up at the tunnel openings, ready for the flow of villagers that were on their way. Once the minecarts were ready, Gameknight freed the hands of the remaining crafters, giving each a sword. His own golden sword drew many curious gazes, but none complained when he gave them an order to quiet down and listen to Crafter.

"We must delay the monsters, so that the villagers can escape through the tunnels," Crafter explained. "But first and foremost, where is your village's crafter?"

An old, gray-haired NPC, clothed like Crafter, stepped forward. Worried lines creased his face.

"I am here," he said with a scratchy voice.

"Excellent," Crafter said. "These monsters are coming here to take you. They don't care about the villagers, but they will kill everyone here to get to you. We must deny the monsters their prize. You must leave through the minecart network, now, before it is too late."

"Leave my village? Never," he protested.

"Listen to Crafter!" Gameknight snapped.

The village crafter looked up at the letters that floated above Gameknight's head, then shifted his gaze to the ceiling. He could see that this was a user, but there was no server thread reaching up into the heavens, connecting him to the Source.

"You are truly the User-that-is-not-a-user," the crafter said in a low voice.

Gameknight999 nodded, then stepped forward to put a reassuring hand on the old NPC's shoulder. "You must listen to my friend," he explained. "I know he looks like a child, but he is a crafter like yourself. We came to this server from another plane, where we battled the monsters that seek to destroy the Source. The battle continues here, on this server, and for some reason, these monsters are moving across Minecraft, capturing crafters. We must not let them take you. You must listen to him."

The old NPC looked at him, his worried eyes boring deeply into Gameknight's. He then looked about the cavern at his villagers, scanning every terrified face. Finally, he brought his stare back to Gameknight.

"Don't worry friend," Gameknight said reassuringly. "We will care for you village and do the best we can."

The old NPC nodded at him, then turned his gaze toward Crafter, nodding at him as well.

"Quickly, you must leave now," Crafter said. "We know these monsters are here for you, and we must not let you be captured. I don't know why they need you, but we must resist them at every opportunity. You *must* leave now."

"But if I leave my village, these NPCs will become Lost. It will force them to leave this village and look for another. Many will not survive this journey."

"The User-that-is-not-a-user and I will not let that happen," Crafter explained. "These villagers will soon be following you in minecarts. We will not let them become Lost." Reaching up, he put his small, child-like hand on the crafter's shoulder. "Beside, if they do become Lost, then I will take them into my village. I will accept all Lost ones and keep them safe. You need not worry, your villagers are in good hands."

The worry faded from the old crafter's face as he nodded to the duo. Moving to a minecart, the old NPC stood next to it, clearly still feeling concerned.

Suddenly, loud noises filtered down into the cavern from the tunnel entrance. It sounded like a huge group of creatures—NPCs or monsters—were moving through the tunnels and headed their way. Gameknight and Crafter turned and looked up at the iron doors that now stood open.

"All of you to the entrance, we must buy your crafter some time," Crafter ordered to those in the cavern that now held swords. He then turned and faced the old NPC. "My fellow crafter, you must leave, now."

And then, Crafter turned and headed up the steps to the entrance of the cavern. Gameknight turned and watched his friend as he led their forces to the cavern doors, then disappeared as they headed into the tunnels. He was so brave. Gameknight wished he had even the smallest sliver of Crafter's courage. Right now, he felt like a container overflowing with fear.

Turning, he saw the village crafter slowly climb into the minecart. The old NPC took one more look at his precious villagers as they charged up the stairway to face the threat that was descending upon them. Then he turned and faced Gameknight.

"Take care of them for me," the crafter said, tears streaming down his face.

"Don't worry, we will do what we can. You will be with them soon, but you must go now or they'll catch you, and we can't allow that."

The crafter nodded, then moved off down the minecart rails, disappearing into the tunnel's darkness. Malacoda had been denied his prize, but there was still one more crafter here. *His* Crafter.

Turning toward the cavern entrance, Gameknight charged up the steps, hoping to reach Crafter, then escape. At the top, he sprinted through the open iron doors and entered the large, round room, identical to the one where he had first met Crafter. It was crowded with armed NPCs, the torches on the walls casting pointed shadows on the ground because of upheld swords. Crafter and the village NPCs, now soldiers, stood ready. Gameknight could taste the fear in the room; the first battle was always the most terrifying. But he knew that the NPCs were not nearly as terrified as himself. He could already see the pointed claws of the zombies reaching out at him through his imagination, the fireballs of blazes seeking his flesh. He shivered.

Moving to Crafter's side, he whispered into his ear. "The village's crafter is safely away, but we have to get you out of here as well. Malacoda can still use you for whatever he is planning. We have to escape before it is too late."

"Not until we help the other villagers get out," Crafter said, courage resonating in his voice. "We don't know what that ghast will do when he finds the crafter gone. He may kill everyone that stays behind. We must help them."

Gameknight leaned in closer. "Crafter, this isn't our battle," he whispered.

"What are you talking about?" Crafter snapped, moving back a step. "All of this is our battle. This entire world is our battle. We're here to stop these monsters and save Minecraft, and anything we can do to resist Malacoda's plans *is* our battle. Now draw your sword and get ready."

Crafter's admonishment shamed him into drawing his weapon. Gameknight was terrified at the thought of facing off against the monsters of the Nether, but he was even more frightened of failing his friend. Standing with the defenders of this village, he waited.

I hate being this afraid, he thought to himself. *I hate it! Why can't I stand tall and be brave like Crafter?*

The shame of his cowardice chipped away at him from within, his fear wrapping around his soul like a hungry viper, ready to strike.

Come on Gameknight, get with it! he screamed at himself, his thoughts sounding mockingly pathetic. Frustration started to grow within him.

He was so scared.

Come on, stand tall and be brave, he thought— no, pleaded...*STAND TALL AND BE BRAVE!*

"STAND TALL AND BE BRAVE!!!"

Oh no, did I say that aloud?

A cheer rose from the NPCs as blocky hands patted him on the shoulders and back, the feeling of courage and bravery visible now on every face.

"That's right!" Crafter yelled. "Stand tall with the User-that-is-not-a-user and be brave. We will face these beasts and save your village!"

Another cheer rose from the round room as the sounds from the tunnel before them started to get louder.

Someone or something was coming.

They could hear the shuffling feet as if only a few were coming, but then the noise became louder. The shuffling of many feet echoed down the tunnel.

A *lot* of somethings were coming.

Gameknight gripped his sword firmly and looked around the room. He could see the iron doors that led to the crafting chamber standing open. It took every ounce of strength for him to keep his feet still and not bolt toward those doors and run away.

I hate being afraid!

Gripping his sword even tighter, he turned back toward the tunnel and the approaching mass of bodies. They could now see shapes moving about in the tunnel—many of them—as the running figures approached the room.

Would it be monsters...zombies and creepers and spiders?

Just then, a crowd of villagers burst into the room, all of then sprinting, unibrows creased with worry. A relieved sigh filled the room. It wasn't the monsters...not yet.

"Quickly, follow the path down to the cavern floor," Crafter directed. "Get into the minecarts and escape through the tunnels. There are enough for everyone...quickly now."

The villagers looked in surprise at the small boy who was talking, but the voice of command echoed within his words. Crafter moved forward so that they could see his clothing. They instantly recognized him as a crafter and did as he instructed. The flow of villagers was nearly constant, with parents leading children while neighbors helped the elderly and the sick. Everyone was running to the salvation below: the minecart network.

Just then, the smell of smoke started to trickle down the entrance of the tunnel. At first, it was just a hint, like someone striking a match nearby, but then it grew stronger and stronger. Slowly, the tunnel filled with a smoky haze, the acrid aroma started to bite at the back of Gameknight's throat with each terrified breath.

The monsters...they were coming.

The last of the villagers came running out of the tunnel covered in soot and ash, some of them with clothes partially burned.

"They're coming," one of them said in a terrified voice. "Blazes, lots of them."

"And ghasts and zombies and magma cubes," another said. "There're hundreds of them...maybe a thousand, and that lone woman holding them all back with her bow."

"Lone woman?" Crafter asked. "Who?"

"I don't know who she is," the last villager said as she headed toward the stairway that led to the cavern floor. "I never saw a village woman with red hair like that, but she's keeping the monsters from getting into the tower with her bow. When she runs out of arrows...she's dead."

"You hear that?" Crafter said to Gameknight. "We have to help her. Come on everyone, the battle is up there."

And then Crafter charged forward through the smoke-filled tunnel to the ladder that led up to the surface, the other village soldiers following their young leader, leaving Gameknight standing there wrapped in fear.

He wasn't a hero. He was just a kid that liked to play Minecraft, but he couldn't let his friend, his only friend on this server, Crafter, face this threat alone. He had to help him, even though fear blanketed his mind and the courage he'd felt on the last server was a distant memory. Moving toward the tunnel, he could hear the clash of swords echoing out of the tunnel...Crafter.

Sprinting with all his might, he shot down the

tunnel, through clouds of smoke that choked the passageway, his golden sword help up high. Ahead, he could see the flash of iron against gold; their soldiers were engaged with zombie-pigmen. Pushing through the crowd, he attacked a zombie, its rotten flesh hanging off its body in flaps, part of its skull and ribs exposed where skin was missing; it was an attractive target for his razor-sharp sword. This was something he'd done many times; sometimes he'd been fighting monsters, other times he'd been attacking other players. His cyber bullying history was not something he was proud of, but his experience served him well at the moment as he dodged attacks and drove his sword through zombie bodies. Gameknight999 had become a killing machine, acting without thought, his mind lost in the heat of battle. With practiced efficiency, he tore through the monsters, slashing his sword under armored plates and blocking lethal blows as he danced through the battle lines with a deadly grace.

Attacking monster after monster, Gameknight fought through the clash of bodies, wanting to get to his friend. He could see him in the distance, the young boy slashing out at legs with his iron sword, ducking under attack and taking advantage of his diminutive height. Kicking one monster away, Gameknight999 drove his sword through another, its rotting body disappearing with a pop as its HP was consumed. Spinning to block a golden blade, he slashed at a black furry spider. Knocking away dark claws, he slashed at the zombie, then stabbed at the spider, killing both. Hacking at one after another, the User-that-is-not-a-user fought from pure instinct, carving a pathway through the tunnel. Finally, he reached his friend.

Crafter was facing off against a zombie-pigman

that was armored, its golden coat looking like melted butter on the monster. Moving with lightning speed, Gameknight slashed at the armor's weak points... under the arm...near the neck...at the waist. He attacked at the points where the armor plates met, and maneuvered his sword so that it slipped in and found soft flesh. In moments, the creature was destroyed, giving him time to talk with his friend.

"Crafter, we have to get you out of here."

"Not 'til we save Hunter," Crafter objected.

"But Malacoda wants you just as badly as any other crafter. You're what he wants right now, not these few NPCs. Come on, we have to get out of here."

Just then, Hunter appeared, covered in soot. Part of her clothing was singed, the edges of her smock still smoking a bit. Her face looked as if it were made from stone, grim determination mixed with unbridled hatred carved deep into her skin.

"Oh good, you're here," she said quickly. "Any of you got any arrows? I'm kinda getting low." She gave them both a grin, her eyes filled with excitement and a thirst for battle.

"What are you doing? We have to get out of here!" Gameknight yelled over the din of battle.

Just then, a zombie-pigman lunged at them. Hunter deflected the golden blade with her bow as Gameknight hacked at the creature's side, hitting it quickly with three well-aimed attacks. The monster evaporated, leaving behind small glowing balls of XP that flew to him.

"Nice," Hunter said with a quirky grin. Then she spun and fired another arrow down the dark tunnel, striking some monster in the distance.

Suddenly, a fireball streaked out of the darkness and burst above their heads.

"Blazes, or worse," Gameknight said, unease

edging his voice. "We have to get out of here."

"I think you're right," Hunter said.

"EVERYONE FALL BACK TO THE MINECART NETWORK!" Crafter yelled, his high-pitched voice piercing through the sound of battle.

The villagers began their retreat back to the crafting cavern. The zombie-pigmen were confused at first, but then quickly ran after their prey. Gameknight and Crafter were able to attack them from the back of the group, hacking away at their backs and legs, killing them in an instant. Arrows streaked past Gameknight's head as Hunter sought out targets of her own, killing monsters farther down the passage. In minutes, they'd killed the remaining zombies in the tunnel, and followed the villagers toward the minecarts. Sprinting into the crafting chamber, they bolted down the steps to the cavern floor. They'd only just reached it when balls of fire streaked into the room, striking one villager after another, causing them to burst into flame, their HP diminishing quickly...and then they were gone, dead. More balls of fire flew into the chamber as an army of blazes burst through the twin iron doors at the chamber's entrance. They were creatures of flame and smoke, with glowing yellow rods spinning about their center, a bright yellow head floating atop the body of fire. Their dead black eyes glared down at the surviving villagers with a look of unbridled hatred. The blazes launched the flaming projectiles at the NPCs, the burning spheres crashing into NPCs and consuming HP in minutes They were carefully aimed to steer clear of Crafter, Gameknight and Hunter benefitting from still being at his side.

"Quickly, get on the minecarts!" Crafter yelled. "If you're the last one, break the track behind you... GO!"

The surviving villagers headed for the minecarts, Gameknight and his companions doing the same. Suddenly, a noise came from the cavern entrance. It was a terrible sound, like the yowl of a wounded, moaning cat. It was a sound made by a creature that was filled with unspeakable despair mixed with a thirst for vengeance on those who were happy and alive. Few ever heard this sound and lived, for it came from the most terrible of Nether creatures: a ghast.

Gameknight turned and saw a large white creature slowly float down from the cavern entrance. Nine long tentacles hung beneath the large, bone-white cube, each one writhing and bending, itching to grab hold of its next victim. This was not a normal monster. It was the biggest creature Gameknight had ever seen in Minecraft, much larger than the standard ghast. No...this was something different... something terrible. This horrific ghast was the King of the Nether—this was Malacoda.

Gameknight was petrified with fear. This was the most terrifying creature he'd ever seen, and easily made Erebus seem like a child's toy. This monster was the incarnation of hopelessness and despair tied together with the rusty wires of anger and hatred. This was the face that nightmares feared; this was the face of terror.

The moans from Malacoda brought an eerie silence to the room. The villagers turned toward the sound, and their mouths fell open in shock. They had never seen such a terrifying thing in their lives, and it instantly caused all of them to panic. NPCs collided with NPCs as they all bolted for the minecarts, almost climbing on each other in an effort to escape.

The King of the Nether struck out at one of the

remaining villagers, throwing a gigantic fireball at the hapless victim and engulfing the doomed soul in a firestorm that mercifully consumed his HP in mere seconds.

Malacoda laughed. "Ha ha ha ha," the ghast boomed. "Now that one went up quick."

Scanning the chamber for his next victim, Malacoda launched a fireball at another NPC, then another, and another, until his burning red eyes fell on Crafter, Gameknight, and Hunter, and stopped his attack. The villagers took advantage, those remaining jumping into minecarts and escaping, leaving the three comrades to face the King of the Nether.

"Now what do we have here?" his glowing red eyes scanned Crafter with meticulous care. "A child that is more than a child...this is interesting." His malicious voice filled the chamber as he pointed at Crafter with one of his serpentine tentacles. "I've been looking for you."

"You won't get a crafter from this village, demon!" Crafter yelled back at the monster.

"Is that so?" Malacoda said.

He flicked his tentacles toward a group of blazes. The burning creatures slowly floated toward the trio, sparks and ash flying from their glowing bodies.

"Quickly, to the minecarts," Crafter said. "I'll go last. They won't shoot any fireballs and risk hitting me."

Taking three quick steps, Hunter leaped into a minecart and shot down the tunnel. Then Gameknight and Crafter jumped into the last minecart, just as Malacoda fired a huge fireball at the tunnel, hoping to cut off their escape. Their minecart sped down the tracks just ahead of the incendiary ball, the back of the tunnel erupting in explosive flame. The tunnel collapsed just behind their minecart, thankfully sealing it off.

They'd escaped, but just barely.

As they sped down the tracks, Gameknight could hear the ear-splitting screams of frustration from Malacoda, the ghast king yelling at the top of his lungs.

"I'LL GET YOU YET..."

CHAPTER 11

NIGHTMARES REVEALED

Crafter and Gameknight crouched close together as they sped down the tunnel in the minecart. The heat from Malacoda's fireball still filled the passageway, making beads of sweat trickle down their faces and sting their eyes. A subtle smoky haze filled the air, but gradually cleared as they sped down the tracks.

"That was close," Crafter said, patting his friend on the shoulder. "Malacoda seemed a little upset at our escape."

"Upset?" Gameknight snapped. "He was insane with rage, a killing rage that was focused directly on us, and probably still is. I don't know if we'll be so lucky next time."

"Perhaps."

Gameknight looked away, staring down the minecart tracks. The tunnel had led straight away from the crafting cavern, but was now slowly going uphill. The beat of the wheels on the crossbeams created a hypnotic effect on him, the *ka-chunk, ka-chunk, ka-chunk* driving the horrifying images of Malacoda from his mind.

Then suddenly the minecart plummeted downward on a steep slope. It turned left then right, then left again as it jogged its way through the flesh of Minecraft. Gameknight knew that the tracks were going around sections of the rail network that had stopped working correctly, a portion of the system becoming visible to the users for some reason. When that happened, the NPCs converted that section of the track to an abandoned mine and filled it with the occasional chest of items: a sword here, food and tools there. It was what the NPCs did—kept the mechanism of Minecraft working. He wished they were just going straight, because the sudden turns were affecting his stomach and the rumbling didn't feel so good. But just as he was about to complain, the track straightened out again. Sighing, he relaxed a little.

Quite suddenly, the stone wall of the tunnel curved away and opened up, showing a gigantic crevasse that stretched up to the sky, the bottom of it plunging far below the level of their rails. Looking up, Gameknight could see blocky clouds drifting across the narrow slice of sky visible through the opening of the crevasse. At the bottom he could see a narrow river flowing down its length, the occasional blossom of lava spilling into the watery stream. The combination of water and molten rock formed dark, midnight blue obsidian that sparkled with purple flecks in the distance. Shadows covered the floor of the valley; the sheer walls and narrow span shielding the crevasse from sunlight except at noon. These shadows allowed the monsters of night, the mobs of the Overworld, to mill about without bursting into flame. He could see zombies and skeletons clustering right next to the vertical walls, still fearing the openness of the floor and the burning sun that would emerge midway through the day.

The scene instantly reminded him of the dream he'd had days ago, the dream where Erebus had first appeared to him...the beginning of the constant nightmare. Shuddering, his face froze as the terror of that dream replayed itself through his mind, his eyes wide, mouth frozen slightly open. Expecting to see green, decaying arms reaching out at him from the shadows, Gameknight's eyes darted about, checking both sides of the tunnel while at the same time trying to stay completely motionless in hopes that the monsters in his mind wouldn't notice him.

He was snapped out of this trance-like state by a hand on his shoulder, a voice ringing in his ears.

"Gameknight...are you alright?" Crafter asked. "What's wrong?"

"Ahh...well...it's...ahh...nothing, it's nothing."

"I think it's time you started telling me the truth," Crafter demanded, his unibrow creased with concern.

"Well...I've been having these dreams," Gameknight confessed. He felt a little ridiculous talking about... nightmares.

"Dreams? NPCs rarely dream when we sleep. We just go dormant. I guess the code that runs us in Minecraft pauses and lets the CPU resources go somewhere else. I've only known one NPC who said he had a dream, and it was my Great-Great-Uncle Carpenter. He used to call himself a dream-walker, though I never really understood what that meant." He paused for a moment. His face looked excited, almost childlike. "What's it like...you know...to dream?"

Gameknight sighed. He could see the excitement on Crafter's face, but knew he had to tell him the truth.

"They aren't really dreams, exactly."

"Not exactly...what do you mean?"

Suddenly, a shaft of sunlight streamed into the tunnel. The wall fell away again, revealing another cavern, open at the top. They could see more monsters milling about at the bottom, staying in the life-preserving shadows. Images of Erebus erupted in his memory.

He shuddered again.

"They aren't dreams. They're nightmares. I'm having nightmares about Erebus." His voice cracked with emotion. Swallowing, he continued. "The first nightmare was a few days ago. It was kinda like this tunnel. I was on a minecart, hurtling down the tracks, and then I saw the caverns like we just saw...and then the minecart stopped."

He paused to see if, somehow, the minecart was going to mimic his dream and slow to a stop. Instead, it continued to plunge down the tracks, the tunnel wall closing in again as the cavern fell behind.

With a sigh of relief, he continued. "I was surrounded by a strange fog in the dream. There were monsters in the fog all around me. I couldn't see them very well, but I knew that they were there. And then they started reaching out at me with their razor-sharp claws and pointed fangs, zombies and spiders flowing toward me from all sides. I couldn't fight back...I was too scared, so I just stood there and let the monsters attack me. The pain was terrible, like every nerve in my body was on fire. I cried out for help, but there was nobody there—just me and all those monsters." He shuddered as the images replayed through his mind, then continued. "But then suddenly it all stopped."

Pausing to take a breath, Gameknight could feel his heart pounding in his chest, his mind lost in those painful memories. He looked sideways at Crafter. The old young NPC sat motionless, his entire being riveted on what his friend was saying, so he continued his account.

"The monsters all backed away and I thought that maybe the nightmare was over, but then I heard chuckling, a spine-tingling cackle that caused waves of panic to flow over me. I knew that laugh, that maniacal, evil laugh.

"It was Erebus," Gameknight said in a low voice, his eyes darting to the shadows that now surrounded their minecart. "He's back."

"But how could that be true? You said he was killed in that explosion on the last server."

"I know, but he must have crossed over…collected enough XP to respawn on the next server plane, like we did. He doesn't look completely solid, more insubstantial and transparent than physically present, but he still terrifies me to death."

"So you think he's here?"

"I'm not sure. I don't really know what the dreams mean, or if the dreams are real, but what I do know… Erebus is becoming more solid with every nightmare. He's becoming real, and that scares me."

Gameknight reached up and rubbed his throat, the skin still scuffed and raw.

"Is this what you were dreaming about last night, when Hunter had to knock you out of the bed?"

Gameknight sighed. Looking down the tracks on a long straightaway, he could see another minecart in the distance, a tangle of vibrant red hair flailing in the breeze; it was Hunter. He wished he had her strength, her courage.

Nodding his head, he continued. "The last dream was the most real of all. I dreamed I was back at home in the physical world. Actually, I thought I *was* home, and all this had been a dream, but then a portal opened up in my basement, right next to my desk. Monsters started coming through: zombies, spiders, creepers... right into *my* basement. They went straight up the stairs and into our home. I heard some kind of fighting but didn't know what was happening."

He lowered his voice, ashamed. "I was afraid to go up and look. They could have been attacking my parents, or...maybe...my sister." A boxy tear trickled down his face. "But I was too afraid to leave the basement. I just crawled under a desk and hid in the shadows. I couldn't do anything. I didn't have any weapons—no armor, nothing. What could I do?"

He paused, waiting for some kind of answer, but Crafter remained silent, listening, empathy showing on his face. The minecart made a sudden turn, lurching to the left, then straightened again. The sudden jolt shocked Gameknight back into his story.

"And when I thought it couldn't get any worse, Erebus came out of the portal. He seemed to know that I was there. He pushed aside the stuff I was hiding under and picked me up by my shirt, holding me up in the air like I was some toy. Then he started to choke me.

"I could feel that I was dying. I couldn't breathe, so I started to panic. I was so terrified I couldn't even think. I just hung there in the monster's grip as my life slowly ebbed away...and then you woke me up. You saved me." He paused to let the terrifying images slowly recede from his mind. "But there was one thing that I noticed in the dream, something that seems important."

"What was that?" Crafter asked softly.

"Erebus looked more solid than in the first dream... more present than not. I think he's almost here."

He reached up and rubbed his neck again where Erebus had choked him. He didn't really believe that the dream had caused his sore neck—maybe he didn't *want* to believe it—but for some reason he kept this fact to himself.

"Crafter, I'm so afraid all the time. When we went down into that first crafting chamber, I was terrified. And when you wanted to look for survivors in Hunter's village, I almost didn't follow you because I was so frightened. I'm on the verge of panic every second...I'm not a hero...I can't do this, battle Malacoda and all his Nether monsters. And now it seems that I have to battle Erebus as well." He sighed, then wiped a tear from his cheek. "I can't fight these epic battles anymore, defeat these powerful monsters and conquer all their mobs. I'm not a hero, I'm just a scared, cowardly boy."

At that, he fell silent.

Crafter stared at him for a long moment, a look of calm understanding in his eyes, his unibrow curved into a sympathetic arc. Reaching out, he put a blocky hand on Gameknight's shoulder. As he was about to speak, the minecart did another of its abrupt course changes, zigging to the right, zagging back to the left, then plunging down a steep incline some twenty blocks deep before straightening out again.

"I understand that you're afraid. We all are."

"Not Hunter," Gameknight snapped with a tone of self-recrimination.

"Hunter is on a dangerous path that will only lead to violence and death. She needs to kill monsters to cover the anguish that resides in her heart. She is not courageous; she seeks death. But you, User-that-is-not-a-user, you are something more."

"But I'm too scared to do heroic things."

"Do you remember Digger, at my old village?" Crafter asked.

"Of course I do," Gameknight answered solemnly. Gameknight had caused the death of Digger's wife when he'd been a griefer, a person that played Minecraft just to destroy things. His reckless behavior had broken a family, just for the pleasure of watching monsters kill NPCs. How he regretted his past. It was a guilt that he'd carried with him since he'd met Crafter and come to learn about the lives within Minecraft and the war that was brewing here. "I remember all too well."

"Well, his son was terrified of the water. He couldn't swim, but loved fishing. All of his friends would go out in boats onto the lake near the village, to catch fish to help feed the village. But Digger's son couldn't go with the other kids...because he couldn't swim. He used to come to me, crying, when some of the other children teased him, but still he was deathly afraid of the water."

"What does this have to do—" Gameknight interrupted. He was silenced by Crafter's raised hand.

"Then one day, one of the other kids brought home a really big fish, and the village was so excited. It was the biggest fish anyone could remember. Digger was so impressed that he complimented the other child in front of everyone, which brought his son to tears. There Digger's son stood, listening to his father talk so proudly of another boy's accomplishments. It made him feel worthless. He felt ashamed for being afraid of the water, for being too afraid to learn how to swim. And so he ran off without telling anyone."

Crafter paused and looked at Gameknight, his bright blue eyes holding his gaze unflinchingly.

"Well?" Gameknight999 asked. "What happened? You can't just go running off all by yourself without any weapons. That's dangerous in Minecraft, especially for a child. Did anyone follow him?"

"Yes...I did, but I didn't let him know I was there. I followed him through the woods, and then through the rocky pass until he led me to the lake. And do you know what I found there at the lake?"

Gameknight looked at him with a questioning look, getting slightly irritated. *Was he ever going to finish this story?*

"What did you find?" he snapped.

"A hero," Crafter answered with a smile.

"Ahh...what?"

"I found a hero at the lake, and it was Digger's son. You see, he saw the respect in his father's eyes at the sight of that fish, and he knew he had to do something or forever feel the shame of *not* trying. So I found Digger's son, later named Fisher, diving head-first into the lake."

"What happened? I thought he was afraid of the water. How does that make him a hero?"

Crafter leaned in closer so that the User-that-is-not-a-user could hear him over the clatter of the minecart wheels. "You see, Fisher's fear of the water was overwhelming. It had paralyzed him beyond the ability to think, made him shake with fear and weep at just the thought of wading into the water. He had to fish from far up on the banks of the lake, using an extra-long fishing pole so that he could cast his line out to catch anything. The other kids used to tease him about the pole, asking if he were trying catch a squid or some other deep sea creature. But Fisher would just return the insults with silence, feeling that the abuse was warranted.

"Well, the day of the huge fish was the last straw. He couldn't bear it anymore, so he went down to the lake and confronted his demon...and it was the bravest thing I'd ever witnessed in all my years in Minecraft. I saw a scared little boy square off against the thing that terrified him the most, the thing that turned his spine to jelly and his feet to stone. I saw him grapple with his demon, using a strength he didn't know he had. For you see, something had changed within Fisher, something very important."

Crafter stopped talking to look at the track ahead. They could still see Hunter in front of them, just at the edge of the darkness that enveloped them, her brilliant hair flowing like a flag of freedom...or a banner of war.

"What...come on Crafter, what changed?" Gameknight asked.

"He began to accept the possibility that he might be able to do this great thing, conquer his fear of water and learn to swim. He began to imagine himself overcoming this obstacle...he started to believe."

Gameknight threw his hands up in the air, exasperated. "How does that make him a hero... because he started to believe? How does learning to swim—something as insignificant as that—make him a hero?"

Crafter leaned even closer so that Gameknight could feel the importance of his words. "Fisher finally stopped being a victim and faced his fear, and that's what made him a hero. You see, it isn't the task that makes a hero, it's the obstacle that must be overcome. Sure, a person that slays an enderman could be called a hero, but would you call Hunter up there a hero because of all the monsters she's killed?"

Gameknight pondered this...Hunter. Her courage was remarkable, her skill with a bow probably legendary, but no, he didn't think of her as a hero. He thought of her as someone who was reckless, killing things out of an insane desire to seek revenge, as if that would somehow make her feel better. No, Hunter wasn't a hero. She was reckless and violent, doing for herself and not others, and ultimately, she was just a crazed killing machine.

"You see, Fisher's fear of the water, fear of drowning, was overwhelming," Crafter continued. "He had become ruled by his fear to the point that he had become only a shadow of his true self. He always tried to hide his insecurity and fear from others, making excuses, concealing his real self. But when that huge fish was brought into the village, when his own father admired the other boy for what he'd done, something inside Fisher snapped. The walls of fear that had barricaded his courage started to crumble, chipped away by the hope that he felt, the realization that he *could* learn to swim. And the belief that he could overcome his fear is what allowed him to try. When he faced his demon— his fear—and stood up to it unblinking, unwavering, and confident...that's the moment he became a hero."

"Did he learn how to swim?" Gameknight asked, now on the edge of his seat.

"He became the best swimmer in the village, and the best fisherman, too, much better than full-grown men...the envy of the other fishermen." He paused and let the story sink in for a moment. "Deeds do not make the hero, Gameknight999," he said in a loud voice, as if trying to tell the entire world. "How they overcome their fear does." Then he fell silent.

Gameknight closed his eyes and considered these words as they echoed off the tunnel wall, penetrating him from all sides. And as they reverberated within his mind, he felt the smallest morsel of understanding. He didn't notice the end of the tunnel filling with light as the minecart approached another crafting chamber; another village, this one peacefully calm. Focusing on Crafter's words with his entire being, he felt that there was something important there for him—for all of them.

Opening his eyes, his stream of thought was broken by the feel of the village they'd just entered. He could tell that this was the place they all needed, the focus of the conflict that was about to crash down upon this digital realm. He could somehow sense all of the anger and hatred from the monsters of the Overworld and the creatures in the burning Nether. All of their rage would soon be focused on this point...on him. He was confident that this was where the Last Battle for this server would start.

"Crafter," the User-that-is-not-a-user said softly, "this village...I can tell that this is where we will make our stand. This is where the Last Battle will be fought on this server. This is the place."

The young NPC with old wise eyes stared at Gameknight and nodded, then turned and looked at the crafting chamber they had just entered.

"Somehow," Gameknight continued, "we have to bring all of our forces here—all the NPCs of this land. But how?"

"Leave that to me."

Crafter jumped out of the minecart and drew his sword. Holding it with both hands, he held it up high, then plunged it straight down into the stone floor. When it hit, a loud crack sounded that stopped all activity in the chamber and brought all eyes toward the duo. Sinking to one knee, he kept his grip firm on the sword's handle, then closed his eyes and concentrated. Gathering all of his crafting power, the NPC reached out across the server, along all the digital lines of code that held this plane of existence together, and called his villagers. Driving his powers even harder, he reached out even farther, calling all NPCs, all of the Lost to this location...to the Last Battle. And as he gave out his silent call, he started to glow an iridescent, shimmering blue that lit the crafting chamber a subtle indigo hue.

A hushed silence filled the chamber as every NPC watched the spectacle, all of them knowing that something big was happening, though they didn't know that the battle for this server had just begun.

CHAPTER 12

NIGHTMARE TURNED REAL

Acrackling of light, like a highly focused lightning storm or the sparks from a million static shocks, started to form over a beautiful grassy plain. The glowing, whirling ball of light pulsated like some kind of electric heart. Its form contracted and expanded ever so slightly, then became more pronounced and amplified. The pulsations made the sparkling, snapping ball of light appear to writhe as if in terrible pain, balls of crackling fire shooting from its depths. The sparks and flame scorched the earth, killing all life that they touched and charring a black, diseased stain onto the surface of Minecraft. A rotten, decaying odor came from the ball of light, a smell that assaulted the senses and offended nature itself. It was such a vile and disgusting aroma that it drove away any animals nearby, and made the very blades of grass want to lean outward.

Then something started to emerge. First a pair of long, dark legs came forth, then a small torso with equally long and lanky arms, and finally a dark head, its eyes burning bright red with a hatred for all living things.

Erebus had come to Minecraft again.

The King of the Endermen gazed around this new land with a look of disdain about all of its beauty. His tall frame towered over the animals nearby, his thin arms and legs making him seem even taller. Cows mooed in the distance. A group of pigs oinked nearby. Sheep walked by the enderman, unconcerned, their bleating driving Erebus into a rage. With lighting speed, he struck out at the nearest sheep, driving a hard fist into the fluffy creature and killing it instantly. The sheep just popped out of existence, leaving behind a square block of wool.

Smiling, Erebus turned toward the distant, rocky mountains. He knew he'd find passageways there into the bowels of Minecraft. That would be where *his* monsters resided. They didn't know that they were his—not yet—but they would soon come to understand that he was their king...or they would perish. Purple particles started to form around him as he focused his teleportation power, and then, at the speed of thought, he was at the foot of the mountain.

Gazing across its slopes, he quickly spotted an opening that would lead him underground. Teleporting to that position, he materialized at the opening. Walking casually into the tunnel, he chuckled his eerie, maniacal laugh. He knew that it would draw the other monsters to him; it always did. As he plunged deeper into the underground warren, he found zombies and spiders hiding in the corners, the ever-present creepers always lurking about. Drawing them to him with his very will, he continued deeper underground, his mob growing with every step. Many of his brother endermen materialized in the tunnels, teleporting from some unknown place, appearing to join his cause. Going deeper and deeper, Erebus traveled through the maze of tunnels that led steadily downward. At times, he had to open a sealed tunnel that blocked his progress. Ordering a creeper to stand near the rocky wall, he commanded the green-spotted beasts to detonate; they always did as he willed. The explosive end of their lives easily opened the blocked passages, and allowed his growing army to continue on their path.

Finally, after traveling to the deepest parts of the Overworld, he reached the lava level and finally felt at home. He had led the horde of monsters into a gigantic cavern that had a waterfall at one end, a large lava lake at the other. Where the two met were bands of cobblestone and obsidian—the result of mixing lava with water. Reaching out with his Enderman powers, he called on all of the monsters in the area to come to this chamber and bow to him. The monsters, being poor of wit and rich with a hatred of living things, flocked to him and his promise of destruction. In twenty minutes—an hour at most—hundreds of monsters had come to join the existing rabble.

Teleporting to a rocky outcropping that would allow him to stand above his subjects, the King of the Endermen gazed down at his army, then raised his long black arms, commanding silence.

"Brothers," he screeched with his high-pitched voice. "The time has come for the end of Minecraft. The Last Battle is coming, and the Prophecy draws to its conclusion, with you, my brothers, taking over everything."

The mobs cheered at this, the moaning of the zombies mixed with the clicking of the spiders, the bouncing boing-boings of the slimes and the cackles of the endermen. Creepers hissed and started to glow as they initiated their detonation process only to turn it off again—their only way of making any sound.

A few withers floated over the crowd, their dark eyes glaring down at the lesser monsters with disdain before looking to Erebus. A rattling, echoing sound came from the three-headed monsters as they drifted through the air; it sounded like a bag of bones was being shaken inside an empty stone room. The echoes lingered as they moved, making the other monsters move back a step. With three skeletal heads and a body that was only the torso of a skeleton; they were fearsome creatures. The three skulls looked about in all directions at once, their cold, dead eyes scanning the room for threats. They sat on a collection of skeleton bones that were blackened as if they'd been rolled in the ashes of some ancient fire. The spine and ribs of the skeletal torso were completely exposed, as with their Overworld cousins, the skeletons, but these creatures had no legs, just a stubby spine sticking out at the bottom of their bodies. To move, the withers floated through the air on unseen legs, able to soar high up into the air, the bony protrusion of their spine never touching the ground.

They were horrible to look at, but even more terrible to face in battle. They could throw flaming poison skulls—called wither skulls—a great distance while hovering far off the ground, making them extremely difficult to kill. With each of their boney heads focused on different targets, or perhaps on a lone user or NPC, they proved to be fearsome opponents on the battlefield. Erebus knew all of this and nodded his dark, blocky head as he saw them float through the air; they were a powerful addition to his army.

These withers will make excellent generals for my army, Erebus thought to himself as he watched the other monsters move away from the floating creatures. A thin, eerie smile spread across his face.

"It is the hour of the monster on this server, and soon, on all servers. We are one step from the Source, and that too will be ours, soon."

The creatures cheered again, this time louder.

"I have seen the Gateway of Light. I know its existence is real, and also that it is almost within our grasp. Before long, we will leave the confines of these digital planes and flow into the physical world, where we will conquer all living things and extend my rule to encompass everything."

"But why should we follow you?" yelled a witch that was standing near the sea of lava.

She looked like any number of NPC villagers, with her arms linked across her chest and a bulbous nose dominating her face. She had long, midnight black hair that reflected the light of the nearby lava lake, so that it had a wavy sheen and sparkle. Her cone-shaped hat, the symbol of her station, leaned slightly to one side on her head, the brown cap formed by tiny little cubes.

Erebus snapped his head toward the voice, then teleported instantly to the witch. With a quickness that made the attack on the sheep seem lethargic, he struck out at her with three fast, devastating punches. Each strike pushed her back a few steps, the King of the Endermen teleporting forward a step with each punch to continue his attack. The last punch drove the witch over the rocky ledge and into the sea of lava. She perished quickly. He turned and gazed at those closest to him, then teleported back to the outcropping.

"Make no mistake. I was the King of the Endermen on that last server, where I ruled all. And now, I am the King of the Overworld here, on this server. I claim this land by my right and might. I AM YOUR KING!!!" His voice echoed throughout the chamber, almost making the wall shake. "Are there any objections?"

Erebus waited for the next doomed soul to speak up, but none dared to defy him. "As I thought," he said, satisfaction in his voice.

Gazing across the army of monsters that stood at his feet, he glared into the eyes of every one of them. These creatures wanted to destroy those that lived up on the surface: the NPCs and users that infested Minecraft. They could almost taste the fear up there; the pathetic villagers going about their pathetic lives, always afraid.

Erebus grinned a wry, evil grin.

Well, I'll give those NPCs and users something to really be afraid of, he thought, as his smile grew wider. *They will learn why they fear the night.*

Using his teleportation powers, he silently issued commands to his mob, whispering into every monster ear nearly simultaneously, telling them to disperse. They would follow the tunnels that would take them to the nearest village—the first target in their campaign of terror and destruction.

He would cleanse this server of all living creatures, and then the monsters would rule. Closing his eyes, he could imagine the wave of destruction that he would bring crashing down onto Minecraft; it would be an unrelenting, merciless flood of pain and despair, and only one thing—one person—stood in his way: the User-that-is-not-a-user. Erebus had seen this so-called Gameknight in his dreams, and knew that he was no longer a threat. Something had happened to the User-that-is-not-a-user when he moved up from the last server, and now he was consumed with fear; there was no way that coward would stop him. Soon, the King of the Overworld would have this Gameknight kneel before him, and he would force the User-that-is-not-a-user to witness his triumph over all living things. And just when his hopelessness was the greatest—when he no longer had the strength to beg for his own death—then Erebus would destroy him, and his victory over the living would be complete. Reaching out with his teleportation powers, he searched for his adversary. Combing the landscape with his mind, he felt for Gameknight999, and then suddenly found him. But as in the dream, he was a terrified little kid, not the great warrior that had defeated his army on the last server. He was pathetic and weak...all the better.

Smiling a terrible, fearsome smile, Erebus chuckled a murderous laugh that filled the chamber with echoes. His cackles rippled outward from the lava-filled cavern and into the very digital fabric of Minecraft.

"I'm coming for you, User-that-is-not-a-user," he said aloud to no one...to everyone.

CHAPTER 13

CHOOSING A PATH

A strange chill settled over Gameknight999. It felt like tiny flakes of snow were being sprinkled across every inch of his skin, while at the same time he burned up from the inside; beads of perspiration formed on his arms and neck. It wasn't just the physical feelings that concerned him, but the emotional as well. He felt as if he were in the throes of battle; his heart rate accelerated, breathing strained, and veins pumped with adrenaline. Simultaneously, however, he was petrified by a fear that felt very familiar, and he knew exactly where these feelings came from...a dream—no, a nightmare.

"Gameknight, are you alright?" Crafter asked. The young boy with old, wise eyes, moved quickly to his friend's side. "You look pale...and your breathing... you're out of breath. What's wrong?"

They were in the village that sat over the crafting chamber their minecart had led them to, taking up residence in the castle-like tower that protected the cavern's entrance. Gameknight had been gazing out the window that overlooked the village when the feeling had struck him.

"Come, sit down," Crafter said as he led his friend to a blocky wooden chair that sat in the corner of the room. "Tell me what's wrong."

Gameknight just sat and stared at the cobblestone wall, trying to sort out the emotions that were flooding into him. And then he started to shake ever so slightly, fear rippling through every nerve in his body. A sound from the floor below drew Crafter's attention away from his friend. Someone had entered the tower, and was now ascending the ladder to the top floor. The sounds of hands and feet on the wooden ladder grew louder and louder as the visitor approached. Just then, Hunter's red hair appeared through the hole in the floor as she climbed the rest of the way up and stepped into the room. She stood there next to the ladder, confident and strong, watching the scene.

"Gameknight, tell me what is happening," Crafter said, concern in his voice.

"He's here," Gameknight mumbled.

"What?"

"It's him...he's here," he moaned.

"Who?" Hunter asked from the doorway.

Sensing danger, she notched an arrow in her bow and moved quickly to the window, scanning the village for threats.

Gameknight shook violently for just an instant as the cold fingers of dread squeezed his heart, but then the terrifying sensation fading away.

"Erebus...he's here, somewhere on this server."

"Erebus, who's Erebus?" Hunter asked as she put away the arrow but kept the bow in her hand, always ready.

"He cackled that eerie enderman laugh he has," Gameknight said, his voice still trembling a little. "I could feel him. And I could tell that he could feel me, too. He knows I'm here, on this server." He paused to force himself to take a slow, calming breath, the strange feeling having passed, but the sensation of fear still present. "He's coming, and he can feel my fear."

"Gameknight, it's alright, it will—" Crafter began but was interrupted.

"Fear...fear is a good thing," Hunter said in a strong voice. "Fear means that you still have something that needs killing. You don't need to be afraid of this Erebus character. One enderman is like the next, just another monster that needs killing."

"You don't get it," Gameknight snapped. "This is Erebus, self-proclaimed King of the Endermen. He leads an army of monsters that are vicious and ruthless. They will attack village after village until they destroy everything on this server. We were able to stop him on the last server, but we had help. We had famous Minecraft users to help battle the mobs. Now, we only have villagers...they won't be enough to turn back the tide, not here. Besides, we can't fight Erebus here in the Overworld, and also fight Malacoda in the Nether. We don't know if they are working together or separate, but either way, they probably have too many monsters for us to face."

He stood, finally feeling better, and moved back to the window to gaze across the serene village. He could see NPCs going about their lives, blissfully ignorant of the destructive wave that was about to crash down upon them. Turning around, he looked at Crafter, hoping the young boy had some answers hidden within that aged mind.

"We need information," Crafter said as he stood and crossed the room to stand at Gameknight's side. "We need to know what Malacoda is doing so that we can figure out which threat is most pressing: the

King of the Nether or the King of the Endermen. We must choose a path and face one of these threats *now*." He paused to look at Hunter, whose eyes were hungry for adventure, for killing, and then glanced back at Gameknight. "We must travel to the Nether."

"The Nether..." Gameknight moaned. He knew what that meant: zombie-pigmen, blazes, magma cubes, and of course, the dreaded ghasts. It was a dangerous place, a living nightmare...he was frightened, but then Crafter's words flickered in his mind like a candle being lit in the darkness. *"Deeds do not make the hero..."* There was much fear for him to overcome here, but the deed seemed great as well.

"We either do that," Crafter advised, "or wait for Erebus to come, and then possibly be forced to face two armies."

The image of two great armies filled Gameknight's mind: a massive horde of Overworld creatures on one side and the monsters of the Nether on the other. The thought made him shudder, and he knew that Crafter was right. Looking around the room, he admired the two NPCs that stood before him; there was Crafter, with his stout friendship and ever-present wisdom and compassion, and then there was Hunter, with her overwhelming, and at times irrational, bravery. They each had something Gameknight desperately needed: confidence and courage.

Sighing, he realized that he knew the path he needed to follow, and where it would lead.

"OK Crafter...to the Nether."

"You two are insane," Hunter interjected. "The Nether is filled with nothing but fire and death. There's enough death in the Overworld, why go looking for more?"

"Because we *have* to know what Malacoda's plan is," Crafter said. "You saw all those Nether beasts

in the last village. He's mobilizing an army and collecting crafters for some reason. We *must* know what's going on."

"Well, you can count me out," she snapped. "There are enough things to kill here in this world. I don't need to go to that burning, nightmarish world to find things to shoot with my bow. You two can go without me."

"We could use your help," Gameknight said softly as he looked at the ground, ashamed to ask for her assistance.

"Not gonna happen," she replied, her brilliant red hair flying through the air as she spun around and moved to the hole in the floor. She grabbed the rungs and dropped down the ladder, sliding to the ground.

Gameknight and Crafter watched her slide down the ladder and slam the door below as she headed out into the village.

"I'm guessing we shouldn't count on her for any help," Gameknight said, a half-smile on his face.

Crafter laughed and slapped his friend on the back. "Maybe not...come on, let's get this done. We're just going to take a peek and see what's going on down there in the Nether. We'll be back in no time."

Nodding apprehensively, Gameknight followed Crafter to the ground floor, shadowing him down the secret ladder that led to the crafting chamber.

Once there, Gameknight's ears were assaulted by the commotion and noise. They had convinced the village's crafter to have the NPCs start making weapons and armor, iron swords by the hundreds and armor for the masses that would soon be called upon to stand up against the destructive tide that was about to flood this server. All across the crafting chamber, there now stood NPCs, each one making the devices of war. Piles of armor and weapons were shoved into corners and under minecart rails, chests overflowing.

As they crafted, Gameknight could see the numerous minecarts move into the cavern with NPCs riding within, some of them with an optimistic look on their faces; whole communities answering Crafter's call. But some of the NPCs had a look of despair on their faces. These were the Lost, villagers that had lost their crafter and were looking for a new community. Crafter had quickly become something of a legend amongst the NPCs; the homeless, village-less NPCs were flocking to this town to be adopted by Crafter and become part of a community again.

When they reached the cavern floor, the new NPCs flocked to Crafter, all of them wanting to lean against their new leader. Gameknight stepped back as the NPCs surrounded his friend. As he watched, Gameknight saw Crafter glow with a soft blue light as he accepted these new NPCs into his care, their faces now filled with jubilation and pride.

Gameknight999 smiled.

Moving to inspect some of the swords that were being crafted, he watched as Crafter talked quietly to the village's crafter, the young boy and old NPC both dressed alike. But the village's crafter clearly showed respect and deference to Crafter's years of experience and wisdom. After their quick discussion, Crafter ran up the steps and approached Gameknight.

"The diggers will start mining for obsidian," Crafter explained.

Gameknight could see a group of twenty NPCs with iron pickaxes over their shoulders moving down a mine shaft, a few with swords following close behind. It was always dangerous to go down to the lava level; that was monster territory. The miners and warriors glanced over their shoulders at Gameknight, then stood up a little taller as the User-that-is-not-a-user waved to them.

"We'll need the obsidian to make a portal to the Nether," Crafter said. "I'll supervise here. You should try to get some sleep. You look terrible."

"Gee, thanks," Gameknight said with a smile.

"Besides," Crafter continued, "I think we'll need every ounce of strength when we travel to the Nether. Go get some rest. I'll be up as well, after they get the portal started."

Gameknight nodded, realizing how tired he truly felt.

The Nether...the thought of going to that terrible land of smoke and flame filled him with trepidation. But he knew he couldn't just hide here in this village and wait for Erebus to find him. He had to do something to change the equation, or they'd all be doomed. With a sigh, he turned and headed back up the steps that led to the surface. He was going to get some rest, even though as he walked he could already feel the monsters of the Nether sharpening their claws in anticipation.

CHAPTER 14

NEW NIGHTMARE

Gameknight999 tried to look through the silvery fog, but the swirling, damp mist was just too thick for his vision to penetrate. He could feel its moist kiss on his arms and face. It gave a cold and soggy feeling to his shirt and body that chilled him to the bone.

Strange shapes moved in the distance, shadowy forms appearing and then disappearing as they maneuvered through the thick clouds, their bodies only fuzzy outlines—unrecognizable. An icy fear began to saturate his awareness as the apparitions moved through the fog; there was an undefined presence here, a dark, shadowy form that floated through the silvery clouds and filled him with dread. The creatures moved about him as if to tantalize his senses and tickle his imagination, his own fears filling in the blank images with frightening details. He started to shake with fear.

"Where am I?" he asked the shadows. "What is this place?"

His voice echoed through the cloudy vapor and came back to him from all directions, making him feel as if he were surrounded. Laughter then began to percolate through the mist, beginning as the faintest wisp of an angry giggle and building to a maniacal uproar that etched away at the last vestiges of his courage. The noise assaulted him from all sides, forcing him to put his blocky hands over his ears, but that didn't seem to help. If anything, the movement seemed to make the sound grow louder, as if it were coming from within him rather than from the silver, terrifying fog.

And then suddenly, the laughter stopped.

Gameknight looked around, trying to discern why the noise had abruptly disappeared, but no matter what, he was grateful for the respite. Still, he felt in the deepest part of his soul that the silence was likely just as dangerous and terrifying as the laughter had been. The mysterious shapes within the fog had all stopped moving, and were now standing perfectly still; these ghostly statues encircled him.

Then it started...a soft purring that melted away some of the icicles of fear that had been lodged in his soul. The soft, reassuring sound filled him with a warmth that spread throughout his body. He could tell that the purring was coming from his left. It was as if a massive collection of cats was out there somewhere within the fog, their contentment resonating with each breath. Their satisfaction brought a faint smile to his face. Then, the sound started to change. A whisper of a cry mixed with the soft purring, like a baby that was far away, desperately crying for his mother. The crying became louder and moved closer, but as it neared, the cries changed subtly. It no longer sounded just like a child missing his mother. No, the crying sounded angry and spiteful, as if the child had been punished for some terrible wrong and now sought revenge. The cries accentuated the feelings of anger and malice.

A shape started to form within the fog; it was clearly the source of the yowling wails. It was a large, square shape, with dangling things hanging underneath its massive body. Gameknight999 felt that he should recognize this shape, but knew that he was in the dream world again, and things like memory and reason didn't always work here. One thing he did know was that he was afraid of this thing, the fear growing to terror as the monstrosity approached.

And then the gigantic creature pushed through the fog. A huge, square, childlike face emerged through the haze and stared down at him, angry tears staining the skin under the terrifying eyes; it was Malacoda.

"Welcome to the Land of Dreams, User-that-is-not-a-user," he boomed, his deep voice reverberating with echoes. "I have been waiting for you for some time now."

"What is this place?" Gameknight asked, looking up into the terrible face of the beast. "This isn't real...you aren't real. This is just a dream."

Malacoda's face brightened as a sinister smile spread across his face, then he burst into an evil, thunderous laugh. The sound was instantly joined by the laughter of the other forms within the mist, some of them now glowing as if aflame.

"Users are so ignorant of things within Minecraft," Malacoda boomed. He flicked one of his tentacles to silence his cohorts. Their laughter instantly died away, leaving only a mechanical wheezing sound. "Things in the Land of Dreams are as real as the dreamer makes them. Haven't you figured that out yet, User-that-is-not-a-user?"

"I...ah..."

Reaching out with lightning speed, Malacoda shot a tentacle toward Gameknight, and wrapped the clammy appendage around his body, pinning his arms to his side. With excruciating slowness, he drew Gameknight toward his huge bone-white face, lifting the User-that-is-not-a-user off the ground and raising him so that they were eye to eye. Gameknight struggled against the thick tentacle, but it was like cold iron: unyielding and solid.

"I have brought you here to give you a chance to escape your death," the King of the Nether explained. "You see, you cannot stop me. I will take my army to the Source and destroy all of these Minecraft worlds, whether you try to resist me or not. You and that little toy of a crafter are nothing compared to me. My forces will sweep this world clean, then do the same to the Source, and there is nothing you can do about it. Your only hope is to run and hide. Enjoy the last few days of your life. Your death is inevitable."

Fear sizzled through Gameknight999 as those words burned into his soul. He imagined his sister standing at the top of their basement stairs, screaming as the monsters slowly flowed up and out, all because of him. He could almost see her in the fog, her silent terrified screams stabbing at him, at his fear. As these thoughts played through his mind, Malacoda smiled an evil, knowing smile, as if he could see what Gameknight was thinking.

"A sister," the ghast boomed. "You have a sister... most interesting. I can't wait to meet her. Ha ha ha."

Malacoda filled the air with his booming laugh. "Let me show you how it will be with your sister and the rest of your family."

Images played through Gameknight's mind then, as if he was watching a movie, but it was one that he was unable to look away from. He squeezed his eyes shut, but it made no difference. The images were playing within his mind.

He saw Malacoda emerge from the portal his father's digitizer had formed, the massive creature barely able to fit through it. He knocked over piles of boxes and stacks of books as Malacoda floated through his basement. When he reached the steps, one of his tentacles shot upward and grabbed something at the basement door, slowly drawing his prize in. Gameknight could see that it was his sister, her face pale with fear, tears streaming down her face. Malacoda held her firmly as he floated up the steps. The monster squeezed through the basement door and into their kitchen. Blazes and zombie-pigmen followed their king as he moved through the house, looking for other victims. Quickly, Gameknight's parents were herded into the living room by some skeletons, their sharp arrows pointed at the adults' defenseless backs. Striking out with his long tentacles, Malacoda also grabbed Gameknight999's parents and held them tight, drawing them near their daughter. Their struggles made no difference; they were prisoners, and completely helpless.

With the flick of another tentacle, Malacoda had some blazes blast open the side of their home. Fireballs from the flaming creatures smashed into their living room wall, blasting it to a million pieces, their sofa and chairs instantly aflame. Smoke started to billow out of their home as Malacoda drifted out into the street, a constant flow of monsters following their king. With the flick of his tentacles, he had his forces attack all the homes nearby. Zombies smashed in doors and creepers exploded walls, letting giant spiders and skeletons into the homes to attack the defenseless inhabitants.

The scene replayed itself all across his neighborhood, then his city, then his state, the attacks relentless. The citizens were unable to resist the flood of monsters that were flowing from the Gateway of Light in his basement. With his defeat in Minecraft, Gameknight999 had unwillingly caused all this destruction; it was his fault. Looking over at his sister, he saw her terrified face staring up at him, expecting her big brother to somehow take care of all this and save her. He felt like a failure and wriggled to get free. Malacoda held Gameknight's family tightly within his tentacle grip, forcing them to watch the destruction of their world; the ghast was saving these three for last.

Gameknight tried to push the images from his brain, but he was helpless. Malacoda seemed to be in control of his mind.

"Noooo," he moaned, tears streaming from his rectangular eyes.

Malacoda laughed. "Yes, I will save your family for last and force them to watch the extermination of their species," he said, his deep voice resonating with pride. "Then I will extinguish their useless lives and become ruler of everything. My army will sweep across the physical world like an unstoppable storm, cleansing everything in its path."

"Noooo," Gameknight cried again, his eyes now stinging.

"Yes, I am certainly looking forward to meeting that sister of yours."

The monster laughed again as icicles of fear cut into Gameknight999's heart. He thought about the look of complete terror on his sister's face and shook uncontrollably. She was terrified, and I was supposed to protect her, *he thought.* I'm her big brother, and that's my job—to keep her safe!

Anger started to well up within him, not directed at the hideous monster that had its cold tentacles wrapped around his body, but focused inwardly on himself.

I can't fail her. I refuse.

"And by the way, User-that-is-not-a-user, tell that runt of a crafter that I'm coming for him next," Malacoda said with an especially vile tone, his tentacles squeezing a little tighter, making it hard to breathe. *"I'm building something special, and it's almost complete. There is a place of honor reserved for him."*

Just then, images of the Nether flooded into Gameknight's mind. He could see a massive fortress, built out of dark stone, standing atop tall columns, raised walkways stretching out around the massive structure. Gameknight's view of the fortress sped before his eyes as if he were flying, his point of view slowly drifted across the landscape. He realized that he was still within Malacoda's icy grip. The monstrosity was floating about the fortress within the Land of Dreams, peering into raised balconies and through barred windows. Gameknight was shocked by the size of the structure. It must have been at least two hundred blocks tall, if not more.

Malacoda suddenly flew to the massive tower at the center of the fortress, plunged through an open balcony, and emerged within the structure. Before him stood a large square room made of netherrack, barred windows dotting the exterior. Gameknight could see people within the structure—sad figures garbed in black with long gray stripes going down their fronts: crafters.

"Behold your friend's future home," Malacoda said in a sinister voice. "He will soon be a guest here, but his true place of honor will be elsewhere."

The ghast then spun around and shot out of the massive tower. Without breaking any blocks, he passed through the wall of the fortress and emerged outside. Floating up high, he moved out over the massive lava sea and turned back to look at his mighty citadel. Gameknight could see a massive opening at the foot of the fortress, with steps leading up to the entrance. Countless numbers of creatures moved in and out of the citadel, some of them being NPC prisoners forced into labor. The entranceway yawned open toward the massive sea of lava that extended out into the distance, the opposite shore not visible through the smoke and haze. Narrow bridges stretched across the molten sea, reaching out to a circular island of stone. Around the edge of the island, he could see twelve obsidian blocks placed evenly apart, positioned on the island like the numbers on a clock. Atop most of the dark obsidian blocks sat a single bluish block of some kind—something that looked like a crafting bench but was not. It was different yet familiar at the same time. Gameknight noticed that not all of the obsidian blocks had this new thing on top, but most were capped. At the center of the island stood a large structure that was perhaps four blocks tall, with steps leading up from all sides; all of them were made of obsidian. And this was where Malacoda brought Gameknight.

"I wanted to show you where your defeat will come. This is where I will take my vengeance on you and destroy that little thing of a crafter you call a friend. His downfall will pave the way for my victory, and when I no longer have any use for him, I will crush him to nothing."

The tentacles around Gameknight999 squeezed a

little tighter, making breathing even more difficult.

Crafter...I can't watch him die again like on the last server.

His anger started turning into a burning rage, now, while images of flames filled his mind. And in that instant, he looked down and saw that he was literally on fire. Strange bluish, iridescent flames danced across his body. They were the same color as an enchanted weapon, something between blue and purple, but had a feeling of power within them. As his rage increased, the intensity of those sapphire flames rose as well, their kiss starting to make Malacoda's tentacles twitch and writhe.

Gameknight suddenly realized that the flames were coming from him—his imagination, his dream. This realization filled him with a glimmer of hope. He was overwhelmingly afraid of Malacoda, the King of the Nether, who was now in his nightmares, but something Crafter had said trickled into the back of his mind: "Deeds do not make the hero, Gameknight999, how they overcome their fear does."

His friend's young voice filled his head, driving the images of his sister and family back into the darkness; they had been banished from his head.

No, *he thought.* I will not let this happen!

Deeds do not make the hero...

His blue flames burned a little brighter, making Malacoda's tentacles spasm more strongly, his grip still firm, but loosening.

NO, I will not play the victim anymore, *Gameknight thought. The flames started to burn brighter, forming a blue circle around him within the mist.*

How they overcome their fear does...

"NO...NO!" *he said aloud.*

Suddenly, he was a blazing sun of blue fire, his flames biting into Malacoda's tentacles like an enchanted diamond sword. The ghost released him in an instant, then floated upward, out of reach.

"So, the cub learns," Malacoda said sarcastically, the smile on the square face replaced by an evil sneer. "All the better. Now, let me give you a little lesson of my own, but remember that Minecraft is mine. Soon, your world will be mine as well, and there is nothing you can do about it."

A huge, orange fireball started to form between Malacoda's tentacles. It burned brighter and brighter until it completely overwhelmed Gameknight's blue flames. Malacoda then hurled the fireball at Gameknight with lightning speed. In an instant, he was enveloped by the ball of fire, pain resonating through every nerve, his mind feeling as if it were ablaze. And when he thought he could bear the pain no more, the fire went out, and Malacoda's face was directly in front of his.

"You will fail, User-that-is-not-a-user," the King of the Nether said. "And then you will be mine."

And with a flick of his massive body, Malacoda's tentacles shot toward Gameknight's head, hammering him with a mighty blow. Then the darkness enveloped him.

CHAPTER 15

SHIFTING THE TIDES OF WAR

ameknight woke with a start; it felt as if something had jolted him awake.

Are we being attacked? What's happening?

Where am I? Thoughts rocketed through his head as the fog of sleep gradually evaporated from his mind.

Sitting up, he looked around. Cobblestone walls surrounded him. Torches placed on each of them cast a circle of golden light that filled the room. Looking to his left, he could see Crafter sleeping in the bed next to him, the young NPC's breathing a steady rhythm. He was still asleep.

Slowly getting up from his bed, Gameknight crossed his small room and looked out the window. It was nighttime. He could see monsters lurking about, zombies and skeletons looking for the unwary. But this village was well prepared. Blocks of stone had been placed in front of wooden doors to keep zombie fists from smashing them in. Torches had been placed all throughout the village, keeping the light level high; this kept monsters from spawning within the village. But with all the preparations they'd made, there were still monsters close at hand. There were always monsters close by at night.

As he looked out the window, Gameknight could feel that something was different. Something had changed. The music of the world had somehow been altered, so slightly that it was almost imperceptible, but nevertheless the grinding electronic mechanism that ran the world was playing a subtly different tune tonight. He could feel the difference, even though he couldn't quite see it. It felt like the rules of the game had changed, as if there had been some kind of software update, but the effects of the upgrade were still unseen. Gameknight followed the movement of a zombie as he tried to sort out these changes, attempting to identify what was different. He had no luck; it seemed that the new music of Minecraft held its secret close. He sighed.

Closing his eyes, he tried to concentrate on the sounds of Minecraft—the grinding sounds from the mechanism that drove this electronic world—the music of Minecraft. But instead, memories from the dream surged into his mind. The crafters trapped within that netherrack cell and that circle of stone on the lava sea, these images seemed important, really important.

"Gameknight, is everything OK?"

Turning, he found Crafter standing next to his bed, his iron sword drawn. "Yeah," he answered. "I just thought I heard something."

Crafter took a few steps closer, then suddenly stopped as his eyes grew wide with concern. "Your jaw...what happened?"

Reaching up with his blocky hand, Gameknight rubbed his jaw. It was sore, slightly swollen, and bruised.

What did I do to hurt my jaw?

And then the end of his dream came back to him in horrific detail...Malacoda. The King of the Nether had punched him with a great tentacled fist, the blow knocking him into unconsciousness and sending him out of the Land of Dreams. This was the second time he'd been hurt in the Land of Dreams: first from Erebus choking him, and now by Malacoda punching him.

What did it all mean?

"I had another dream," Gameknight said slowly, the images still trickling through his brain.

"Erebus?"

"No...this time it was Malacoda."

Gameknight rubbed his jaw again as Crafter stepped closer to get a better view. "Crafter, he showed me what he was going to do...to my family...to my sister!" He paused as emotions choked his voice. Small, blocky tears flowed from his eyes as the dream repeated its agonizing performance in his mind. Shaking his head to force the images away, he continued. "He told me about the crafters. He has them down there in his fortress in a prison cell."

"What? In his fortress?"

Gameknight nodded. "He has them in a prison cell. But there's more." He rubbed his jaw again as he looked down into his friend's bright blue eyes. "He said that he was looking for you, and that he had a special place for you. It was on this stone island on a lava sea. There were these strange blocks all around the island, like crafting benches but made of diamond. I think there were maybe ten of them, maybe more, and they were…"

Crafter gasped, his eyes wide with fear. "What did you say?" the young NPC asked, taking a step closer.

"I said that there were maybe ten of them all around the island and…"

"No," Crafter snapped, "before that. What kind of blocks did you say they were?"

"I'm not sure. I've never seen anything like them. They looked like diamond crafting benches, but that doesn't make any sense at all. How could they be—"

"Twelve," Crafter interrupted. "There will be twelve of them, and then one at the center."

"Yeah, that's it. How did you know that?"

"There is an old Prophecy—the monster's Prophecy—and it seems it's being lived out in the Nether," Crafter said in a low voice, his eyes cast to the ground. "Our Prophecy tells us of the User-that-is-not-a-user coming to save us during the time of trials, when the monsters of the Overworld will try to take over everything and get to the Source. But there is another prophecy…the Lost Prophecy.

"All crafters know of the Lost Prophecy. It tells us about the creatures of the Nether and a ring of diamond blocks, specifically diamond crafting benches. They can only be crafted by a full-fledged crafter, and are made at the expense of a crafter's life. When twelve of these crafting benches are activated in a ring, with a thirteenth at their center, a portal will be formed to take the Nether creatures directly to the Source."

Crafter paused to take a breath and let his words sink in. Raising his gaze, he looked up at Gameknight999, a look of uncertainty and fear apparent on his square face. Sighing, he continued.

"If he finishes this portal, then he can take his army straight to the server that houses the Source and try to destroy it." He paused for a moment, lost in thought, then continued. "Did he have a large army?"

"I saw lots of monsters around his fortress, but I don't think his army is that big—not yet anyway," Gameknight said. "However, the thing that concerns me is the number of spawners I saw. He has hundreds and hundreds of them. In a week or two, his army will be so big that it *will* be unstoppable."

"If they finish what they are doing down there and make that giant portal, Malacoda will move *all* of his monsters to the Source," Crafter said, his voice now sharpened with a hard edge. "And if he continues to grow his army, then..." A look of desolation covered the young NPC's face. "We have to do something...now."

"What can we do to stop Malacoda?"

As soon as he'd spoken, an image popped into Gameknight's head, an image of Malacoda screaming in rage upon finding his obsidian prison cell empty, its precious contents stolen and ushered back to the Overworld. A smile slowly grew on his face.

"I know what we have to do," the User-that-is-not-a-user said proudly. "We'll steal the crafters from him. That will stop him...for now."

"Of course," Crafter exclaimed, patting his friend on the shoulder. "It's time we shift the tides of war. We're going to bring the war *to* Malacoda instead of just reacting to him, and I know just how to do it. Come on...to the crafting chamber. We need supplies and the portal to the Nether. Let's check on the miners."

Crafter sprinted to the hole in the floor and slid down the ladder to the ground. Gameknight watched his friend leave, but hesitated.

The Nether...do I really want to go to the Nether? he thought. *But what choice do I have? I can't let Crafter go alone. I have to be there to help.*

Images of zombie-pigmen and blazes and wither skeletons and ghasts filled his mind—all the creatures of the Nether that would love to kill the User-that-is-not-a-user. And, of course, the thought of facing Malacoda paralyzed his feet, making it impossible to move. Malacoda...he was Gameknight's new nightmare, someone that actually made Erebus seem almost insignificant. He would have never thought there would be a creature in Minecraft that could be more terrifying than the King of the Endermen. But Malacoda...he was the most terrifying thing Gameknight had ever imagined.

What am I going to do? he thought as an overwhelming sense of terror coursed through his body, making him shiver.

Suddenly, a small head popped up out of the hole in the floor, two bright blue eyes staring up at the User-that-is-not-a-user.

"Hey...Gameknight...you coming?" Crafter asked.

"Yeah," Gameknight999 answered, and moved toward the opening in spite of the fear roiling through him.

CHAPTER 16

EREBUS' RAGE

Erebus howled in anger; they had come upon yet another village without any villagers...what was happening? He wanted to kill NPCs, needed their XP so that he could move up to the next server and get closer to the Source, but he wasn't making any progress. Someone or something was getting to these villages first, emptying them out before he could come and kill anyone. That was filling him with a burning rage.

"Where are they?" he screeched, his high-pitched voice scratching at the ears of those nearby.

"We don't know," one of his wither generals responded.

Erebus looked down on the floating half-skeleton. The creature was difficult to see in the darkness of night. During the daytime, its dark bones would have stood out in stark contrast to the rolling grassy hills that surrounded this village, but the dark embrace of midnight made this difficult. The King of the Endermen could just make out the three skulls that sat atop its bony torso, two of them scanning the area in all directions, looking for threats, while the center head focused on Erebus.

"This is the third village our scouts have found abandoned," the wither general reported. "They were all completely empty, with no evidence of battle. It's like all the NPCs just moved out."

"Some of these villages housed at least a hundred NPCs. Didn't you see their tracks on the ground and follow them?" Erebus asked, his rage barely held in check.

They stepped into one of the houses, the blacksmith's shop, and looked around, Erebus having to stoop so that his head wouldn't hit the ceiling. At one end of the room sat a chest. The top was flung open and the contents gone, as if someone had left in a hurry...but to where? Erebus teleported from the doorway to the open chest and looked inside, then slammed the lid closed, the box shattering upon the force of his blow. Wooden splinters flew into the air and rained down on him, making the boiling rage within him even greater.

Swallowing his anger, Erebus moved back outside. He could see the tall, castle-like tower at the center of town, its tall structure looming over the area. He headed toward it. Every village had one of these structures; it was their lookout post. The memory of Gameknight999 standing atop one of these towers on the last server during that terrible village battle still haunted the enderman's mind. That annoying User-that-is-not-a-user had actually gotten the villagers to somehow fight back. He had stood up there at the top of the tower as Erebus' own army of monsters had approached the fortified village. Erebus could remember the burning hatred he'd felt for him almost immediately, and his own defeat on the last server had only fanned the flames of his anger.

"I'm coming for you, User-that-is-not-a-user," Erebus said quietly in his screechy voice, to no one in particular.

He reached the tower quickly, the monster horde following at a distance, never wanting to be too close to their easily angered leader; only withers dared to be within arm's length. Erebus could still hear Gameknight's mocking laugh from the end of that battle, as well as the insults he'd cast at the King of the Endermen; the memory was still vivid. All the villagers had stood on the walls they'd erected around their village cheering for the User-that-is-not-a-user, many of them also mocking Erebus as he watched the remains of his army retreat back into the shadows. The memory made him angrier and angrier. This tower was clearly a symbol of that defeat. It had to be destroyed... NOW.

"Creepers, forward," he commanded.

A group of mottled green creepers scurried forward, their tiny feet a blur of motion. They all ran up to Erebus and looked up at him with their cold, black eyes, their perpetually frowning mouths agape.

"I want twelve creepers inside that tower right there," he commanded. "Look for any villagers. Keep looking until I order you to come out."

The creepers, knowing refusal was fatal, moved quickly through the open door and crammed themselves into the ground floor of the tower. A few started to ascend the steps to the second floor, searching for villagers that the King of the Endermen knew would not be there.

He could still hear Gameknight laughing in the back of his mind—his fury over the defeat at the village still strong. Turning to look at his general, he spoke two quiet words, only meant for the wither commander's ears.

"Ignite them," he said.

"Sir?" the wither general asked, confused.

"What don't you understand, *wither*?"

Erebus disappeared and instantly reappeared on the creature's opposite shoulder, then teleported so that he was directly in front of the three-headed skeletal beast, and again so that he appeared at his back, each time rapping ever so slightly on the monster, letting him know that he could be destroyed at any instant. Returning to his original spot, the King of the Endermen glared down at him again.

"Do I need to repeat myself?" Erebus asked, his rage hanging by threads.

He could still see Gameknight999 standing atop this tower in his mind, smiling a stupid grin at him. The memory drove all sound reasoning away.

"Why are you still just standing there, doing nothing? DO IT!"

And at that, the wither launched a stream of flaming black skulls into the open doorway, striking the nearest creepers and starting their ignition process. The green beasts started to glow white and expand, growing bigger and bigger, their bodies becoming white hot, until…

BOOM…BOOM, BOOM, BOOM.

A chain reaction of explosions shook the village. The creepers that detonated first lit the fuse on the remaining creepers, creating a series of explosions that tore into the tower with an explosive fist. Blocks of cobblestone rained down across the village as a mighty gash was torn into the surface of Minecraft. When the blocks settled and the smoke cleared, Erebus stared at the remains of the tower with glee. The thing that reminded him so much of that humiliating day, that terrible defeat, was gone, and now only a deep crater remained.

"Wait a minute…what is that?" he asked, pointing into the crater with one of his long, dark arms.

At the bottom of the smoking crater was a dark hole that plunged straight downward. It was clearly something built by the villagers, the shaft cut perfectly vertical, with the remnants of a ladder dangling on one side. Erebus teleported to the bottom of the crater, a cloud of purple particles floating about him for an instant after he'd materialized. The ground was still warm. The acrid smell of sulfur floated all around him, the wafting remains of the creepers filling the air.

He stooped down and peered into the tunnel. The ladder attached to the wall stretched down into the darkness; the end of the tunnel wasn't visible even to the keen eyes of an enderman.

Clearly this was made for those foolish NPCs to go from their pitiful village to something underground, he thought to himself. *But why? What is down there?*

Standing, he found that his army now ringed the crater; zombies, skeletons, creepers, endermen, spiders, and slimes were all looking down at him. One of the withers floated to him, its blackened skeletal form standing out against the gray stone and brown dirt that lined the pit.

"What are your orders, sir?" the wither asked with a dry, crackling voice.

Erebus' eyes scanned his troops on the crater's rim. Spying a group of skeletons, he motioned them to come near. The monsters glanced at each other, their featureless black eyes still somehow looking terrified. Slowly, hesitantly, the group of four skeletons moved to their leader, the sound of clattering bones echoing through the air.

"Go down this ladder and find out where it leads," Erebus commanded. "Once it is known, one of you will return and report to me while the others stay behind to keep everything secure."

Moving quickly, the skeletons clambered down the ladder, disappearing into the darkness. After about ten minutes, one of the skeletons returned, its head sticking up out of the tunnel like a disembodied trophy.

"There is a great chamber below," the skeleton said, its rattling voice sounding like the grinding of bone against bone. "Perhaps twenty crafting benches cover the cavern floor and a series of minecart tracks lead off into tunnels. They go in all directions—maybe thirty or forty tunnels in all, with minecarts lying about in open chests."

"So this is how they do it," Erebus murmured.

"What, sir?" asked his wither general.

"The NPCs," the King of the Endermen answered. "They were able to quickly communicate with the other villages, move people from one place to another without walking across the landscape. They must have had a minecart network."

His voice started to crackle with indignation. He suddenly realized that this network was part of his defeat on the last server, and this knowledge filled him with boiling anger and a desire to kill.

"Do the minecart rails look to be in working order?" he asked, his screechy voice conveying his vexation.

"I believe so," the skeleton replied meekly, knowing that if he were wrong, it would likely cost him his life.

"Very well," Erebus replied, then turned to address his troops. "The villagers have been keeping this secret from us, the mobs of the Overworld. While they can move from village to village underground, we must risk traveling across the landscape, always in fear of being caught in the sunlight—something that we all know is fatal to some of our brothers and sisters. These NPCs kept this secret from us, knowing that it would cost many of us our lives."

Some of the mobs started to mumble amongst each other, clearly agitated. Erebus disappeared, the reappeared at the crater's edge, his body surrounded by sparkling purple teleportation particles. He stood before a group of zombies.

"These NPCs would gladly see all of you suffer the flames of daylight so that they can have more of the Overworld to themselves. They delight in your suffering, revel in the knowledge that we, the monsters of the Overworld, must live underground, only getting a morsel from the banquet table that is Minecraft."

More mumblings of discontent from the mob could be heard as their anger grew, but they weren't where he wanted them to be yet, so he continued.

"We have shared the smallest slice of this world for too long," he screeched. "And this minecart network will allow us to move across this world with impunity, free from the ravages of the sun."

The zombies and skeletons started to snarl and cheer, followed by the clicking of the giant spiders. Excitement and anger were both about to boil over.

"My army will flow across this world like a flood, drawing savage revenge upon the NPCs and users until all are extinguished. Once they are all dead, we will cross over to the Source and free ourselves from Minecraft's limitations and take over the physical world!"

His army was now cheering, and the chant, "Destroy the NPCs...Destroy the NPCs...Destroy the NPCs..." echoed across the landscape.

"Now, my friends, FOLLOW ME TO OUR DESTINY."

And at that, Erebus teleported to the tunnel opening and dove into the darkness, his army of monsters flowing down into the crater, a relentless flood of angry monsters with only one thought in mind: destroy.

CHAPTER 17

THE CLASH OF KINGS

Erebus and his army moved from village to village through the minecart network, unconcerned about the time of day. The first village they came to was empty, the crafting chamber completely deserted, discarded belongings scattered across the stone floor. Erebus sent some of his sun-resistant monsters to the surface, only to have them return with reports of an empty village.

Erebus grew angry... *Where were the villagers?*

The mob gathered about the minecarts and piled in again, moving to the next village, and the situation repeated itself; the village was abandoned.

Erebus grew even angrier... *What was going on here?*

"Perhaps we should split up," his wither commander suggested. "These villagers pose little threat to us."

"No," snapped Erebus. "The User-that-is-not-a-user is out there, somewhere, and he is preparing his pieces in this game. We cannot risk dividing our forces."

"But the villagers cannot fight back," the wither insisted.

"They can, you fool. Don't you know anything? The presence of the User-that-is-not-a-user changes everything, even the rules of war. He cannot be underestimated. I made that mistake once. I will not make it again. We stay together."

The monsters piled into the minecarts again, the withers and endermen going first, followed by skeletons, creepers, spiders, zombies, and slimes protecting their rear. Erebus was at the column's head, acting as the tip of the spear. The army easily flowed through the minecart tunnel, their discontentment building with every deserted village they encountered. Erebus could sense some kind of pattern here—could feel Gameknight's involvement.

"I'll find you soon, User-that-is-not-a-user," he said to himself as he zoomed through the minecart tunnel, the darkness comforting him.

And then he could see it...a dim light at the end of the tunnel. Turning backward, he motioned to the withers behind him, signaling them to be ready. As they burst into the brightly lit chamber, Erebus was greeted with a wonderful, joyous sound that was simply the best music to his ears...screams of terror.

"Mobs in the crafting chamber!" yelled one of the NPCs. "Everyone, RUN!"

Before anyone could leave, Erebus teleported to the other end of the chamber. Grabbing the dirt blocks on which the minecart rails were attached, he removed the blocks, making the rails fall to the ground, closing off that avenue of escape. Teleporting from rail to rail, he destroyed all of the tracks that led out of the crafting chamber, sealing off the inhabitants, escape route.

The withers then entered the chamber and began throwing their deadly black skulls, the flaming blocks slamming into the NPCs without remorse, killing the recipients and damaging those nearby. More monsters flooded into the chamber as the terrified cries of the NPCs filled the air. The clattering sounds of bones started to echo throughout the space as skeletons entered the fray, their pointed barbs of death streaking through the air and biting into flesh.

Just as the rest of Erebus' army flowed out of the minecart tunnel, an explosion shook the ground—a massive explosion—followed by the *thud, thud, thud* of smaller explosions. And then suddenly, the door at the top of the chamber burst open, and Erebus couldn't believe what he saw…a ghast with blood-red eyes.

"What is happening to my prisoners?" the ghast boomed, its feline voice filling the chamber with fear.

A mass of blazes surged out of the blasted doorway as the ghast slowly moved out into the open air, hovering up high near the ceiling, its nine long tentacles twitching with excitement. Following the blazes were zombie-pigmen, then wither skeletons, distant cousins to Erebus' wither commanders. The room was choked with monsters, all of them confused and unsure about what to do.

"These NPCs are not your prisoners," Erebus snapped. "I am the King of the Endermen, and these victims belong to me."

Malacoda's gaze quickly snapped to Erebus, a venomous rage on his deceivingly innocent-looking face. "Listen to me, enderman," Malacoda said with a sneer. "You don't know what's going on here. There is a war raging across Minecraft, and you are interfering with my plans."

"Of course I know about the war, *ghast*." Erebus stepped forward, allowing three glowing balls of XP to flow into him. The feeling of increased power was exhilarating as he leveled up. Smiling, he glared back at the creature. "I have already faced the User-that-is-not-a-user in battle on the last server plane and have followed him to this server to finish him off. I am going to drain this world of XP, then take my army to the Source, and you are in *my* way."

Malacoda slowly moved through the air, then shot downward toward Erebus with a speed that most would have thought impossible for such a large creature. Wrapping his long tentacles around the enderman's body, he floated back up to the ceiling, holding the struggling King of the Endermen high above the ground. A purplish glow started to envelop Erebus, but it was suddenly extinguished as the enderman was stopped from teleporting away.

"You cannot teleport while in my presence, *enderman.* I control the workings of all portals that are nearby, and your feeble teleportation skills are no exception."

Malacoda waited to make sure that all eyes were on him. He wanted to make sure the Overworld mob knew who was in command here. His troops continued to move into the chamber as he held the King of the Endermen aloft, the blazes taking up strategic positions around the greatest threats, the withers.

"Now, I will release you, *enderman.*"

"The name is Erebus."

"Fine...I will release you, *Erebus*, and then you will do as I command or suffer my wrath. Do you understand?"

Erebus grunted a high-pitched, screechy consent that sounded like the creaking of a rusty hinge, then stopped struggling. Malacoda floated downward a bit, then released him, allowing Erebus to fall the rest of the way. As he fell, Erebus tried to teleport away, but found that he was still being blocked, likely because of his proximity to the ghast. He hit the ground hard, taking some damage to his HP. A gasp of shock came from his troops.

Standing quickly, he shouted out orders. "Withers, attack the ghast NOW!!!"

Before any of the three-headed monsters could even move, a barrage of fireballs rained down onto them. The blazes were firing from their positions around the chamber. Then the smaller ghasts that had entered the room opened up, their fiery balls of death also seeking out the black, skeletal three-headed monsters. In seconds, ten of the withers were dead and small piles of coal and bone littered the cavern floor. The monsters of the Overworld all took a few steps back, lowering their gazes, hoping to avoid being the next example.

"Now let me explain to you how it is, *Erebus*," Malacoda said, his loud, purring voice making the NPCs in the cavern cower with fear. "I am Malacoda, King of the Nether, and I am leading this war. I will share with you my plans for this world and for the Source, but only after you prove your worth to me."

One of the skeletons moved to stand next to Erebus, a look of defiance on his bony face. Malacoda was there in a flash, wrapping his pale tentacles around the creature. Rising high up into the chamber, the King of the Nether squeezed and squeezed. Everyone in the chamber could hear a cracking sound, like a pile of sticks being stepped on by some giant...and then the noises abruptly ended. Releasing his prey, Malacoda dropped a pile of bones onto the ground, the small pieces scattering across the cavern floor, all disconnected. All eyes looked down at the remnants of the skeleton, then fixed back on the ghast.

"But my first command to you is to stop this foolish killing of NPCs," Malacoda continued. "Instead, you will collect them for me, especially the crafters. I have a need for more laborers in the Nether, and you will gather them for me. You may kill some of them to encourage the others to obey, but do not harm the crafters...they are special and cannot be injured."

Malacoda pointed one of his tentacles toward the village's crafter; the black-robed NPC was standing in the corner, surrounded by iron-clad villagers. A group of blazes pushed through the crowd and surrounded the crafter, the other villagers cowering in fear.

"All you monsters of the Overworld," Malacoda

boomed. "I am preparing a way to the Source that can include all of you, if you serve me well. Your pitiful *King* will act as one of my generals and help to accelerate the collection of NPCs and crafters. Everything depends on the collection of crafters, and they are becoming scarce, for some reason. You will all help me, or meet the same fate as those bones on the cavern floor."

Monstrous eyes shifted from the floating ghast to the pile of bones that hovered on the cavern floor; they also surveyed the smoky outlines of three-headed withers that were forever burned into the stone surfaces. They then shifted their gazes back up to their new leader.

"Those villagers that are strong and healthy will be taken back to the Nether to work for our cause. The weak and infirm can be dealt with as you wish." Malacoda then scrutinized Erebus. "Bring me villagers and crafters, and you will be rewarded. Disobey, and you will be destroyed. I will be sending blazes and ghasts with you to make sure my orders are followed." He then floated down so that his massive, square face was level with Erebus. "Understand?"

Erebus stuffed his rage into the deepest, darkest place within his soul and swallowed. He bit back his pride and nodded his head.

"Good," Malacoda replied. "Bring me my villagers and my prizes quickly. I want you to personally deliver them to the Nether. The blazes will show you the location of my portals." He then leaned in closer and spoke in a low voice so only Erebus heard him. "Do not delay if you wish to avoid being punished."

And at that, the King of the Nether turned and headed back up to the chamber entrance, a circle of ghasts following close behind, the crafter in tow.

Erebus glared at the ghast's back, completely outraged. *How dare that creature treat me like this? I am Erebus, King of the Endermen.*

He paused, then grinned ever so slightly as a thought percolated up through his evil brain. *Just when that floating monstrosity doesn't expect it, I will have my revenge...but first, the User-that-is-not-a-user...then this fool of a king...and then the Source.*

The pieces of the puzzle started clicking in place within his violent, twisted mind, and a malicious smile crept across his face.

CHAPTER 18
RESCUE

The crafting chamber was a bustle of activity as groups of diggers expanded the cavern, making room for all the NPCs that were flocking to this village, Crafter's call still resonating within the music of Minecraft. There was a nearly constant flow of NPCs arriving by minecart, and the homes on the surface were full. Diggers were carving out new tunnels and excavating rooms off the new passages for the newcomers—homes for the new warriors for Minecraft.

Not only were diggers expanding the crafting chamber, but many were also mining deep down into the ground. Gameknight watched with curiosity as the NPCs emerged from the mine, each carrying a massive load of stone, iron ore, and coal. Those who had been digging deeper emerged with small amounts of diamond and obsidian. They had been at it for days, carving their way into the bowels of Minecraft, looking for rare materials. Of course, obsidian was the main target of their efforts. This was the fundamental block needed to build a portal to the Nether, and the safest way to get it was to dig down to the lava level and mine it with diamond picks.

Once pockets of lava were found, the miners dug passageways around the molten stone, marking its perimeter. NPCs with buckets of water then created flowing water sources and carefully allowed the streams to flow over the lava. As soon as the flowing water met the lava, it quenched the molten rock and formed the dark purple blocks. Then the miners went to work digging up the newly formed obsidian with their diamond pickaxes—the only tool that was strong enough to break those precious cubes.

As the miners trudged from the mineshaft with their prizes, the portal gradually began to take shape. Builders first set two obsidian blocks into holes in the ground, then added three blocks piled up on either side of the inlaid pair, and finally capped two black obsidian blocks across the top; ten blocks were used in total, and the ring of stone slowly became complete.

Gameknight was amazed at how quickly the miners found the materials. As the ring was formed, he moved nearer to look at the beautiful obsidian. The dark blocks, with their purple flecks of color, stood out in dark contrast to the gray stone that covered most of the gigantic crafting chamber. They seemed to call out to him, the flashes of color reminding him of the dancing particles that always surrounded an enderman.

Walking right up to the silent ring, he reached out and placed his hand on its smooth surface. The obsidian felt cool to the touch, but also seemed alive with energy. He could feel power pulsing within the stones: the power of fire and water—a remnant from the violent clash during the block's creation.

Reaching out with his senses, he wasn't sure how, Gameknight could feel something on the other side of these blocks—not behind them, but on the other side of the dimension they were about to open. He knew white hot anger lurked in that parallel dimension— raging heat, either from the ever-present lava flows that crisscrossed the Nether or from the ferocity of the Nether creatures' hatred for those in the Overworld. And then suddenly, he felt a violent burst of malice from the shadowy stone, the specter of something vile and malignant on the other side sensing his presence. It tried to reach out to strike at him, though the portal was not yet complete, the image of a pale snake-like tentacle flashing through his mind.

Malacoda.

Swiftly pulling his hand back, Gameknight stepped away from the obsidian ring, checking his blocky fingers for scars or burns. Glancing around the room, he looked to see if anyone had noticed. With the bustle of activity in the chamber—miners coming up from the mines, NPCs crafting armor and weapons, blocks of iron ore being smelted into ingots, minecarts traveling in all directions on the crisscrossing network of rails— no one noticed his reaction except for Crafter.

"What was that?" the young boy asked, his old eyes showing a hint of worry.

"Nothing," he lied. "I was just feeling the stone before the portal became active."

"Well, it's almost time. Are you ready?"

A thousand thoughts popped into Gameknight's mind—all reasons why he wasn't ready—but he knew, deep down, that these were just excuses to avoid going. None of those reasons were real; they had all just been fabricated by the fear that had enveloped his mind. Looking to his friend, he could see the hope in Crafter's bright blue eyes, the confidence reflected in his young, square face, and knew he couldn't let Crafter down. He had to see this through.

"Yeah, I guess I'm as ready as I'll ever be. Let's do this thing."

"Not yet," Crafter said. "First, we need to dress you properly."

Gesturing to a group of NPCs nearby, he motioned for the village's crafter. The NPC stepped forward and stood before Gameknight.

"I'm sure you're used to better, but this is all we could prepare for you on such short notice," he said in a low, gravelly voice.

Reaching into his inventory, he produced a suit of iron armor and tossed the pieces onto the ground at the User-that-is-not-a-user's feet. The armored plating bobbed gently up and down in front of him, and for a moment Gameknight wondered why things did that in Minecraft, why the creator of Minecraft, Notch, had programmed it to be so.

Now was probably not the time to answer that question.

Gameknight999 picked up the pieces of armor and put on the chest plate, leggings, boots, and helmet as they were retrieved. He instantly felt more confident, the metal coating lifting his spirits a little. Flexing his arms and legs, he was surprised by how light armor felt. He had long ago discarded his own iron armor, the metal having become cracked and gouged by the numerous monsters that had felt compelled to leave their marks. But this armor was something different. It had a fine crisscrossing weave of steel wire near the neck and waist, and elaborate designs across the knees and shoulders. Small rivets held it together with, a band stretching across the chest. The overlapping plates were covered with chain mail to close off gaps that would otherwise allow sharp points to seek flesh. In all, it was an incredible example of Minecraft workmanship. He felt honored to be given such a fantastic gift.

"Does that feel better?" Crafter asked.

Gameknight nodded and smiled.

"Give it to him," Crafter said to the village crafter.

The old NPC turned around so that his back was to Gameknight, then reached into his inventory and pulled out a long, metallic thing that seemed to shimmer and give off an iridescent blue radiance. Turning back around, the crafter held out an iron sword that glowed a warm, cobalt blue, waves of enchanted energy flowing across its deadly sharp blade. Holding it out handle first, he extended it toward the User-that-is-not-a-user. Gameknight looked down at the blade and could see the incredible weight of responsibility that came with the weapon. He was afraid and took a step back.

"I apologize, User-that-is-not-a-user, but we had to use all the diamond we found for the pickaxes," the crafter said. "We had ample iron for this sword, and all the miners donated their XP so that you would have a proper blade. It has *Knockback 2* and *Sharpness 3*."

Gameknight reached out to take the sword, but then hesitated. Crafter saw the trepidation flash across his friend's face and stepped close to him.

"My Great-Uncle Weaver once told me about the first great zombie invasion of Minecraft back in the old days," he said softly as he moved closer. "He said that the monsters nearly overwhelmed all of the villagers on our server, but there was one thing that kept the NPCs from being destroyed—hope. Weaver told me, 'Hope is a powerful weapon, even for those without a sword or bow. Hope keeps people from giving up and surrendering to their fears. It lets the terrified masses believe in something bigger than themselves.'" He paused to let the words sink in, then continued. "Hope is the dream that something better is possible."

Crafter moved nearer. He was so close that his lips brushed Gameknight's ear as he whispered ever so softly, so that only Gameknight could hear his words, "All of these people have just accepted the possibility that they *might* prevail. Before this moment, they all thought they were doomed, Malacoda and Erebus and their two armies just too much to overcome. But now, with the User-that-is-not-a-user before them, they have accepted the idea that it *might* just be possible for Minecraft to be saved. And accepting the idea that success is a real possibility, even though it may still be difficult to achieve, is the first step toward victory." Crafter paused for a moment and looked about the room, Gameknight following his gaze. Bright, hopeful eyes were focused on him, smiles starting to creep out from behind worried faces. "Accepting that you *can* do something makes that thing doable, no matter how hard it is, and you have given this gift to these people. You have given them hope."

If only I had the same hope for myself, Gameknight thought to himself, but he knew he couldn't let Crafter and now these other NPCs down.

Reaching out, he curled his blocky, stubby fingers around the hilt that was still extended toward him, and squeezed it tight. Gently lifting the blade from the crafter's hand, he held it up high, pointing it to the ceiling. A cheer filled the crafting chamber, the walls almost bulging outward with the ferocity of the jubilant cries. Gripping the sword determinedly, he could feel magical power pulsing through the weapon, its keen edge ready for battle. As he looked about the room, Gameknight realized that maybe, just maybe, they *could* win this final battle and save Minecraft.

As he lowered his sword, a couple of NPCs approached Crafter, their arms filled with TNT. They deposited the red and black blocks at his feet, and the young crafter quickly picked them up, putting them into his inventory.

"What's the deal with all the explosives?" Gameknight asked.

The young boy turned to look up at his friend as he stuffed the rest of the TNT into his inventory. "Something else Great-Uncle Weaver taught me," he explained. "He said, 'Many problems with monsters can be solved with some creativity and a little TNT.' I figure we might run into some monsters in the Nether, so it's probably best to bring *a lot* of TNT, just to be safe."

Gameknight looked down at Crafter, but did not smile. The feeling of overwhelming responsibility sat heavily on him, like a leaden cloak. Shuddering, he tried to push away his anxiety as he turned to face the silent portal. Walking up to the obsidian ring, he sheathed his blade as the village crafter pulled out a piece of flint and steel. With a quick flick of his wrist, a spark leaped off the flint and hit the dark blocks, and in an instant a purplish field formed within the dark ring. Plum-colored sparks danced in the air before the gateway, the same kind that were always present near endermen when they teleported. The particles floated around the opening to the portal, then slowly drifted into it, as if pulled by some unseen current, the teleportation field coloring the dull gray walls of the crafting chamber with a flickering lavender hue.

Suddenly a voice could be heard yelling from the cavern's entrance. The words were unintelligible, but the tone was clear. Someone was angry and in quite a fit of rage; Gameknight could easily guess who it was. Turning from the portal, he looked up at the two iron doors that stood open at the crafting chamber's entrance. Hunter burst through the doors, her red hair flowing behind her as she ran down the steps to the cavern floor.

"Get out of my way!" she shouted at other NPCs as she moved down the steps that led to the crafting chamber floor.

She walked across the chamber with her enchanted bow in her hand, headed directly toward Crafter and Gameknight, her iron armor clinking and clanking as she walked. The sea of workers parted for her as she strode confidently to them. Most NPCs wanted to keep their distance from her. A person that had a thirst for killing was a good person to avoid.

"Are you two insane?" Hunter barked as she came near, making no attempt to keep her voice low. "Going to the Nether with just a handful of troops is madness!"

"Hunter, I know how it might seem, but many of us have talked, and we feel that this is the best path," Crafter explained. "We're going to sneak in with about fifty NPCs and free the crafters from Malacoda's fortress. With only fifty, we can move about the Nether relatively unseen. With a large army, we'd be spotted right away. This is the best course; sneak in quick and quiet."

"You're insane," she snapped, then turned from Crafter to glare at Gameknight. "Do you agree with this ridiculous plan?"

"Well...ahhh...I think that..."

"Well...ahhh..." she mocked. "I think that *you're* an idiot."

Just then, a group of NPCs entered the crafting chamber, each wearing a full suit of iron armor, blades shining brightly in their hands. They approached Crafter and Gameknight but stopped a few paces away, wary of Hunter.

"Shhh," Crafter snapped. "We're following this path for good or ill. I'm tired of reacting to Malacoda.

If we continue to stay one step behind the King of the Nether, then he'll win. I know what he's building there in the Nether, and he must be stopped or all will be lost. It's time we took the initiative and took the battle *to* him." Crafter looked at his fifty ironclad volunteers and smiled, then put an arm around Gameknight. "It's about time we attacked the monsters of the Nether and let them know that we won't go quietly into the night," he said in a loud voice, so that all could hear his words. A cheer rang out through the chamber. "This is our world! These are our families, our friends...our community, and we won't let them take it from us. Now is the time to push back and say NO MORE."

Crafter looked up at Gameknight and smiled, the User-that-is-not-a-user smiling back, knowing the part he was expected to play. Drawing his enchanted sword, Gameknight held it high overhead, the shimmering light from the magical blade filling the area with its peaceful blue illumination. He then looked at Hunter and gave her a nudge with his elbow. Rolling her eyes, she held her bow over her head and squeaked out a meek battle cry.

"Yay," she said unconvincingly.

"For Minecraft!" Gameknight yelled.

"FOR MINECRAFT," the chamber replied, the battle cry shouted at the top of everyone's lungs. The walls of the cavern vibrated slightly.

"COME ON, FOLLOW ME!" Crafter shouted, and ran toward the portal that glowed ominously at one end of the crafting chamber.

Turning to look over his shoulder, Crafter gave a wry smile, then sprinted into the portal, Gameknight at his shoulder and Hunter following close behind.

"I don't have a good feeling about this," she said as she leaped through the portal and disappeared from the Overworld, the wave of ironclad troops at her back.

CHAPTER 19

THE BEST LAID PLANS

They emerged from the portal expecting the monsters of the Nether to be waiting for them. But to their surprise, there were none, just the overwhelming heat of the land hammering them in the face, the acrid smoke stinging their throats.

"Quickly, spread out," Crafter commanded. "Kill any monsters you see fleeing; we cannot let word of our arrival reach Malacoda. But touch none of the zombie-pigmen. We don't want all of those creatures falling on us out here in the open."

The warriors spread out, making sure the area was secure. Smoke and ash filled the air, stinging Gameknight999's eyes and making him want to cough. Clearing his throat, he looked down the steep hill. He could see zombie-pigmen moving about in their aimless manner, their golden swords shining bright in the orange, fire-driven glow of the Nether.

Surveying the area, he saw that they were on a high plateau that was maybe a hundred blocks above the distant plain. To one side was a gently sloping hill, which extended off into the distance. It would be a long way down in that direction. To the other side were tall cliffs that likely could not be scaled, but just to his right, Gameknight saw what they needed. There was a deep ravine that was carved into the landscape. From this distance, it looked like a terrible wound gouged into the surface of the Nether, like the remnants of some terrible war between giants, the steep walls of the crevasse and shadowy interior looking sinister and dangerous.

Beyond the ravine, in the distance, sat Malacoda's fortress, the dark, ominous structure seeming to emanate malice and hatred. Small shapes could be seen moving about it, some of them glowing as if aflame, while others seemed to trudge about, backs bent in hard labor. Looking carefully, he could tell that the latter were villagers forced to work on the mighty structure, expanding the fortress to likely hold more monsters. Near the doomed villagers were blazes, their guards, and likely their executioners, when exhaustion made it impossible for them to continue working.

Poor souls, he thought.

"Like what you see?" said a mocking voice over his shoulder.

Turning, Gameknight found Hunter standing next to him, her dark brown eyes boring into him. Her curly red hair seemed to glow in the light of the Nether, making it seem as if a burning red halo floated around her head.

Just then, he noticed the iridescent blue glow of her bow.

"Where did you get that enchanted bow?" he asked her.

"I took it off a skeleton that was lurking around near the village," she replied with delight. "You'd think that creature would be able to shoot accurately with such a fine weapon, but it just confirms that a weapon is only as good as the wielder."

Gameknight nodded understanding.

"In fact," she added, "I was able to get one for you, just like mine. It has *Power IV, Flame I*, and *Infinite I*." Holding up the shimmering weapon before her eyes, she gazed at the bow as if it were alive and part of her. "I love this bow. I hope you can do it justice."

She pulled another bow out of her inventory and tossed it to the User-that-is-not-a-user. Gameknight picked it up quickly, grateful to have such a fine weapon. He remembered his enchanted bow from the last server and missed it like an old friend, but this one would have to do, for now. Smiling, he patted her on the shoulder, and she smiled back, showing an unexpected amount of camaraderie.

Suddenly Crafter was at his side, followed by one of their NPC warriors.

"All secure, our presence is still a secret," the NPC stated, his eyes darting to Gameknight, then Crafter. He was unsure of who was really in command here.

"Excellent," Crafter said. "User-that-is-not-a-user, are we ready to go?"

Gameknight turned and faced his friend. He found their company standing behind him, the wall of ironclad warriors all looking at him expectantly.

"It's time," Gameknight said, trying to muster as much courage in his feeble voice as he could. "Let's go get our people back."

A cheer rang out from the NPCs as he turned and headed down the hill, toward that terrifying ravine, the soldiers following close behind. He moved, when he could, from cover to cover, hiding behind a tall hill of nether quartz, then crouching down near a small hill of netherrack, trying to keep himself from the prying eyes that he knew were down there in that fortress. Looking back over his shoulder, he could see that their troops were following his example, also stooping and crouching to hide their presence for as long as possible.

It was slow going, moving by foot down the slope. Having to stay concealed made it even slower, but in general, NPCs and users, were slow when they crossed a battlefield. And that was a weakness in their plan. He knew from playing games like *StarCraft*, *Command & Conquer*, and *Age of Empires* that in battle, speed was life. Those that had the greatest mobility and could react the quickest could change their tactics in the heat of battle. The phrase "no battle plans survive first contact with the enemy" had been proven in history over and over again, and Gameknight had learned the truth of that statement many times in online battles. Here, their plan had two critical components: speed and stealth. They had to get to the crafters quietly, without being noticed. Once they broke through their prison walls and freed the captives, there would likely be alarms sounded, and then all that would matter would be speed, and luck.

All the aspects of this plan terrified Gameknight. The thought of having to face Malacoda and his horde again brought chills while simultaneously making him sweat. Fear ate away at him and made him want to just dig a hole and hide, but he knew that he couldn't. Those captive NPCs down there were depending on him, as were the friends that followed him right now. He had to see this through, though the anticipation of the battle that he knew would come seemed to wring out his courage until there was none left. Pushing away those troublesome thoughts, Gameknight concentrated on the moment—on this very instant—and focused on taking another step forward. He determinedly ignored the images of the coming battle, of Malacoda and the monsters that would eventually confront them. Instead, he simply thought about putting one foot in front of the other. And surprisingly, his anxiety receded a little. The images of the King of the Nether and his minions faded away as he pushed these thought of what *might* happen out of his mind.

Maybe I can do this.

Sprinting out of a small recess in the netherrack, Gameknight moved quickly to the opening of the ravine, the ground sloping downward. The steep walls of the ravine gave him a feeling of security, and of knowing that the spying eyes of the mobs would have a harder time seeing them here. Moving about fifty blocks into the ravine, he stopped and waited for his friends. Crafter quickly reached his side, sheathing his sword and pausing to catch his breath. Hunter then ran to him, but instead of stopping, she continued down the ravine, sprinting past them as if on some mission of her own. The rest of their troops entered the ravine and also stopped to rest for a moment, the clanging of armored bodies bumping against each other echoing in the air.

"Shhh," Crafter said in a soft voice, looking at his warriors.

They instantly stilled and spread out a little, giving a bit of literal breathing room between the panting bodies. The only sound they could now hear was the squeaking of bats, the black creatures flitting about, some of them flying high up into the air and over the top of the ravine. In a few moments, Hunter returned, sprinting back up the pathway. There was a look of violence about her, her whole body tensed and ready to lash out at anyone and anything that got in her way. The look in her eyes, like black holes in the sky, was an unquenchable rage; it was as if she had seen her family suffer under the hateful claws of the mobs again.

"What are you doing?" she demanded of Gameknight and Crafter.

"We need a brief rest," Crafter replied.

"You don't rest until you know your position is secure," she snapped. "Put a few warriors in front and behind." She then turned to face the warriors. "Don't just bunch up, you fools. A single fireball from a ghast could take out most of you."

Gameknight and Crafter looked at each other, both ashamed of their carelessness.

"To successfully fight an enemy, you must think like them. If I wanted to catch this group of idiots, I'd put a ghast in front of us and behind us, and catch us in a cross fire." She faced the warriors again. "You three, pull out your bows and go back up the ravine to cover our backs. You four," she said, pointing to another cluster of NPCs, "use your bows and scout ahead. Kill any blazes or ghasts you see. Remember, you'll likely only be able to get off a shot or two before they fire back, so you all must aim for the same target. Now GO!"

The warriors looked at Crafter and Gameknight, their eyes seeking permission.

"You heard her," Gameknight said. "Go."

They nodded and ran off down the pathway, the other three going back to cover the rear.

"Now, let's move," Hunter commanded. "The quicker we get this foolishness over, the quicker we can get back home." Spinning quickly on one foot, she turned and started heading down the ravine. "MOVE OUT!" she shouted without looking back.

Crafter and Gameknight looked at each other and shrugged, then followed their companion, the rest of the troop on their heels.

"Spread out," Gameknight said, looking over his shoulder. "Do as Hunter commands."

The warriors nodded and spread out into a long, thin, ironclad line, following as silently as their metal armor would allow, eyes cast up at the top of the ravine, looking for threats.

They moved along quickly without incident, gradually descending down the winding path that was carved through the ravine. At its lower end, the passage opened onto a massive plain that stretched out across the landscape. Gameknight could see zombie-pigmen walking about, their golden swords standing out against the rusty background. Their rotting flesh almost looked lifelike in the rosy hue from the many rivers of lava that crisscrossed the scene. The mindless creatures shuffled around without purpose, their golden swords glowing bright.

In the distance, Gameknight999 could see a gigantic sea of lava, the scorching mass of molten stone glowing bright orange. Smoke and ash floated up from the boiling sea and created a gray haze that obscured any features on its far shore, making it appear impossibly endless. The thought of all that lava stretching out into the infinite chunks of Minecraft gave him a feeling of dread.

How could there be that much lava in any one place? he thought to himself as he stared out along the bubbling sea.

But the most terrifying thing before him was the gigantic fortress that sprawled across the terrain. Dark towers capped with burning blocks of netherrack stood out against the rusty orange landscape. They stretched up high into the air, like the burning claws of some titanic beast. The menacing towers were connected with elevated walkways, many of them completely enclosed. The dark nether brick from which they were constructed gave them the appearance of something shadowy and sinister. Glowing torches dotted the sides of the massive structure, casting circles of light here and there, but the illumination made the fortress seem no less terrifying.

It was the biggest structure Gameknight had ever seen in Minecraft.

The raised walkways stretched out in all directions,

spreading out across the land. But the most amazing and terrifying part of the entire structure was the main central tower. It was a huge square building that extended up into the air at least a hundred blocks, if not more. Jagged crenellations dotted its top, with flaming blocks of netherrack decorating the peak. On its sides, Gameknight could see balconies jutting out here and there. He knew that these balconies housed multiple monster-makers known as spawners; it was something he'd seen in his dream. Hundreds of monsters were being brought to life on those balconies, their angry voices adding to the moans and wails that already rode on the hot winds. This fortress brought feelings of hysteria to the User-that-is-not-a-user, because he knew that this was the thing that threatened the electronic lives that he was struggling to protect.

Pulling his eyes from the fortress, Gameknight brought his attention to the plain before him. A wide, exposed space stood between the opening of the ravine and Malacoda's fortress, the landscape dotted with flaming blocks, lava rivers, and countless zombie-pigmen. Rough hills of netherrack could be seen to the left and the right, their blocky, steep sides standing out against the gently sloping plain.

Suddenly a bat streaked by, the black shape flitting erratically about as it flew toward one of those hills, likely its home. He could hear it screeching as it flew, the heat probably making it uncomfortable. Bats were cave dwellers, the small animals used to cold and damp spaces underground. Here, in the Nether, it was neither cold nor damp, and the creature was likely considerably stressed.

Cautiously, the party moved out, sprinting across the open plain as they threaded a sinewy path around zombie-pigmen, whose sorrowful moans filled the air. Taking the most direct path possible without aggravating any of the rotting monsters, the group sprinted as fast as possible, trying to reach their destination: the fortress.

The massive structure filled their entire field of view, stretching from the tall hills in the hazy distance, across the sloping plain, and down to kiss the shore of the lava sea. Gameknight could see the terrifying circle of stones sitting on the surface of that boiling expanse of lava, the dark pedestals of obsidian just barely visible from this distance. He felt anger and violence emanating from the island; all of the dissonant, grinding feelings in the workings of Minecraft were focused on that location.

It'll all be decided on that island, Gameknight thought to himself. He knew that all their fates would be determined there. Anticipation and fear started to creep into his psyche as the thought of some terrible battle being fought on that mass of stone started to cloud his mind. And then he remembered something his father had said to him once. It hadn't made much sense at the time, but for some reason...in this situation...it clicked.

"Being afraid of something that has yet to happen is like a snowflake being afraid to fall from the sky because of its fear of summer," his father had said. "The poor snowflake would miss the joys of winter: of being formed into a snowman or thrown in a snowball fight. It would miss being alive because of the fear that was consuming it. There is enough time to fear something when it comes. Don't waste a second being afraid before then. The anticipation of a thing can sometimes be worse than the thing itself. Think about *the now* and release the fears that are reaching into the future. Focus on *the now...the now...the now...*"

His father's words echoed in his memory, filling him with warmth and courage. Pushing aside his thoughts of that impending battle, he concentrated on *the now* and on what was around him... Crafter...Hunter...their warriors...blazes...

What...blazes?

"BLAZES!" Gameknight shouted, pointing to the rough netherrack hill.

An army of blazes and magma cubes were coming from behind the hill on the left, heading straight for them. Pointing to the threats, he turned his head to find Crafter on his right. He noticed the young leader pointing off to the right, toward the other tall hill. Another army composed of blazes, skeletons, and zombie-pigmen were emerging from behind that mound, also heading straight for them.

The now was suddenly filled with monsters, all of them thirsting for their destruction. The air began to fill with the clattering of skeleton bones, the clicking of spiders, and the mechanical breathing of blazes; it was a symphony of hate.

Gameknight could feel panic and terror surging through every nerve like an electrical shock.

Looking behind him, he judged the distances. These two armies would reach them before they could get to the fortress. And even if they could release the crafters, there would be no getting back home; they'd be trapped in the fortress with enemies before them and Malacoda's monsters from the fortress at their backs.

The rescue was a failure.

Looking at his friend, he saw the look of defeat on Crafter's face as well, his unibrow furled with sadness and regret.

"We failed," the young NPC said despondently. "I'm sorry, my friends."

Gameknight wasn't sure if he was talking to those around him or the poor imprisoned crafters within the fortress, but it didn't matter. What did matter was getting back to the Overworld safely.

But how?

As it was, they would barely make it back to the ravine before the monsters reached them. Would there be another army at the other end of the ravine, closing off their retreat back to the Overworld? They needed to move faster down here in the Nether, but their blocky legs were not made for speed.

"What are we going to do?" Crafter asked, his voice filled with uncertainty.

"Many problems with monsters can be solved with some creativity and a little TNT," Gameknight muttered to himself, then spoke louder and more confidently, *the now* driving his courage. "Crafter, you still have that TNT?"

"Of course I do," Crafter replied, his voice still weak.

"Me too," came from some of the other warriors.

Gameknight looked at Crafter and saw the indecision reflected on his face. He then turned to Hunter and could see her itching to run off and face these armies all on her own, but that would be a wasteful course of action, and would certainly end in her death. At this moment, in *the now*, his troops and friends needed him, needed Gameknight999...and as the pieces came together in his mind, he knew just what to do.

"COME ON, EVERYONE FOLLOW ME!" he yelled as he put away his iron sword and pulled out his own enchanted bow. "Back to the ravine!"

"But we'll be trapped there," Crafter said, his legs moving sluggishly.

"No, we won't," Gameknight replied. "We're going to solve a monster problem at the mouth of the ravine. COME ON!"

CHAPTER 20

FIREWORKS

T he party sprinted back to the ravine, taking a straight-line path and ignoring stealth; clearly they had been spotted. How the creatures had known of their presence was still a mystery that bounced around within Gameknight's brain. He felt that this tidbit was important, but not now, not in *the now*. He would ponder this turn of events later, if there *was* a later.

They quickly reached the mouth of the ravine.

"Half of you go back to the entrance of the ravine and make sure that we aren't trapped in here," he commanded, his mind working in automatic mode to solve the puzzle that lay before him. "The rest of you, I need a platform and walkway on both sides of the ravine—high up so that the monsters can't reach it."

The warriors leaped into action, one group digging up blocks of netherrack, while another built stairs into the walls, climbing up about twelve high. Then they started forming a long, straight walkway, only one block wide. As they built the causeway, other NPCs brought the blocks up to the builders.

"Quickly," Gameknight encouraged. "Diggers, we need as many blocks as you can dig up. Don't stop until the horde gets here. Crafter, we need a little surprise for the opening to the ravine. You think you can make something your Great-Uncle Weaver would be proud of?"

Crafter smiled, his spirits lifting. Here was something he knew he could do, and do well. Pulling out his own pickaxe, he started to dig holes around the ravine opening, then dug holes in the walls as well; they were strategically placed under the soul sand that was nestled within the netherrack blocks.

"They're coming!" Hunter yelled. She ran out to meet them, firing flaming arrows high up into the air.

"Hunter, get back here!" Gameknight commanded. "You over there—" He gestured to the handful of NPCs that were doing nothing but worrying. "Start digging holes in the ground and place blocks of TNT in them. If you don't have any, get some from Crafter. I know he always brings lots of TNT with him."

Crafter smiled as he placed explosives around the ravine opening.

"But we don't have any redstone to trigger them," one of them complained.

"Don't worry, Hunter and I will take care of that. Now go."

The group of NPCs flew up the ravine, digging holes as they went and placing blocks of explosives into the ground. The striped red and black cubes of TNT stood out bright against the dull brown of the netherrack. *Good, they'll be easy to see*, Gameknight999 thought to himself.

"You," he said to one of the diggers, "place a block of netherrack in front of every block of TNT so that the mobs can't see them, but they can still be seen from behind. Then put a few random blocks down where there is no TNT. We can't let the monsters know where our little presents are until they're ready to pop."

The warrior nodded his understanding, put away his pickaxe, and then ran off, placing a dull, brownish cube of netherrack before each hole in the ground.

"They're almost here," Hunter shouted as she ran back to the mouth of the ravine.

Gameknight could now smell the approaching mob,

the rotten smell of decaying flesh from the zombies and the acrid smoke from the blazes being the first volley in the battle that had just begun.

"Quickly, up the steps to the walkway," he said, gesturing to the far wall. "If any of you have bows, go up the walkway as well. But those who still have netherrack blocks must go up first. Those with swords, you're the bait. You have to make sure that the mobs come into the ravine. Now move!"

A handful of NPCs quickly put away their picks and ran up the steps that had been placed on the sheer walls. Three warriors then followed, worried looks on their faces and bows in their hands. They stared down at the twelve warriors that stood at the ravine opening, their swords drawn and their expressions grim. Crafter stood at their head, his childlike frame dwarfed by the ironclad adults around him.

"Crafter, come on, up here!" Gameknight yelled.

"NO. My place is here, with my troops," he replied. "We'll slow them down and make sure they take the bait. I hope this plan of yours will work—whatever it is."

"Me too, my friend," Gameknight yelled down to him. "But there is one more thing we might need."

Crafter looked up at him, clearly confused, and the other NPCs also stole glances at the User-that-is-not-a-user.

Gameknight reached into his inventory, pulled out a stack of something, and quickly tossed it down to Crafter, who caught it deftly. The young boy then put it quickly into his inventory before any of the others could see, a smile growing on his face.

"Your father always said 'be prepared when going to the Nether,' right?" Gameknight said, remembering one of Crafter's many stories. "You never know what you'll need."

Crafter only smiled, then drew his sword again and turned to face the approaching horde.

Gameknight could feel the tension building, the trepidation of the warriors below and the archers above starting to boil over. The thirst for destruction from the approaching monsters was palpable, the moans of the zombies and the mechanical wheezing of the blazes filling the air. Forces were about to crash down upon each other, and lives would be lost. He had taken whatever steps he could, and had unleashed the dogs of war. Nobody could stop what had begun, and for many their fates were signed, sealed, and would soon be delivered to oblivion. He shuddered as *the now* came smashing down upon him.

The magma cubes came first, the gigantic bouncing monsters looking like they were made of jello with burning embers of fire at their gelatinous cores. They leaped upward, their bodies extending like accordions as they sprang up, then reassembling when they landed back on the ground. The glowing creatures made squishing, bouncing sounds when they landed, the *boing-boings* adding to the symphony of monstrous moans and wails. Gameknight knew that the death of one of these creatures would only create two smaller magma cubes; they always divided themselves when killed, then divided again and again as their smaller selves were slain. If his troops attacked these creatures, they would quickly be overrun and surrounded. He hoped that Crafter would realize this, and was gratified when he saw the warriors withdraw deeper into the ravine rather than slice up the glowing beasts.

But flaming arrows streaked down from the other side of the ravine. Hunter was shooting at the magma cubes from her walkway.

"Hold!" he shouted, holding up a hand to keep his archers from firing.

Crafter and the remaining warriors pulled back farther into the ravine, drawing the monsters toward their little surprise, but still remaining visible to the rest of the horde.

"Hold!" he yelled again as Crafter withdrew a little more.

And then Crafter stopped backing up and got ready to hold his ground.

"Come and get me, you cowardly insects!" the young NPC yelled at the top of his lungs. He then scratched a line in the ground. "This is where you will be stopped. YOU CAN GO NO FURTHER!" He then casually placed his sword over his shoulder and stood nonchalantly, waiting.

This made the approaching army wail with anger. They charge forward with uncontrolled rage, the dam that had been holding back all their violence and malice finally shattered. As the mass of monsters reached the ravine opening, Crafter looked up at User-that-is-not-a-user, an expectant look on his blocky face.

"Hunter, the TNT...NOW!" Gameknight yelled.

Flaming arrows streaked down from both walkways, landing amongst the blocks of TNT that Crafter had strategically placed around the entrance to the ravine. Gameknight fired at the explosive targets from his side as Hunter did the same, her shots always landing true. Black and red cubes started to blink as the monsters surged forward. The magma cubes, realizing what was happening, all turned around and tried to escape the trap. Their massive bodies smashed into the oncoming wave of Nether creatures, causing a major traffic jam at the ravine entrance. The magma cubes tried to push past the monster bodies, but it was too late.

BOOM!

The ground suddenly shook violently, then raised up into the air as the TNT detonated. Huge balls of fire blossomed as the explosives came alive, enveloping massive numbers of blazes and skeletons in the flaming grip of the blast. The walls of the ravine fell in on them, the soul sand flowing down to the ground, burying many of the attackers. But more importantly, the ground was now covered with the slowing sand. The monsters that survived the blast struggled to move through the thick sand, their ability to walk or run severely hampered as the soul sand slowed their every movement.

Crafter's forces charged through the cloud of smoke and attacked the survivors near the front. Once those had been killed, the NPCs sprinted to those creatures struggling on the soul sand, staying on the netherrack so that they could still move quickly; mobility meant life in battle. Arrows streaked down from the overhead walkways, the sharp, pointed projectiles raining down onto the monsters with a vengeance. A few fireballs streaked up toward the attackers, but Hunter and Gameknight's flaming arrows quickly silenced the blazes with a vengeance.

Gameknight999 wasn't thinking about what was happening or which monster he should shoot at next, he was just reacting, living in *the now*. He was an automated machine of death, his arrows seeking out the flesh of his enemies as fast as he could draw his bow. Glancing across the ravine, he saw Hunter doing the same, her enchanted bow moving in a blur, her face set in grim determination. Moving with surgical precision, she tracked each target, snapping her body about quickly and decisively, her brilliant red hair glowing like a majestic battle flag. Then a fireball burst over his head. Ducking, he spotted the attacker and quickly drove three arrows into the flaming body of the blaze.

More of the monsters had now reached the ravine

opening, the advance party thinned significantly by their trap and blades. Gameknight could see the massive horde, and knew that they could not stay there and hope to survive.

"PULL BACK!" Gameknight yelled as he motioned those on the walkway to head deeper into the ravine. "Crafter, plant more little gifts."

"I don't have anything to ignite them with," the old voice said from the young face.

"We'll take care of that," he replied. "Just plant the TNT and get back."

Crafter nodded then withdrew, leaving the monsters to struggle through the soul sand. As he ran, he placed blocks of TNT in the holes that another NPC had dug, a cube of netherrack positioned on the ground to hide its explosive presence. The troops sprinted across the ravine floor, running up the gently curving pathway as they headed back to their salvation: the portal. Just then, fireballs streaked through the air as a group of blazes emerged from the soul sand and rounded the bend. Flaming balls of death struck at the soldiers and two of them were enveloped, their screams echoing in Gameknight's brain.

That could have been Crafter...it could have been me, he thought to himself. *What will happen when we get to the other end of the ravine? Will it be blocked? Will it...*Fear ran wild through him as he thought about what *might* happen rather than what *was* happening.

"'Anticipation of a thing can be worse than the thing itself.'" His father's words echoed in his mind. They brought him back from the *what if* and to *the now.* He had to focus on what was happening right now, and not worry about what would happen when they got to the other end of the ravine or the portal. If they didn't survive the *now,* then nothing else mattered.

Moving back farther on the walkway, he fired at

one of the TNT cubes just as the oncoming blazes came near. The block exploded, tearing up the floor of the ravine and, fortunately for them, taking with it many of the blazes, though a few still remained. Hunter fired her deadly projectiles into the beasts, and the archers behind her added their own arrows, bringing down the survivors within seconds.

Clouds of smoke started to choke the ravine, making their targets hard to see, but also protecting the villagers from the blazes. Gameknight999 and Hunter's flaming arrows looked like glowing specters as they streaked through the hazy air, striking the smoldering blazes. The flaming monsters' internal fire made them easy targets in the smoke and confusion, and every archer took advantage of that.

"Move back farther!" he shouted. "Crafter...move!"

They moved back again and repeated the process: retreat, draw the enemy near, fire at the TNT, and tear up the terrain and kill a few monsters in the blast. They continued this strategy while they slowly retreated back through the ravine toward the upper opening which lead to their portal. Their strategy worked a few more times before the monsters finally caught on and started to hold back, sending smaller and smaller parties of monsters forward to trigger the explosives, mostly the slow-moving zombie-pigmen— the dim-witted creatures were obviously considered expendable. Their plan was losing its effectiveness.

Suddenly, there was a clatter of noise came from the other end of the ravine. Turning, Gameknight saw the rest of their forces returning, the ironclad troopers sprinting down the pathway to join the others.

"What about the other end of the ravine?" Gameknight shouted as he continued to inch his way along the walkway. He could see the end of the walkway approaching, the NPC at the end of their column quickly placing more blocks on the raised path, but not faster than they had been retreating.

"No monsters are near," one of the warriors replied. "In fact, they all just sorta disappeared—all of the zombie-pigmen left the area. It looks clear all the way back up the hill to the portal."

Suddenly, a massive fireball fell from the sky and enveloped the soldier, his HP quickly dropping to zero and his body disappearing in a pop, leaving behind his armor and weapons. Gameknight glanced upward and felt his soul freeze.

Ghasts...at least ten of them.

Fighting one ghast was hard enough, but ten of them...they were doomed. Fireballs started to rain down on the NPCs, each one claiming a life. The warriors scattered, trying to avoid the fiery balls, but there was nowhere to run in the cramped ravine. As the balls of fire rained down from above, smaller balls streaked out from the blazes that now approached.

"PULL BACK, RETREAT!" Gameknight yelled, the taste of defeat on his lips. "Archers, push the blazes back."

The archers on both sides opened up, launching as many arrows as they could toward the approaching monsters, covering the retreat of the ground forces while balls of death rained down on them from above. Gameknight noticed that one of the NPCs was placing blocks of TNT as they withdrew, but he was not Crafter. Where was Crafter? He scanned the floor of the ravine, looking for his friend, but was soon distracted by something streaking upward into the air at the edge of his vision.

Suddenly there was an explosion of light in the sky, a burst of color that made the battle in the ravine pause for a moment: Crafter's fireworks. Another missile streaked up into the air, sparkles trailing behind its path before it exploded and a shower of green sparks outlining the face of a creeper looking down on those locked in battle. It had detonated right between two of the ghasts, the hot embers driving the floating monstrosities back in an attempt to avoid being burned. A dozen fireworks then shot into the air, all of them exploding directly over the ravine, forcing the ghasts back even farther. This drew a cheer from the warriors on the ground, invigorating them and making them fight even harder.

Another block of TNT exploded on the ground, Hunter's flaming arrow having set it off. It drew Gameknight's attention back to the battle below. Seeing another explosive cube, he sent one of his own burning shafts into it, making it explode just when a cluster of wither skeletons surrounded it. Their dark bones rained down on their companions.

"YEAH!" someone shouted.

The warriors surged forward, pushing the massive army of monsters back a few steps.

"NO, keep pulling back!" Gameknight yelled. "We have to get back to the portal."

He knew that they would never win this battle. The only thing that was keeping them alive at the moment were the narrow walls of the ravine, but once they were out in the open it would be a race for survival.

They continued to withdraw through the ravine, the TNT on the ground tearing at the attacking monsters, while Crafter's fireworks kept the ghasts slightly at bay. Looking over his shoulder, Gameknight could see the top of the entrance to the ravine, four warriors guarding their exit. Seeing the pitched battle, these last four ran toward their comrades and threw themselves into battle. The ground was covered with skeleton bones, blaze rods, and golden swords, but there were also piles of iron armor that were no longer needed, iron swords and bows scattered on the ground—the belongings of those now dead. This monster horde had done its damage, probably reducing their size by half if not more, but still the villagers fought, unwilling to give up, for surrender meant death.

He could see Crafter now, the young child planting a huge collection of fireworks at the opening of the ravine, readying their escape.

The elevated walkway was now only four blocks off the ground as the ravine had slowly sloped upward. Gameknight motioned for the builders on both sides to make some steps so that they could get to the ground without taking any damage.

"Hunter...to the ground!" he yelled over the din of battle. "Lead the way back to the portal."

She nodded and leaped to the ground, her red hair flowing wildly as she jumped. Landing like a graceful cat, she streaked to the ravine opening.

"Everyone, follow Hunter!" he yelled. "RUN!"

The warriors turned and fled from the battle lines, sprinting to the upper ravine opening that led to the flat plateau and their portal. They knew there would be ghasts out there, but speed was their only weapon now. The NPCs sprinted with desperate haste, the sounds of the murderous rabble growing louder as the monster horde left the ravine and started to spread out across the sloping hill. Gameknight and Crafter brought up the rear, the young NPC still planting blocks of TNT and fireworks behind them, hoping they would cause some confusion amongst their attackers. Crafter didn't bother to try to hide the little surprises, just placed the TNT on the ground and the rocket on top of that.

Watching over his shoulder, Gameknight would wait until the monsters approached, then spin and fire, launching a flaming arrow at the TNT, setting it off as well as igniting the firework. The detonation caused some damage to those on the ground while at the same time the firework shot up into the sky. Hopefully it would hit one of the ghasts in the air.

Since Gameknight and Crafter were at the end of the column of warriors, he feared the ghasts would use them for target practice, but none of the fiery balls came down on them. The floating monsters instead fired balls of death at their men, the burning spheres enveloping villager after villager, rending their HP to nothing so that the NPCs disappeared without a shriek, a yell, or a goodbye. The ghasts slowly whittled down their forces from the fifty that they'd started with, to now only twelve...*BOOM*...make that eleven still alive.

Gameknight shuddered and wanted to weep; all those lives had been lost for what? To his left, he could see Hunter running backward. Her enchanted bow was firing burning shafts of fire at the floating giants, the projectiles striking them, one...two...three times before they would die, dropping a crystalline ghast tear. Other warriors saw Hunter's actions and spun to add their fire to her attacks. More arrows streaked through the air, sinking their pointed teeth into the floating, baby-faced creatures, the ghast tears starting to fall down like rain.

Gameknight focused his shots on the TNT that Crafter was dropping. The striped blocks were not only wreaking havoc on those that pursued them, but more importantly at this point, also tearing up the landscape, making pursuit more difficult. But their party was just moving too slow. They desperately needed to move faster, because he could see that speed was the key to survival in the Nether. Gameknight could feel that this was an important puzzle piece, but he didn't have time to ponder it. All he could do right now was concentrate on firing his bow as fast as his arm could draw back the string.

A cheer rang out from the surviving warriors, drawing his attention upward. The last of the ghasts had been killed, the rocky ceiling of the Nether now clear of threats. Looking back to the soldiers, he saw them all start to sprint again, not having to fire backward any more. The massive quartz hill that marked the location of their portal now stood before them, but he knew that the horde of monsters at their backs was still hot on their heels. Looking over his shoulder, he was surprised to find that the creatures had halted their pursuit; they were now just glaring at him with their dead, hateful eyes.

"Why did they stop?" he asked Crafter.

"Who cares?" the young boy replied as he continued to sprint.

Gameknight didn't like this, but he knew that whatever the monsters were doing, it was better if the soldiers didn't have to try to fight them. And so he too continued to sprint as he put away his bow and drew his enchanted iron sword. Maybe they *could* survive this after all.

The party sprinted up the hill, gradually rounding the gigantic mount of nether quartz, the reddish blocks sparkling with embedded crystals, their shining facets reflected the fiery light of the Nether. Looking toward the front edge of the survivors, he saw Hunter sprinting forward, her shimmering bow still in her hand. She looked so confident, so brave...he wished he was more like her. Maybe he could be, someday, if he...

Suddenly she stopped and drew back an arrow, the pointed top burning with enchanted fire. But she did not release it. The rest of the warriors caught up with her and also came to a quick stop, their apprehension quite apparent. Gameknight and Crafter continued to sprint as they finally rounded the base of the nether-quartz hill. They pushed through the few remaining survivors and stood next to Hunter. Looking in the direction her deadly bow pointed, Gameknight's heart gave a sickly beat.

They were doomed.

Between them and their portal stood a sea of tall, lanky black creatures. Each had a set of angry purple eyes that glared at them with unbridled hatred. At the center of the shadowy group stood a single island of dark, dark red, a creature that emanated a thirst for violence that could never be quenched: Erebus.

All hope left Gameknight999, and he was filled with the bitter taste of defeat.

CHAPTER 21

THE LOSS OF HOPE

A sea of endermen stood between them and the portal, with Erebus at the front, his dark red form glowing with purple teleportation particles, ready to disappear and reappear anywhere his mind could fathom. Their tall, dark forms stood out in stark contrast against the reddish netherrack on which they stood, their black bodies and long arms making them seem even taller. Behind Erebus, the other endermen started to emit their own ender particles, creating a purple haze around the deadly creatures.

Erebus chuckled his creepy, spine-tingling enderman laugh. It made the warriors cringe.

"So, User-that-is-not-a-user, we meet again," Erebus screeched, his high-pitched voice piercing through the moans of the monsters that stood downhill.

Gameknight started to shiver, the terrible memories

from his dreams flooding back into his mind. He could still feel those cold, clammy arms squeezing his throat as Erebus' fearsome, blazing red eyes bore into his soul.

"What do we do?" one of the warriors asked. "User-that-is-not-a-user, tell us...lead us."

It sounded less like a question and more like a plea, but he knew he could do nothing. Here was the living incarnation of his nightmare standing before him, waiting to kill him. Fear overwhelmed his mind as he numbly stood there, unsure what to do. Hunter moved to his side.

"Quickly, we have to do something." she said, her voice still sounding courageous. "Gameknight, snap out of it."

"I...ahh...we can...ahh," Gameknight stammered, indecision and fear keeping him from taking any decisive action.

"I have an idea," Crafter said. "Hunter, they want me alive for some reason. They won't raise a hand against me." He pulled out a block of TNT and held it over his head. "Ready your bow. If they attack me, I want you to shoot this block. Do not hesitate, do you understand?"

Hunter's brown eyes looked down into Crafter's blues, and she nodded. Pulling a handful of red hair from her face, she tucked it behind an ear, then notched an arrow. With her free hand, she patted the young NPC on the shoulder, then moved to the front of the significantly diminished group of warriors.

Crafter moved to Gameknight's side and spoke softly, for his ears only.

"Remember what I have told you, User-that-is-not-a-user...remember Fisher." And then he whispered, "Deeds do not make the hero, how they overcome their fear does."

Then Crafter stepped forward, moving directly toward Erebus, the red and black striped block of TNT held high over his head.

"What is this, a little present?" the King of the Endermen screeched.

Crafter did not reply. He just slowly moved toward the crimson monster.

"What are you doing?"

Crafter again remained silent, moving slowly but surely forward. Now Hunter stepped forward, a flaming arrow drawn back, her bowstring stretched tight.

Hesitantly, the other endermen started to back away, their purple eyes all focused on the block of TNT. Crafter continued on, his eyes focused on the ground, the explosive block held up high, making it an easy shot.

Gameknight felt blocky hands push him forward as the few remaining warriors slowly moved forward as well, their swords now sheathed. They all knew that their weapons would do little against this many endermen.

The scene began to come into focus as Gameknight surveyed the situation. He could see Crafter out in front, the TNT held over his head. He could vaguely remember Crafter saying something to him—something about deeds...the words were still obscured by his fear. But slowly, his fear faded into the background as he recognized his inevitable fate. A cold, calm reasoning spread over him as he realized that this would be the place of his death.

Shaking the hands from him, Gameknight moved forward on his own alongside the few survivors who had their shoulders slumped in defeat. They too knew that this place would be their final battlefield, all except Hunter. She stood at the head of their party, back straight, blocky chin held high, her flaming arrow trained on the explosive block.

"Hunter, you can't shoot," Gameknight pleaded. "It's Crafter."

"Shut up," she snapped.

"But it's—"

"Be quiet, you fool," Hunter commanded. "Just get up here with me and try to look like a leader for once."

He felt ashamed. She'd seen his cowardice, his acceptance of defeat while she still stood courageous and defiant. Moving forward, he walked slowly next to her. He drew his own shimmering bow and notched an arrow, pointing it in the general direction of Crafter, but unwilling to cause the death of his friend. The flaming tip of his arrow shook as he tried to hold it still; terror and despair still ruled his every muscle.

"Move back, or I will order them to fire," Crafter yelled. "Your master will not be pleased if I am killed, now, will he?"

"I HAVE NO MASTER!" Erebus screeched. His eyes burned bright and deadly with renewed hatred filling his blood-red pupils.

"And yet, you still move back," Crafter said, a wry smile coming across his face.

This made Erebus start to shake with rage, his eyes burning even brighter.

"Careful," Crafter advised. "You don't want to do something you might regret."

"Not killing you right this instant is something I might regret, but there will always be time for you later. The cowardly User-that-is-not-a-user, however— him, I can kill now."

Crafter took two quick steps forward, pushing the endermen back, opening a pathway to the portal.

"NOW!" Hunter yelled. "RUN!"

The warriors sprinted forward, diving through the portal. Hunter stood right in front of the portal, one leg within the purple, wavering field, her flaming arrow still aimed at the TNT. Gameknight stood next to her, unsure of what to do.

"Go through, you idiot," she commanded. "I'll take care of this."

And at that, Gameknight dove through the portal. The purple shimmering field filled his vision as the view of the Nether slowly faded away, only to be replaced by the stone wall of the crafting chamber. He stepped away and turned, facing the purple gateway. One leg stuck out of the portal; it was Hunter's. Drawing his bow, he aimed at it, ready for the flood of monsters that might come through.

"Get ready to seal the portal!" he yelled.

NPCs surged forward, blocks of cobblestone in their hands. Some of them started to fill in the back of the portal, leaving the front open for Crafter and Hunter. Suddenly, Hunter materialized with Crafter next to her. A cheer rang out from the multitudes that watched. It seemed to Gameknight that nearly the entire village was there, hundreds and hundreds of NPCs crowded within the enlarged crafting chamber.

"You made it," Gameknight said, a smile on his face.

The workers started placing cobblestone on the portal opening as Crafter and Hunter stepped forward a few steps, the block of TNT still in the young NPC's hands. But before the masons could place their last blocks of cobble, Erebus materialized within the crafting chamber, his blazing eyes filled with rage. He stepped forward and wrapped his long arms around Crafter's small body, gave Gameknight an evil, toothy grin, and then disappeared in a haze of purple ender particles.

Crafter was gone.

The chamber grew instantly silent as the shock of

what had just happened struck the observers.

"Seal it up," Hunter yelled. "DO IT...NOW!"

Her voice echoed through the deathly still cavern, snapping the workers into action. They sealed the portal with blocks of cobblestone, stopping any further invasion from the Nether.

"Crafter...Crafterrrrrrr!" Gameknight wailed, tears streaming down his cheeks. He fell to his knees and wept, his face held in his blocky hands, bow falling to the ground.

How could this have happened...what have I done?

Overwhelming anguish flooded through him as the last, surprised look on Crafter's face was seared into his mind. It was a look of shock mixed with a grief that struck deep into his heart. His friend had known that this was the last moment of his life, and all hope had left the young face. Erebus had won—no, Malacoda had won.

They were doomed.

One of the surviving warriors looked down at Gameknight, and then slowly raised his hand, fingers spread wide, arm reaching up to the ceiling. The others in the cavern lifted their hands as well, their extended fingers rising from the collection of bodies like flowers on a blocky plain. They stretched their arms up high, each person trying to reach the rocky ceiling overhead, and then they slowly clenched their hands into fists of despondent acceptance of what had happened. They saluted their fallen comrade, their leader...Crafter. As their fingers transformed to fists, the villagers bowed their heads, their knuckles turning white as they squeezed their hands with every last bit of strength left in their strained muscles.

Crafter was gone, and all hope was lost.

CHAPTER 22

THE FACE OF DESTINY

Gameknight slowly raised his own hand, fingers held out wide, but before he could clench his outstretched hand into a fist, offering the salute for the dead, a sound began to bubble out of him. It started deep within his soul, in the darkest recesses of his being, where the shadow of his elusive courage resided. It was a guttural sound, like the moaning of a wounded beast, but it slowly changed into a blazing wail of rage, a refusal to accept the things before him.

"Nooooo." It began as barely a whimper, then louder, almost like a battle cry, "NOOOOOO!" He brought his arm down and stood up, glaring at the villagers in the cavern.

"What are you doing?" Hunter said quietly. "You must honor the dead." Her arm was still raised, her hand in a fist. "We have to *all* honor Crafter's passing before we can move on."

"NO! He is not dead. Malacoda needs him for some reason. HE'S NOT DEAD!" Gameknight yelled, his voice echoing off the cavern walls.

"He's as good as dead," Hunter said, her arm now resting on his shoulder.

"I won't accept it," he snapped. "Put your arms down, ALL OF YOU! Crafter is not dead."

The villagers looked at him, perplexed and a little worried, but they brought down their arms. Some of them murmured to each other, unsure what the User-that-is-not-a-user was doing.

"Gameknight, you must accept that—"

"NO, I will not accept this," he interrupted. "I can feel that this is not over yet. There is more to do here, and surrendering to defeat is not the answer. Crafter is still alive, and we can save him."

A hush drifted across the NPCs in the chamber, sad eyes looking at each other in disbelief. Gameknight leaned in closer to Hunter and spoke, his voice barely above a whisper.

"We know where he is."

"Where? In the Nether?" she replied, her voice loud and challenging.

"Yes...in that Nether fortress. Malacoda has him there, I know it."

The villagers were now listening to the debate, the tension in the room building.

"You think we can just walk in there and take him back?" she asked, her voice edged with mockery.

"Well...I ahhh..."

"You know they'll be waiting for us, and a group of fifty soldiers is going to do nothing."

"I know," he answered, feeling as if he were now defending himself. He was starting to feel frustrated and angry. "But we can—"

"We'd need a plan—a real plan. We can't just sneak down there and hope they won't see us, because they *will*. There needs to be a real plan with real strength behind it. Who's gonna make that plan...you?"

"I've been thinking about how to—" he tried again, his annoyance at not really being listened to building up even more.

"And how are we going to move fast enough to keep those ghasts off our backs? How are we going to stay ahead of all those monsters in the Nether...how?"

Finally, he'd had enough.

"Hunter, would you just shut up and listen to me?" he snapped, his voice filled with indignation.

A gasp sounded across the crafting chamber. He lowered his voice and moved closer to her, speaking only for her ears. "I have a plan," he said. "I've been thinking about the pieces of the puzzle we learned while we were in the Nether. And I almost have it all figured out. But Hunter, I don't have the courage to pull this off. I'm not strong or brave like you. I'm terrified and have been since coming to this server, and I'm so tired of being afraid." He paused for a moment to collect his thoughts, then continued. "I can figure out how to get us to that fortress, but I'm not a leader and never have been. It doesn't matter what name these villagers call me...I'm just not that person."

"You have a plan, huh?"

"Yes, I do, but I haven't solved how we can move fast enough so that we won't be where Malacoda expects us to be. I know the answer is out there somewhere, though...and it's close by. I feel like I just have to open my eyes and find it."

"What do you mean?"

A grating, grinding noise came from one of the many minecart tracks that extended into the dark tunnels. New villagers were arriving; Crafter's call was still resonating throughout Minecraft.

"I'm not sure," he answered as he glanced at the minecart tunnels, the grating sound echoing through the stony passage and filling the cavern.

Many of the NPCs moved toward the newcomers, helping them out of the minecarts and moving them up to the many tunnels overhead, finding the strangers a new place to live. And then Gameknight saw the last piece fall into place. It was the thing that had changed since the last server and would be the key to their success. A small girl, the most innocent of NPC children, climbed out of a minecart with a pet pig, the animal on the end of a leash, and he finally understood what had changed after that nightmare with Malacoda. The servers, they'd been updated, and the leash reminded him of the upgrade preview he'd seen on YouTube, the latest snapshot video. The Source had sent them the solution, and the User-that-is-not-a-user hadn't been able to see it...until now. Smiling at the young girl, he turned and looked at Hunter, his own smile growing.

"I've got it," he said. "I have all the pieces. They're barely connected by the finest of threads, but it's all there. All I need is for you to lead us."

She moved quickly and aggressively across the cavern floor and stood directly in front of him. "I'm not a leader, and you know this," she snapped. "I'm an angry killer, and these people here won't follow me. They fear me...everyone fears me."

Not me...

The room became silent.

"But there is a leader here," she said with a quiet voice.

Gameknight looked about the room, then back to Hunter.

"Where?"

She moved next to him and grabbed his arm, then led him to the corner of the cavern. Villagers moved aside as the duo walked through the crowded chamber, all eyes on them. They parted like a great ocean, expectant faces all looking toward the User-that-is-not-a-user with hope—and a bit of trepidation. Pulling him to the farthest corner, Hunter stopped directly in front of the pool of water that had been put there for the villagers to drink, and pointed downward.

"Leaders do not choose to be leaders, their followers choose them," she said in a firm, confident voice. "Look around you. These NPCs have faith in you. They trust you and are willing to risk their lives to achieve something that is bigger than themselves. They will do this, not because of me...but because of you."

She then pointed down at the pool, gesturing to his reflection. *"There* is your leader," she said, her voice ringing with confidence.

Gameknight peered into the flowing water, expecting to see some sort of hidden mystery unveiled, but all that was there was his own reflection staring right back at him, Hunter at his side. He could see the confident look of expectation on her face, her warm, brown eyes boring straight into him, and then Crafter's last words floated through his mind.

Deeds do not make the hero...

His friend's words echoed within him. *Can I do this? Can I face this threat...face my fears?* He tried to wrap his mind around this possibility and thought about Malacoda and Erebus, the monsters wreaking havoc in his soul. But then his attention was brought back to Hunter's warm eyes, her face ringed by her vibrant red hair. She exuded confidence and faith in him. Drawing his gaze from hers, he stared into his own steel-blue eyes, and deep within those terrified orbs, he could see Crafter's bright blues looking up at him, confident and strong. But how could he save him? He wasn't strong, wasn't a hero. He was just a kid...a nobody.

Deeds do not make the hero...

He could hear Crafter's staunch belief in him resounding within his own mind. His friend was counting on him, and he had to do something to help. He couldn't let Crafter down; he had to save him, even if he was terrified. And then some of the villagers approached him and stood next to him, all of them staring down into the pool of water. Their eyes were looking expectantly at him as well, their faith and hope in the User-that-is-not-a-user something that would not easily abate. *Maybe I can do this.*

But Malacoda...those eyes...those terrible red eyes. How could he face that monster...and also Erebus? He knew that both of his nightmares would be there in the Nether, waiting for him. He couldn't defeat both of them. He wasn't strong enough. But then his attention was drawn back to the villagers standing around him. He could feel more of them coming nearer, pressing their bodies against his in silent support. They all knew now that he was afraid—could see the fear on his face—but they still had faith in him. He was part of a community, and no longer just an individual or griefer. He had people to help him, to carry some of the burden of fear for him and lend him a little courage in return. They were together in this, and for the first time in a long time, Gameknight999 did not feel alone.

Deeds do not define the hero...how they overcome their fear does.

Maybe he could overcome his fear, maybe he could focus on *the now* and be the hero Crafter needed. He felt Hunter's hand on his shoulder, and turned to look at her, her face framed by her glowing red hair.

"You can do this," she said quietly, compassion in her eyes. "*We* can do this...all of us. We just need you to lead us."

He looked about the chamber, the village's supportive eyes all focused on him. He could see the small girl with the leashed pig smiling at him across the cavern, a look of excited hopefulness on her face. Glancing at the leash and then back at her, confidence flooded through him. He could do this... no, *we* can do this...and he looked at Hunter and nodded.

Pulling her shimmering, enchanted bow from her inventory, she held it up high over her head and yelled, "THE USER-THAT-IS-NOT-A-USER WILL

LEAD US IN THE LAST BATTLE!"

The cavern erupted in joyous cheers, and many villagers patted him on the back, raising their own swords in excited jubilation.

"OK, EVERYONE QUIET DOWN!" Gameknight yelled, trying to bring order to the happy chaos. He then cleared out an area on the ground and started placing blocks of stones, each one representing a piece of the puzzle, the different aspects of his battle plan. "We have to move fast so that we can hit them hard where they won't expect it. And the first thing we're going to need is diamond, lots of it. Here's what we're going to do..."

CHAPTER 23

BATTLE FOR THE NETHER

He warriors surged out of the portal like an unstoppable flood. None of them paused to look at their surroundings; they had been told what to expect—a world of smoke and flame—and that was exactly what they saw. Moving off to the right, they headed straight for the ravine—the gash in the landscape that had been the scene of the last fateful battle. This time it would be different. This time they were not just a handful of soldiers, fifty warriors hoping to go unnoticed by the creatures of the Nether. This time, they were hundreds and hundreds of angry villagers, each heavily armed with only one thought in mind: Stop Malacoda and reclaim their crafters.

Watchful eyes saw the mass of Overworlders burst through the portal and moved off to report to their masters. The remaining observers stayed close to the invading army, watching their every move, ready to report anything new. The little watchers flitted behind hills and hid in the few shadows that existed there, silently observing and moving with the army as it flowed into the ravine. What the flying observers didn't see was a second army emerging through the portal after the first had led the watchers away. This new group moved in the opposite direction, away from the ravine and down the long, gently sloping hill that curved around and headed toward the distant Nether fortress.

The main force moved quickly into the ravine, led by one of the new additions to the village: Mason. He'd come from a village that had been destroyed by Erebus and his mob. Having been out building a jungle temple, Mason returned to find his village destroyed, all of the people he'd know his entire life simply erased from the face of Minecraft. He had a natural sense of command about him, and the villagers had quickly chosen him to lead this army, his strong, muscular build making him a formidable presence on the battlefield. His short-cropped brown hair was barely visible under his iron helmet, his balding scalp hidden under the metal cap. A neatly trimmed beard outlined his face and made him seem wise and knowledgeable. In the village, he'd always seemed to have a smile on his face, making his green eyes light up, except when he was working, shaping and carving stone.

Right now, a stern scowl was painted across his blocky face, for he was shaping something less forgiving than stone. Right now, he was shaping a battlefield. Scanning the area with his piercing gaze, he turned to his squad leaders and nodded, signaling for things to start.

Half of the warriors stayed on top of the ravine while the other half moved within its rocky depths, securing both entrance and exit. The NPCs above pulled out blocks of cobblestone and quickly started to build a stone roof over the narrow chasm, sealing it from overhead threats. Those within the ravine built fortifications at the lower entrance, getting ready for the attack that they knew was coming.

Bats flitted about in the area, their little beady eyes taking in every aspect of the fortifications. Some of them tried to carry this information to their masters by flying out of the ravine.

"The bats, shoot them!" Mason yelled.

Suddenly, the air was full of arrows that tore the shadowy creatures to bits, the little flying informants unable to give away any of the NPCs' preparations.

In minutes, the rocky cover over the top of the ravine was complete, those below now safe from overhead attacks. Then they built rocky crenellations around the top of the high plateau—stone spires to hide behind once the battle had begun.

Warriors could be seen running out onto the open plain and digging holes into the ground, only to be followed by other NPCs with TNT blocks in their hands. The striped black and red cubes were placed in the ground, with blocks of netherrack in front to hide their presence from the expected attacking horde. Working as fast as they could, the villagers prepared the battlefield, putting tripwires here and pressure plates there, each tied to little explosive surprises that would tear apart the monstrous horde that was sure to come.

And as they had anticipated, two large groups of monsters emerged from behind the netherrack mounds in the distance. Blazes, wither skeletons, magma cubes, and zombie-pigmen could be seen slowly crossing the smoky plain, gradually and inevitably approaching the ravine while a cluster of terrifying ghasts floated overhead. In the distance, a pair of burning red eyes watched the coming encounter; Malacoda, the King of the Nether, was laughing at this new, foolish attempt to thwart his plans.

The huge army of monsters approached slowly, moving casually across the sloping plain as if they were unconcerned about the threat that faced them. They didn't notice the new features on the plain, or the recently added rocky structures atop the ravine. The villagers could feel the tension build as the monsters approached. Their moaning cries and angry wails filled the air, a thirst for killing resonating strong in their monstrous voices. Remaining completely quiet, the villagers endured the terrible sounds, waiting patiently for the tide of destruction to crash down upon them.

When they were within bowshot, a hundred archers atop the plateau stood from behind stone blocks and opened fire. The sky darkened as a hundred arrows streaked through the air and fell down on the monsters. Painful moans filled the air as zombie-pigmen were hit, their rotting flesh pierced by the steel-tipped rain. Magma cubes quickly split into two as the arrows tore into their gelatinous bodies. The destruction amongst the monsters was terrible, but they continued to advance. Blazes at the rear drove the monsters forward with whips of fire, forcing the mob closer to the attackers.

Another wave of arrows fell down upon them, wreaking more havoc. Moving forward to the front of the mob, the blazes flared and launched a quick volley of three fireballs up at the archers. Expecting this, the archers quickly ducked behind their rocky shields and waited for the flames to hit. As soon as they impacted, the archers jumped out again and fired another round of arrows, shooting as fast as their blocky hands could draw back the string.

On the ground, more archers with enchanted bows started firing at the hidden blocks of TNT. Some of the monsters hit the hidden trip wires and stepped on pressure plates, triggering explosions that added to the destruction. The battlefield turned into chaos. Areas of the netherrack plain had become gigantic craters as the explosives detonated, taking many of the monsters with them, but still the main body surged forward.

The first ranks of zombie-pigmen finally reached the entrance to the ravine. Their golden swords flashed through the air as they tried to push their way through the NPC defenders. The ferocity of their attack, coupled with their massive numbers, forced the defenders to pull back a little.

"NO!" Mason bellowed. "STAND YOUR GROUND!" He looked up at the overhead walkways that Gameknight and Hunter had used in their last retreat. "Archers, fire on the lead monsters. We do not retreat...keep fighting...FOR MINECRAFT!"

"FOR MINECRAFT!" the warriors shouted in return.

The archers fired from their elevated positions, their arrows tearing into the rotting bodies. The swordsmen on the ground surged forward, driving the monsters back, those on the front line refusing to give an inch, using their very lives to hold back the press of the attacking horde.

Some of the archers atop the plateau pulled out blocks of TNT and carefully leaned out over the sheer cliff on which they stood. Between dodging balls of fire from blazes, they placed as many explosive blocks as they could on the exposed edge, the TNT hanging out over the lip of the netherrack wall. Looking straight down, they could see the mass of zombies trying to push their way through the villager's defenses; they had to hurry. Stepping back, one of the archers started lighting the blocks with flint and steel. The TNT instantly began to blink, then released from the cliff wall and fell straight down onto the attacking mobs.

"INCOMING!" one of the archers yelled as the flashing bombs plummeted onto their intended targets.

"Pull back and use bows!" Mason yelled as he notched an arrow and sent it into the soft pink underside of an attacking monster, a grim smile on his face.

The other soldiers at ground level moved back from the attacking horde and drew their bows, firing from a safe distance. They saw the flashing blocks drop amidst the mass of zombies and then detonate. The explosives tore through the attackers with a vengeance, creating a huge crater in the mouth of the ravine. The concussive sequence of explosions was almost beautiful as bright flashes illuminated the area with intense light, one after another. Explosive balls of fire came alive and consumed many zombies, their bodies flashing red with damage as they were thrown into the air.

Once the last block detonated, Mason sounded the charge. "ATTACK!"

The soldiers drew their swords and cut down the surviving monsters from the initial wave, then charged through the massive crater and took control of the ravine opening. Arrows from skeleton archers fell on the soldiers, taking a terrible toll on those at the front. Bodies disappeared as their HP was consumed. Archers from the cliff top answered in kind, aiming for the skeletons. The sky grew dark with arrows flying back and forth, the flying projectiles dimming the light for the blocks of glowstone overhead. The steel-tipped shafts took life after life, but the archers above the cliff were stronger in number. They quickly cleared the area of skeletons, leaving the battlefield littered with pale white bones.

The ghasts howled in rage and started to hurl spheres of fire at the NPCs. The floating gasbags drove the blazes forward, their overwhelming firepower boosting the morale of the monsters and making them fight even harder. Mason knew that these floating creatures had to be eliminated, as their blazing fireballs were wreaking havoc among his men.

"Archers...target the ghasts!" he yelled over the din of battle.

The archers turned their pointed shafts of death toward the floating menaces. Working in groups of six, they targeted the same ghast, simultaneously piercing it with half a dozen arrows and killing the monsters instantly. The spotter for each group directed the clusters of archers to a new target as soon as the last one was killed; the groups were working like intricate machines of death, just as Gameknight had taught them to. They tore through the ghasts like they were harmless balloons, the ghasts' feline cries echoing across the landscape as they died.

With most of the zombies, magma cubes, and ghasts destroyed, the NPC army surged forward, moving out onto the plain to hunt the blazes. Arrows streaked out from above the ravine as archers searched for the remaining monsters, while the infantry charged forward. A large group of warriors led the charge, but they had no weapons in their hands; instead, they held small white balls. As they approached the blazes, they threw the white balls at the flaming beasts. Snowballs fell on the blazes like a blizzard—something the creatures of fire had never experienced before. The snowballs were lethal to the burning monsters, the icy projectiles hammering their HP and extinguishing their internal flames. Balls of fire streaked back toward the warriors as their white balls fell on their prey. It was a peculiar scene, what with white and orange-red balls flying back and forth. Many NPCs succumbed to fiery deaths, but most survived, tearing through the monster lines like a scythe cutting wheat, their snowballs doing more damage than the incoming fireballs. With the blazes occupied, the swordsmen were able to get close enough to finish off the burning monsters with a few quick sword thrusts. In moments, though it felt like an eternity on the battlefield, the blazes were extinguished and had become nothing more than piles of blaze rods lying scattered about with the rest of the battle debris.

Small groups of NPCs spread out across the plain, now, searching out the remaining monsters. They fell on the stragglers, with four warriors surrounding individual monsters in a killing circle, and reducing their HP quickly and efficiently, just as they'd been taught. When the battlefield was finally clear, and the last remnants of the attacking mob destroyed, a cheer rang out across the landscape—something the Nether had never heard.

A terrible scream came from the looming fortress, and Malacoda's rage-filled voice echoed across the Nether. Many of the villagers laughed and jeered at him, mocking him from a distance. They pointed their swords and bows at the ruler of the Nether, daring him to come forth. But not all were celebrating. Many NPCs mourned the loss of a comrade or spouse, scattered inventories the only evidence of their existence. Blocky tears ran down dirty faces of widows, widowers, and parents, their weeping only making them angrier at the King of the Nether.

"Quickly, form up," Mason shouted, his commanding voice stopping the celebration and bringing the soldiers back in line. "Archers, come down and join the ranks."

Scanning the battlefield with his bright green eyes, Mason chose the route for his army to take—a meandering path past pools of lava and around patches of soul sand. He had to choose the quickest path; right now their entire plan relied on speed.

The archers from above sprinted down through the ravine to the sloping plain, joining the main force. They took up position at the head of the column, with groups on either side guarding the flanks.

"TO THE FORTRESS!" Mason yelled, pointing with his iron sword.

The mass of bodies sprinted forward in tight formation, heading directly for the Nether fortress. In the distance, they could all see the circle of stone that sat on the surface of the boiling sea. Multiple bridges now spanned the lava, each one leading from the shoreline to the island, the dark obsidian pedestals dotting its edges. Along the surface of the fortress, Mason could see workers moving about, expanding the dark structure.

Those are our people...my people, he thought to himself.

"We're coming for you!" Mason yelled as they ran forward.

The fortress looked ominous in the distance. He knew it was filled with more monsters—far more than they'd just faced—but felt confident that the User-that-is-not-a-user would be there when they needed him.

As they ran forward, Mason could see monsters started to stream out of the massive fortress—more than he'd ever seen in his life. If their plan didn't work, then everyone in this army would surely die. Looking around him, he saw the brave faces of men and women, confidence in their eyes, and sprinted forward through the Nether and toward what seemed like certain death.

CHAPTER 24

MALACODA'S PLAN

Malacoda screamed in rage.

How could those mindless insects have defeated my army? Where did they get so many warriors? NPCs can't fight!

Floating on a balcony that faced the sloping plain, he focused his attention on the approaching army. He could see their archers shooting any monster that approached, killing it within seconds. One zombie-pigman was shot, drawing all the others on the fiery plain to the villagers, but the NPC archers destroyed the approaching monsters in seconds, clearing the plain of defenders. Onward they ran. They didn't seem to care whether Malacoda could see them or not; they just charged toward his fortress, intent on his destruction.

"They can't possibly win," he mused aloud. "What

could these villagers be thinking?"

"Perhaps they are here to end their miserable lives, Malacoda," screeched a voice from behind him.

Spinning, Malacoda formed a ball of fire and held it within his writhing tentacles. "What did you call me?" he demanded of the enderman that stood before him.

"Ahh...right...I mean, *your Majesty*," Erebus replied.

"That's better," Malacoda snapped, his booming voice filling the stone corridors as the fireball slowly extinguished.

Malacoda floated farther out onto the balcony and looked at the approaching army. He could see hundreds of villagers, all armored and bristling with weapons, charging toward the fortress. A bulky NPC led the charge—a square-shouldered villager running out in front, his dark beard barely visible from this distance.

Curious, I would have thought that fool Gameknight999 would be leading. Maybe his own people turned on him and killed him. That thought made Malacoda laugh.

"What are you laughing about...ahh...sire?" Erebus asked.

"I wonder why the User-that-is-not-a-user is not leading this misguided army," Malacoda said. "Perhaps his NPC pets finally realized that he was insignificant and a coward."

"I learned on the last server that *Gameknight999* is anything but insignificant, and can do the unexpected at the most inconvenient of times. He should not be ignored."

"YOU DARE GIVE ADVICE TO ME?" Malacoda boomed, a fiery ball of flame reappearing within his twitching tentacles.

Erebus quickly teleported from the balcony and

back into the brick-lined hallway, head bowed, trying to look meek and subservient.

"You try my patience, Erebus. You should be more careful," Malacoda advised.

"Yes, sire," the enderman replied, a wry smile creeping ever so slightly across his downcast face.

Floating away from the balcony, Malacoda moved down the steps and into the corridor, the cramped space making him feel claustrophobic. He floated right next to Erebus and glared down at the lanky creature. Feeling satisfied that the monster was properly scared and timid, he moved down the passageway, the burning ball within his tentacles evaporating with a puff. He could see his blaze guards stationed periodically throughout the corridor, their dark eyes scanning for threats.

He moved slowly through it, his tentacles dragging on the ground and creating a noise that sounded like snakes slithering along. Erebus followed obediently behind him, for now.

"Do we have enough crafters?" Malacoda asked Erebus. "Have your foolish Overworld monsters gathered enough for my plan?"

"Yes...ahhh...*sire*. The last batch of captives yielded the remaining crafters you need."

"Excellent," Malacoda said excitedly. "SOUND THE ALARM! It's time to activate the portal and move my army to the Source."

"You mean *our army*," Erebus corrected. "My forces will only follow my orders."

"Yes, yes, whatever," Malacoda replied, anger and frustration leaking into his voice. He gestured with a tentacle to a nearby skeleton. "You, wither skeleton, send for my generals. It is time we begin our assault on the Source."

The dark skeleton nodded once and floated off,

the clattering of his bones echoing through the stone passage.

"What of the approaching army?" Erebus asked.

Malacoda stopped and gave the enderman a scowl.

"*Sire*," the King of the Endermen added rather reluctantly.

"They are not a large enough force to be of any concern. When they reach us, we will be ready with a trap, and then the jaws of death will crush them. They will be destroyed soon enough."

Malacoda then laughed an evil, maniacal laugh that made all the monsters nearby shudder. Then he thought of the approaching army of fools being destroyed just as they opened the portal to the Source and laughed even harder. But then a disturbing thought pricked his vile mind. It was something Erebus had said about the User-that-is-not-a-user...*doing the unexpected and appearing at inconvenient times*...This made Malacoda pause for a moment. He loved it when a plan came together, and this Gameknight999 was an unknown variable, though an insignificant one. But still he wondered—w*here was the User-that-is-not-a-user?*

CHAPTER 25

CRAFTER

Mason drove his force across the smoky land, the burning patches of netherrack and the bubbling lava rivers giving off a black, sooty smoke that covered the landscape, making it hard at times to see. Regardless, the NPC army sprinted through the Nether toward the circle of stones. In the distance, he could see monsters flowing out of the massive fortress, some of them lining up to face them. Most of the monsters, however, were just milling about on the center of the gigantic island, standing there as if waiting for something to happen.

A group of zombie-pigmen suddenly burst at them. Their archers took the monsters down before they could get within striking distance, and the army of NPCs did not slow their advance; they just continued toward the fortress. They knew that Malacoda's eyes were trained on them and that he would be prepared for their arrival...just as they had planned. Their progress was slow, because their short, stubby legs were unable to move any faster. They went from sprinting to running, then back to sprinting again as they moved across the Nether, Mason driving his force hard. They had to be there at the exact time they'd laid out, or their plan would fail.

Scanning the terrain, he looked for some sign that everything was going as arranged. *Where are you, User-that-is-not-a-user? You'd better be there when we need you, or we're all dead,* he thought to himself, a shudder of fear rippling down his spine.

He drove his force even harder, and they charged forward, crossing the netherrack plain in a zigzag path, having to go around lava pools and flaming blocks. The monsters across the plain had now started to avoid them, knowing that to approach this force meant instant death.

As they neared the fortress, they started to hear the creatures that had gathered in front of them. The mechanical wheezing of the blazes, the moaning of the zombies, and the purring cries of the ghasts filled the air. As expected, Malacoda had the blazes and ghasts out front, their long-range fireballs a devastating weapon in the open, which is exactly where they were.

"REFORM!" Mason yelled.

The soldiers changed their formation as they ran, swordsmen to the front, archers and snowball throwers behind. The warriors at the front removed their iron chest plates and replaced them with diamond ones. They then pulled out potions of fire resistance and drank, giving their bodies a subtle sparkle. This was their fire shield. These warriors had to hold long enough to give the archers and snowball throwers time to take out the long-range threats.

As they neared the massive collection of monsters, they stopped and their archers opened up. Wave after wave of arrows streaked through the air, as the archers aimed at the ghasts as they did before, groups of six working in a synchronized fashion, all focusing on the same target, taking it out in an instant. At the same time, a white blur of snowballs flew through the air, raining down on the blazes. They screamed in pain as the balls of ice hit them, their internal flames sputtering and shaking. Some of them threw their deadly fire toward the NPCs, the balls of flame bursting on the diamond-encrusted warriors at the front. A few balls of fire flew over the front line and landed amongst the group of archers. Screams of pain and despair floated up from the army as the villagers' HP was consumed. Many died in the first attack, but when one archer was killed, two stepped forward to take his place so that the flow of deadly arrows continued unabated.

The front rank held after the first volley of fireballs, as the snowballs thinned out the blazes. But then, out of nowhere, a gigantic cluster of ghasts appeared through the smoky haze on their left flank, their evil baby faces lit with rage. They rained down spheres of death upon on the archers, a single fireball enveloping multiple warriors at a time. More attacks came from above, some of them now landing amidst the snowball throwers. Archers turned to face this new threat, but that left the ghasts before them able to attack with impunity.

At that instant, the zombie-pigmen and skeletons charged forward, engaging the swordsmen at the front. The battle quickly degenerated from a carefully orchestrated sequence of attacks into a melee of villagers fighting hand-to-hand with monsters. They were fighting for their lives. The ranks tried to hold, but there were just too many attackers; they were being overwhelmed.

Mason tried to direct his troops to seal up breaches in his lines, but he just didn't have enough NPCs to fight this kind of battle out in the open. The mass of monsters before him were too numerous... *Where is the User-that-is-not-a-user?* He could see his newfound friends and neighbors perishing before him, their lives being sacrificed for their common cause. Screams of agony and misery echoed across the battlefield as more monsters charged forward. He tried to pull his troops back, but groups of zombie-pigmen had gotten behind them.

There was no place to go...they were surrounded.

Where are you, Gameknight999?

Monsters hammered at them from all sides. Fireballs streamed in from the ghasts overhead, smashing into the NPCs who were fighting for their lives. The blazes that had survived the snowball attack pounded away at them, their fireballs streaking in with pinpoint accuracy, every one of them finding a target. A large cluster of magma cubes charged forward, smashing their gelatinous bodies against the front line of diamond-clad warriors. Swords slashed at the bouncy cubes, only to divide them into more and more of the monsters. A large company of zombie-pigmen engaged their right flank, their moaning wails sounding sorrowful but at the same time excited at the prospect of killing. It was chaos. Mason looked around and saw his army—no, his people—perishing around him, their screams of pain and terror adding to the cacophony of battle. It was terrible.

What should I do...what should I do?

And then suddenly, out of the haze of the Nether, he heard a battle cry.

"FOR MINECRAFT!"

The sound did not come from his troops, but from somewhere else. And it was not just a single voice or a hundred voices; it was a thousand angry voices, crying out as one. Leaping through the smoky mist came Gameknight999 himself, clad in diamond armor and sitting atop a mighty steed. But he was not alone; the army he brought was also on horseback, the massive animals leaping through the smoky haze.

The incoming cavalry fired bows from their saddles, striking out at the ghasts from behind, the monsters' HP disappearing before they even knew what was happening. In seconds, Gameknight's thousand-strong army shredded the airborne threats, then turned their attention to the ground forces. Putting away their bows, the horsemen and horsewomen drew their swords and charged toward the remaining monsters. Forming an armored wedge, they drove into the ranks of the monsters, carving a terrible path of destruction through the enemy forces. Monsters tried to flee before them, but the horses were just too fast. They shattered the enemy lines, tearing apart zombie-pigmen in seconds, cleaving great slashes of destruction amongst the blazes, and shattering the wall of magma cubes. They drove their deadly formation completely through the enemy forces, smashing their resistance completely.

Instead of turning for another pass, though, the

mounted army continued onward toward the fortress, leaving Mason's troops to finish off the horde. With the ghasts and blazes now destroyed, the remaining monsters, who had been standing their ground, were quickly destroyed; those that fled were spared their lives.

Gameknight moved like an automated robot without thought or fear; he was in *the now* and nothing would stop him. He was a killing machine, his sword and bow something these monsters would remember for a long time. Looking over his shoulder, he could see that Mason had the remnants of the monster mob well in hand, and turned forward, with his sight set on their next target.

"Mason, catch up when you can!" he yelled, then turned his attention back to the fortress. "Onward to the fortress!"

"FOR MINECRAFT!" Hunter yelled at his side, her black and white horse running with seemingly endless strength.

Others joined the battle cry as they streaked toward the mighty citadel.

In the distance, he could see monsters milling about on the island. Blazes were leading NPCs to the obsidian pedestals, planting them in front of the diamond crafting blocks. A collection of villagers was being held at the center of the island and they were surrounded by blazes—likely hostages to force the crafters to do Malacoda's bidding. And then he saw the gigantic beast himself floating out of the fortress, his tentacles holding something beneath his massive body. Gameknight knew exactly what it was, and spurred his horse for more speed, Hunter right at his side.

"You ready?" he asked her.

"Yep," she replied, then moved her horse closer.

And in a single, dangerous leap, she jumped from her horse and stood on the back of his, her hands resting on his shoulders for support. He grabbed the line to her horse and charged forward, the riderless mount following his closely. "Let's do this!"

They closed the distance to the fortress in minutes. None of the monsters noticed their approach, expecting the army that had been sent earlier to easily deal with the threat, but as they neared, the thunderous hooves drew the attention of the mobs. Alarms sounded throughout the fortress, but there were no more monsters within the dark castle. They were all out on the stone island, clustered together, waiting.

Malacoda deposited his package on the center pedestal; it was Crafter. In the distance, Gameknight could just barely make out the monster's words.

"Now activate the crafting bench before you," the King of the Nether commanded, his voice booming like thunder.

"No," Crafter snapped.

A flick of a single tentacle commanded the blazes to incinerate a couple of the hostages, their cries of unspeakable anguish filling the air.

"DO IT!"

"No."

Another flick. More cries of pain, shortly followed by the pleadings of the survivors. Distress covered Crafter's face as he settled his hands on the crafting bench. He could not bear to hear anyone else suffer because of him. He had no choice. Looking around him, he could see that the other twelve crafters had activated their diamond crafting benches, a ring of glowing blue cubes now surrounding the island. Tears streamed down their faces as piles of possessions scattered on the ground, marking the victims killed to force the crafters to do as they were told. Sighing, he drew on his crafting powers and extended them into the crafting bench, causing the blue cube to suddenly flare into life. It shot out icy cobalt beams of power to the other crafting benches until a spider web of energy had been formed. Then a purple haze started to materialize across the island. Crafter knew what that color meant: a portal...a massive portal.

Just then, a commotion erupted behind him; it was the sound of steel on steel, the clash of bodies in battle. Turning, he couldn't believe what he was seeing. Galloping straight toward him was Gameknight999 on horseback, and Hunter was standing behind him, a massive army of mounted NPC warriors at their back. The cavalry smashed into the monsters, swords flashing out to rend monster flesh. The monsters turned to face off against the approaching force, making them slow their advance...all except Gameknight and Hunter. They crossed the stone island in seconds, their horse pushing aside the monsters in their path as if they were feathers. As they neared, Hunter leaped from the horse and landed atop the obsidian pedestal.

"What are you doing?" Crafter asked, disbelief in his voice.

Without an answer, she drew a diamond pickaxe and hammered away at the blue crafting bench. Malacoda, who was watching from above, was clearly stunned by what was happening.

Before he could react, Hunter had destroyed the diamond crafting bench. Grabbing Crafter by the arm, she looked down then shoved him off the pedestal.

But the destruction of the diamond crafting bench did not stop the teleportation field from forming. The purple field of distortion was getting brighter across the stone island, deep blue particles starting to float about in the air.

Crafter fell and landed on the empty horse with a thud.

"What is this?" he asked Gameknight, who rode at his side.

"A server update gave us something new...horses... and now a cavalry," the User-that-is-not-a-user replied, patting the horse affectionately on its neck. He then looked up at Hunter. "Come on, JUMP!"

Hunter considered the timing, then ran to the edge of the dark pedestal and jumped, flying high through the air, hoping to land behind Gameknight. But before she had completed her arc, cold, clammy tentacles wrapped around her body and pulled her upward: Malacoda.

"So, you've come to join me?" the monster said.

"We've come to stop you, and we did," she snapped. "I destroyed your little diamond crafting bench and your plans."

"You are a fool," Malacoda boomed. "It has already begun. Once started, it will not stop."

Hunter looked down and was shocked at what she saw. The island was now glowing purple, small particles dancing along its edges. She could see Gameknight and Crafter riding through the masses as clawed arms reached out to grab them.

"Run, Gameknight!" she yelled, a tear seeping from an eye. "RUN!"

He looked up and met her gaze, then looked around and saw the transformation continuing. He knew that they had to get off this island, or they would be pulled away with this monstrous horde—and that meant certain death. Sighing, he gave his friend one last look, then charged off the island, their steeds running over any creature that stood in their way.

"EVERYONE OFF THE ISLAND," Gameknight

yelled to his cavalry.

The mounted warriors leaped off the island just as the portal formed. Looking over his shoulder, Gameknight saw the thousands of monsters fall through it, disappearing into the purple mist. Malacoda still floated above the center of the island with Hunter struggling in his tentacles. Drawing his bow, Gameknight stopped his horse, turned and aimed at the ghast, but he couldn't fire while knowing that he might hit his friend as well.

Just then, a mass of Overworld monsters surged out of the fortress and crossed to the island: zombies, spiders, creepers, and endermen, all led by none other than Erebus. The King of the Endermen disappeared in a cloud of mist and reappeared on the obsidian portal at the center of the island, Malacoda floating at his side.

"So, your failure is complete, User-that-is-not-a-user!" Erebus screeched, giving one of his spine-tingling cackles.

Reaching out with one of his long dark arms, he stroked Hunter's curly hair. She shuddered as her eyes locked onto Gameknight's, pleading.

"Shoot," she yelled. "SHOOOOT!"

But he couldn't do it, and lowered his bow.

"Our battle is not over," the enderman cackled. "We will meet again, this I promise you, and then I will finish what I started in the Land of Dreams. Goodbye for now, User-that-is-not-a-user."

The King of the Endermen stepped off the obsidian pedestal and fell into the portal, disappearing from sight, his cackling laughter still filling the air.

Malacoda boomed with laughter as well, glaring straight at the User-that-is-not-a-user. "You have failed, as I have foretold," the King of the Nether said, an eerie smile stretching across his vile, childlike face. "And now, the Source will be mine. Goodbye, fool."

Malacoda then slowly lowered himself into the portal, disappearing into the purple mist and fading from view. All the while, Hunter's terrified eyes were glued to Gameknight's...and then she was gone.

CHAPTER 26

THE SOURCE

The ironclad warriors all surrounded Crafter, sounds of joy and celebration echoing across the Nether. Everyone wanted to pat him on the back, hug him, or just be near him. He had survived the unthinkable as the personal captive of Malacoda, and a huge smile stretched across his face, tears streaming down his cheeks.

Captured NPCs shuffled out of the fortress and joined the group, their clothes tattered, their bodies worn to exhaustion. They had huge smiles on their faces as well, knowing that they would now survive, but many had to be helped to stand, their HP nearly gone.

"Thank you, everyone, for coming for me," Crafter said, his voice cracking with emotion. "We have done a great thing here, and all of Minecraft will hear of this."

A cheer filled the air as swords and bows were lifted high above heads. Mason moved next to Crafter and patted him on the back, a smile painted firmly across his big square face. His green eyes seemed to glow with joy as he looked at Crafter, the stocky, muscular NPC overwhelmed with happiness.

Gameknight stood near the edges of the celebration, his heart heavy. He was glad that they'd saved Crafter, but it had cost him his friend, Hunter, and he grieved her loss. Even though she was frustrating at times, with a temper that always seemed to be lit and ready to explode, he still missed her, and felt like someone dear to him had been taken away. Rage started to bubble up from within—rage at her loss—but it was also coupled with venomous fury toward his enemies: Malacoda and Erebus. He'd failed to stop them, and now they were on their way to the Source.

They have to be stopped, he thought. *THEY HAVE TO BE STOPPED.* His thoughts were like thunder within his head.

"THEY HAVE TO BE STOPPED!"

The joyous celebration abruptly ended as Gameknight's voice echoed across the Nether. They turned and looked at the User-that-is-not-a-user, confusion on their smiling, blocky faces. Crafter came forward, a look of concern on his face, Mason following close behind.

"Gameknight, what is it that you said?" his friend asked.

"I said that they still need to be stopped," Gameknight replied, his irritation barely held in check. "Don't get me wrong. I'm thankful that we were able to save you, my friend, and I am indebted to each and every one of you here, but we also lost someone special...Hunter... and Minecraft is still in danger."

At the sound of her name, hands started to stretch up into the air, fingers spread wide.

"For Hunter!" someone yelled, and more hands sprouted upward.

Crafter looked at Gameknight with compassion in his eyes as he too raised his hand, fingers stretched wide.

Tears streamed down Gameknight's cheeks as he looked across the sea of faces, all focused on him, the villagers' fists in the air. They waited for him to complete the salute to the dead, the closest friend of the deceased always going last. Slowly, he raised his arm, his hand shaking with grief. With his fingers outstretched, he turned and looked at the last place he'd seen her—there in the middle of the portal that still glowed purple. And suddenly, he was overwhelmed with a burning wrath that threatened to devour his soul.

No, I don't accept this, he thought. *I won't let her die.*

Pulling his hand down quickly without clenching it into a fist, he turned back and faced his warriors.

"He refuses the salute," someone murmured.

"Again?"

"What is he doing?"

"Why?"

Questions rippled through the masses as Gameknight looked down at the ground, lost in thought. Contemplating everything that had happened to him on this adventure in Minecraft, he realized that it had all been necessary to prepare him for the decision he was about to make. Learning what it meant to sacrifice for someone else, how to stand up to your fears, how to focus on *the now*, and coming to the realization of what it meant to be a hero; all of these things—these lessons—resonated within him, and he knew what he had to do.

"She isn't dead," he said softly, then confidently raised his voice. "SHE ISN'T DEAD!"

The crowd hushed.

"Just because she was taken by that vile creature doesn't mean that she's dead." He scanned the faces of his army, an angry glare in his steel-blue eyes. "I'm going to save her, and I'm going to save Minecraft. I will go through that portal to the Source, and I will stop them somehow. Who's with me?"

Shock spread across the crowd, everyone taking a few steps back.

"Gameknight, no one has ever been to the Source," Crafter explained. "It is forbidden. It is where the Creator resides, and the rules of our programming do not allow us to go there."

"The Creator...you mean Notch?" Gameknight asked.

Crafter nodded.

Mason looked up and stared at Gameknight, while others did the same.

Crafter moved a step closer to Gameknight999 and spoke in a low voice. "If we go through that portal we will die. Each of us can feel that thing, that obscenity to Minecraft, and we know with complete certainty that it will kill anyone that passes through to the Source. There is no chance of survival for NPC or User. Our journey stops here."

"But those rules aren't real—clearly they aren't. I mean, you just saw a thousand monsters go there. Don't you think they were *forbidden* as well? It seems they could go to the Source without any problems. Now we have to follow them and finish the battle."

"But you don't understand," Crafter said. "Our task was to stop the mobs from getting to the Source... we failed. We reduced their number and did what we could, but we can follow them no further, it would be suicide. For all we know, Hunter is already dead for having gone to the Source and violating that rule. Minecraft itself may have deleted her. You see, in our minds that portal feels like...like death." He looked toward the portal and cringed. "That thing is an assault on everything we NPCs feel as natural and safe. That monstrosity feels like it will devour us in a single bite and we will have no chance for survival. We cannot do this thing that you ask, nor can you, for it would certainly mean your death. Stepping through the portal would be the same as trying to swim through lava." He hung his head down meekly and looked at the ground. "That portal is death."

"I don't believe that, Crafter, or all those monsters would have been destroyed. Listen to the music of Minecraft, does it feel like those terrible creatures perished when they went through? No! They're still alive." He stepped closer to his friend and looked down into his blue eyes. "When all of those behind you left you for dead, I still had hope. No one believed that you could be saved, except for me and Hunter, and we still tried, no matter the risk." He turned to glare at the sea of faces that were now focused on him. "Our friend is out there, and it's not just Hunter, it's every living creature in Minecraft. We can't stop trying to save them. That would mean giving up...and I'll never give up to Malacoda and Erebus."

He paused to let his words sink in, hoping for a response. The silence that filled the air was thunderous...oppressive...hopeless.

Gameknight sighed.

"It has been an honor to be chosen at the apex of this great conflict to be a part of Minecraft history forever, to stop the monsters of the Overworld and the monsters of the Nether and save everyone on the server planes. All of you here agreed to risk your lives to come to the Nether and save Crafter; now, I'm asking you to do the same for Hunter and every living creature in Minecraft. We have to go to the Source and stop the mobs."

Crafter looked up for a moment, then looked back to the ground, shaking his head. Many of the NPCs followed his lead and also cast their gazes downward.

"Gameknight, we want to continue the fight, but it would be certain death, all of us know it. Sometimes, it is necessary to stop and be thankful for your accomplishments. Nobody blames you for this failure. It just is what it is," the young NPC said with a sad voice.

Gameknight stepped the rest of the way across the stone bridge and moved up close to Crafter. "Sometimes we can be greater than we thought we could be. You taught me that. But first we have to accept the possibility that we *can* overcome what lays before us, and that we *can* be successful. Once we accept the possibility that we *can* do something, the all we have to do is figure out how to do it."

Stepping back, he noticed that Mason had moved closer, his large, blocky frame leaning close to the User-that-is-not-a-user. A wry smile creased his stern face, his green eyes lighting up a bit.

"You see, Crafter," Gameknight continued, this time a little louder so that others could hear. "Anyone can be a hero, even a griefer like me. You just have to accept that it's possible. Remember, deeds do not make the hero, it's overcoming your fears that makes a person great." He paused for a moment and looked around at the sea of blocky faces that were now looking toward him. "An NPC that I respect, whose friendship I cherish more than anything, whose lessons have taught me to be a better person; he told me this." He paused and then continued, raising his voice even louder. "You can be what you want to be, and do what you want to do, all you have to do is accept that its possible, and keep trying until you succeed." He then leaned forward and spoke in a whisper, only for Crafter's ears. "Like Fisher."

Crafter looked up. "Gameknight, do not do this

thing. I don't want to see you die, for I'm not sure if I could bear that. Stay here on this server with us... please."

The User-that-is-not-a-user just shook his head as he stared at the defeated army, then turned his gaze on Crafter. His friend looked up at him, then sighed and lowered his eyes to the ground, a tear running down his cheek.

Gameknight999 sighed again. Reaching out, he lifted Crafter's chin and looked into his eyes. For the first time, they did not seem to glow with that bright blue twinkle of hope. Instead, they were dull and faded with sadness and regret. Another tear rolled down the young NPC's cheek as he tore his gaze from Gameknight and looked at the ground, his shoulders slumped. Glancing across the NPC army, Gameknight999 saw the same thing; eyes that had once been bright with hope were now pale with defeat; they had given up.

The last one to look away was Mason. He stared at the User-that-is-not-a-user with a stony glare, his close-cropped brown hair and beard glowing slightly red by the light of the nearby lava sea. The thin smile had now faded to a grim determined scowl, his unibrow creased as if he were fighting some kind of great internal battle. He looked at Crafter, then glanced back at Gameknight, his eyes filled with bright rage, but then they seemed to fade as well as the internal battle was finally lost. The big NPC slowly lowered his head and stared at the ground, defeated.

Gameknight was alone.

He could feel the tension from the collection of NPCs, but no one was willing to follow him and tempt destruction. Fine, then he'd have to do it on his own.

I started this adventure on my own, he thought. *I'll just finish it on my own.*

But then a lone voice spoke out; it was that of a

child. Looking for the source, he could see a young girl walking through the crowd. Her clothes were tattered and torn from forced labor in Malacoda's fortress. Though she looked exhausted, she stood tall as she walked through the crowd, pushing her way past warriors and tall horses. As she came to the front, he saw that she had long, curly red hair like Hunter's, a pair of deep brown eyes looking up hopefully at him.

"I'll go with you," she said in a weak voice.

A murmur spread throughout the crowd. Some reached out to pull the young girl back, but she pushed her way through the sea of restraining arms, determination etched on her face

"You can't go with me," Gameknight replied as he looked at her small size. "There will be—"

"My name is Stitcher, and I *will* be going with you," she said. "I dare you to try and stop me."

"You can't go," some of the NPCs whispered.

"Your programming..."

"You'll die..."

"You'll be deleted..."

Villagers near her all gave reasons why she couldn't go with the User-that-is-not-a-user, but she ignored their excuses and strode forward.

"I don't care about the rules...about the programs or lines of code," the young girl said. "If I die when I go through the portal, then so be it, but I won't just stand here and watch everything be destroyed."

The young girl glared at the shamed and downcast faces of the adults around her as she pushed through the crowd, daring any one of them to stop her. Boldly, she walked straight up to the User-that-is-not-a-user, a look of determined hope in her eyes.

Gameknight smiled. This little girl had all the ferocity and tenacity that Hunter had, maybe even more. Her matted red hair glowed bright as she pulled some loose strands from her face. And then he knew who she was.

"She's your sister?" he asked, looking down at her.

The young girl nodded and gave him a hopeful smile.

"I won't just let her go after I finally found her again," she said in a confident tone. "I would rather die than do nothing. She's my sister... she's all I have."

He stepped forward and patted the young girl on the shoulder. She could have been the same age as his own sister.

My sister...I miss my sister.

Taking her hand, he led her across the stone bridges and walked to the edge of the massive portal, sparkling purple particles marking its perimeter. Turning around, he looked one last time at the people he'd come to think of as friends, then turned and faced the portal. He could feel teleportation particles being drawn into the gateway, sliding across his skin as they were tugged along some unseen current. Through the purple fog within the portal, he could just barely make out faint shapes: blocky trees, rolling hills, and mountains in the distance. Then the images faded away as the purple mist became thicker and more turbulent.

Glancing over his shoulder again, he saw all of the NPCs watching him—all except for Crafter, whose gaze was still fixated on the ground. Letting go of Stitcher's hand, Gameknight turned and stepped halfway across the stone bridge, then faced directly toward Crafter.

"Crafter, you have been like a brother me," he said, his voice choking with emotion. "I will always cherish our time together, and will remember the many lessons you have taught me... if I survive. That soothing tune you are always humming, I will keep it close to my heart as I step through to the Source, and will sing it when hope seems elusive. Thank you for being my friend."

"If you go through that portal you will die," Crafter said. "Please. Don't do this thing."

"Don't you understand, I have no choice."

Turning back to the portal, he took up Stitcher's hand and stepped forward. Stitcher took one step forward, then hesitated, pulling back on Gameknight's hand.

"Stitcher, are you alright?"

"I'm scared," she said in a quiet shaking voice. "It feels wrong...so wrong. I can hear the portal in my mind and it is terrifying. It sounds like a monster gnashing his teeth while at the same time also like the grinding of broken gears. User-that-is-not-a-user, I think it knows I'm coming...and it is waiting for me to come close." She paused and looked up at Gameknight, her dark brown eyes filled with terror. "I'm so afraid."

"Stitcher, you don't have to do this. You can stay here with the others. It will be..."

"NO!" she snapped. Squaring her shoulders she turned and faced the portal, her unibrow creased with determination. "I won't abandon my sister!"

The young girl took a step forward...and then another...and another until she was on the very edge of the portal, the purple mist of particles circling around her ankles. Gameknight stepped up to her side, then glanced over his shoulder. He saw Crafter slowly raising his hand into the air, fingers spread wide, tears of mourning rolling down his cheeks. Giving his friend one last smile, he turned and looked down at Stitcher. She gave him a weak, terrified smile, then closed her eyes as they stepped into the portal. The instant her foot touched the purple distortion field she screamed as if in terrible agony. Her cries pierced Gameknight's soul, but all he could do was hold on to her hand as pain raked his own body and pray that she... that they... would survive.

CHAPTER 27

ALONE

ameknight999 fell on the ground in a heap, his face buried in blades of grass. He was disoriented and confused. Looking back over his shoulder he instantly understood. The portal back in the Nether had been horizontal, sitting on the ground, but here on this server, it was vertical, standing straight up. Brushing himself off, he looked around.

Stitcher, where is Stitcher?

"STITCHER, WHERE ARE YOU?" he shouted.

He looked around, frantically looking for the young girl, but he saw nothing.

Oh no...

"Here I am," a voice said from within the thick grass.

She stood and pulled tufts of grass from her curly red hair. Gameknight rushed to her and enveloped her in a warm hug.

"I thought you were...you know," he stammered.

"I'm OK," she said. "But I certainly don't want to do that again. That was terrible...it felt like I was dying."

"Well, its over and we're here now. Rest assured, we're gonna find Hunter."

"And save Minecraft?" she added.

"Yeah, that too," he replied, smiling.

They glanced around at their surroundings to

see where they had landed. The portal had deposited them into a new land of grass-covered, rolling hills. Tall, majestic birch trees dotted the landscape, with clusters of flowers here and there adding a bit of color to the green sea of grass that stretched out in all directions. The sun was high in the sky, shining its warmth down onto the land, but the color was somehow off. Instead of the bright yellow he'd come to expect from the Minecraft sun, it had a reddish stain to it, as if someone had spilled a cup of crimson paint across its radiant, square face—or maybe it wasn't paint, maybe it was...He shuddered, not wanting to think about it. He could feel the wrongness of this land. Here, the music of Minecraft was dissonant and strained, like a motor someone had dumped sand into, so that its gears and axles ground against each other in a way that would lead to the inevitable death of the mechanism in a cloud of smoke.

That was how this land felt, and it made him feel sick.

"Can you sense it?" Stitcher asked. "Something's really wrong here."

He nodded and sighed. It was clear that Malacoda and Erebus had already been here with their massive army. Before him lay a swath of landscape that was blackened and disfigured because something terribly evil had moved through it, the vile presence scarring the land and killing everything that it touched. The damaged pathway stretched off in the distance, with small piles of pork, beef, and wool floating along the path. The inhabitants of this area had likely been killed just for sport.

What kind of creature would do this? he thought. *Killing just for sport?* And then he remembered that he had been like that once—killing animals just because he could. But that was a long time ago, when Minecraft was just a game to him. Now he knew better.

Looking at the diseased scar that stretched off into the distance, he knew clearly which way to go. Adjusting his diamond armor, he reached down and took Stitcher's hand once again.

"Don't worry," he said, trying to hide his own anxiousness, "we'll fix it. We'll fix Minecraft."

"Alone?"

"If necessary," he answered. "We won't give up, will we?"

Stitcher shook her head, her red hair flying wildly. Then she gave him a warm, uplifting smile. Holding her hand tight, he started to walk, staying on the green, living grass and off the darkened blemished path.

The silence was deafening. He'd never felt so alone, so vulnerable, so afraid.

"Can I do this on my own?" he asked Stitcher. "Last time I had Crafter and Shawny, but now I'm truly alone. Maybe I can contact Shawny on this server. I should find a village and start building a new army, but how much time do I have?"

"You still have me," Stitcher's high-pitched voice squeaked.

"Of course I do," he replied.

Uncertainty and doubt clouded his thoughts. He pondered all the different options here—using the NPC minecart network, collecting the crafters...the options all bounced around in his head as he tried to figure out what the pieces of this puzzle looked like. He considered trying to find Notch, but where would he be? Maybe he was a user on the server, like Shawny had been. He could try to contact him, but how?

A strange hum started to fill his ears; it was a melodious sound that interfered with his thoughts, but was somehow calming and reassuring. Pushing

away the noise, he focused on the problem at hand…
gather an army…contact Notch…follow the mob ……
WHAT IS THAT SOUND?

And then he realized what it was…someone was
humming a soft, comforting song, in a high-pitched
voice that was filled with joy and courage. The sound
was then mixed with the shuffling of feet across the
ground—not just a single pair of feet, but thousands
of them … and horses, too, lots of them. Spinning
around, he was shocked to see what had followed him.

Crafter!

"Why hello, Gameknight999," the young NPC said,
a smile on his face, his blue eyes once again glowing
bright. "Imagine that, us running into you here…what
a coincidence!"

Gameknight looked beyond Crafter and saw the
hulking form of Mason trailing behind, his smiling
face shining back at him. Behind Mason followed
their entire army, with foot soldiers and cavalry still
flowing through the portal that stood out dark against
the landscape. There were at least a thousand of
them, most armored and carrying a weapon, but some
without armor; they had been Malacoda's prisoners
and slaves, now freed by the army, and had chosen to
join the battle for Minecraft.

Stopping in his tracks, Gameknight faced Crafter,
tears welling in his eyes. "You came to the Source," he
said, choking on his emotions.

Crafter stopped walking and held his hand
up, halting those behind. "We talked about it, and
decided that some rules were meant to be broken," he
explained. "And if the mechanism of Minecraft would
let the monsters invade this sacred world, then it was
our duty to come and help. Besides, we knew we'd be
OK, since we were following the greatest rule-breaker
of them all…Gameknight999."

He grinned, his smile contagious and infecting those near him, Gameknight included. Moving forward, the young NPC wrapped his arms around Gameknight's waist, hugging him with all his strength, the User-that-is-not-a-user fiercely hugging him back. Releasing Crafter, Gameknight moved to Mason and patted the big man on the shoulder, Mason's green eyes glowing with pride. As he moved further into his army, Gameknight noticed the same kind of look from the others; their eyes were glowing bright with satisfaction, the NPCs standing up a little taller. His warriors were bursting with pride at being able to do something for someone else...for *something* else...for Minecraft. They were here to make things right for the sake of their families and friends and people they didn't even know...like Gameknight's sister and parents. And for their sacrifices, he would be eternally grateful. He tried to speak, tried to put into words how appreciative he was, but all he could do was smile and brush aside the tears that ran down his cheeks.

A small hand settled on his shoulder, pulling his attention from the masses.

"Are you ready to go or what?" Crafter asked. "We're tired of waiting around for you." Those near him chuckled, the laughter rippling through the army, while Crafter's words were being quietly repeated for ears farther away. "Come on, we have a server to save—no, we have countless servers to save. So let's get going!"

"FOR MINECRAFT!" Gameknight yelled.

"FOR MINECRAFT!" the voices thundered at his back.

Someone came forward with horses for Gameknight, Crafter, and Mason. Swinging up into the saddle, Gameknight sat tall, surveying his forces.

Reaching down, he pulled Stitcher up into the saddle with him, her small form sitting in front of him. He was proud of every one of these NPCs, and clearly from the looks on their faces, they felt the same.

But uncertainty about what to do still plagued Gameknight's mind. He couldn't see the pieces of the puzzle here yet as he did back in the Nether. And that uncertainty filled him wth dread. They had to stop the monster here...somehow.

Mason must have sensed Gameknight's uncertainty because he started to issue commands, sending out scouts in all directions. He positioned squads of warriors at their flanks and instructed a group of horsemen to take up the rear guard. With their forces deployed to his satisfaction, he looked at the User-that-is-not-a-user and nodded. Gameknight, unsure as to what their plan was, did the only thing he could think of, he moved forward. Urging his horse forward, he followed the diseased path that had been gouged into the flesh of Minecraft.

With his friends at his side, Gameknight traveled with newfound confidence and thought about his other friend, Hunter.

"I hope you're OK, Hunter," he said aloud. "We're coming for you."

"Yeah, we're coming for you, sis," Stitcher echoed.

"*All* of us are coming for you," Crafter added.

"And for Minecraft," Mason said with a booming voice, triggering a response from the troops.

"FOR MINECRAFT!"

Their upraised voices echoed across the landscape, driving doubt and fear from their minds. The army of NPCs moved forward with Gameknight999 at the helm, prepared to relentlessly pursue their enemy, and they would not stop until everyone in Minecraft was safe.

READ AN EXCERPT
FROM THE NEXT
GAMEKNIGHT999
ADVENTURE!

CONFRONTING THE DRAGON

CHAPTER I

THE LAST BATTLE

ameknight999 floated through a silvery mist, a feeling of dread pulsing through every nerve. Something was about to happen . . . something bad, and somehow, he knew that he could not avoid the deadly consequences of what was about to transpire.

Gradually, the cloud started to clear, and he found himself on a large plateau atop a huge mountain of bedrock. As the silvery fog settled to the ground, figures started to emerge from behind its misty veil . . . NPCs, all of them armored and carrying weapons; they were the surviving defenders of Minecraft.

Sensing a presence next to him, Gameknight turned and found Crafter and Mason standing next to him. They talked quietly to each other, their faces grim with determination. They glanced out across the plateau to the vast plain that sat at the mountain's base. Something seemed to be moving through the shining fog that obscured the ground . . . angry things . . . hurtful things.

Does the mist mean this is a dream? *He thought.* That shiny fog seemed to be in all of the strange dreams I've been having lately.

He couldn't explain it, but something inside told Gameknight he was looking at the future . . . that he was seeing his own future. And somehow, a feeling from within made him shake with fear as he realized the truth about what was going to happen.

He was about to witness his own death and the end of Minecraft.

Shuddering, he turned to look at his friends. Next to Mason, he found Hunter standing rigid and strong, enchanted bow in her hand, and now he knew for sure that this was a dream. She looked haggard and exhausted, almost translucent, but with a look of deadly anger in her eyes.

How could this be the future when Hunter had already been captured by Malacoda and Erebus on the last server? *Gameknight thought.* How was this possible?

Gameknight looked about the plateau, and found that it was covered with what looked like beacons, transparent glass cubes with light emitting blocks trapped within. He could see a whole field of beacons, hundreds of them, maybe thousands. But the curious thing was that they were all dark save for two. One shone bright, sending a brilliant beam of white light straight up into the sky. It was bigger than the rest, in fact it was massive, taller than any of the NPCs, its base surrounded by diamond blocks that also cast shafts of icy blue light up into the sky. It was so bright that its light felt blazing hot, as if anyone that touched the glowing beam would be vaporized instantly. All of the other beacons were normal sized, even though they looked tiny in comparison. Only one of these smaller beacons shone with light, its brilliant beam feeling just as hot and deadly as its larger companion.

What's going on here? *Gameknight thought.* What am I doing here? What's that beacon for? Is this the Last Battle for Minecraft?

Gameknight could see that everyone on top of the

mountain had looks of fear and uncertainty painted on their faces. In front of them was a steep stairway that led from the plains below up to the flat mountaintop where they stood. It was the only way up to the plateau of beacons; the sides of the plateau were sheer and unscalable.

Gameknight watched as Mason peered down the sloping hill and surveyed the landscape. He then turned and focused his green eyes on him.

"They're coming," he said with a grim voice. "There must be five hundred monsters, maybe a thousand, right behind Erebus." He reached up with a blocky hand and stroked his neatly trimmed beard, his eyes scanning the faces of his warriors. "I fear there is no way for us to stop this horde. Minecraft is doomed."

Doomed?! Gameknight thought. If this is the future, does this mean we're going to lose the battle for Minecraft?!

He wanted to yell, tell them to not give up, but his voice would not respond. He felt trapped within his own body, unable to do anything other than be a spectator from behind these helpless eyes.

"Do not despair, User-that-is-not-a-user," Crafter said, his wise voice resonating across the mountaintop. "You did all that could be done. There is no shame in failing after doing your best."

"What are you talking about?" Hunter snapped, her voice sounding dreamlike and surreal to Gameknight. She had a transparent look to her, as if she were not completely there, her fate still uncertain. "If we lose, then we lose. There is nothing to be proud about."

Gameknight turned and looked at Crafter. The young boy with the old eyes gazed up at him, a look of sadness across his face.

"I'm sorry we couldn't do more," Crafter said in a low voice, his words meant only for Gameknight.

"You've seen the horde below. You know we cannot defeat Erebus and the monsters of the night this time. We have barely a hundred soldiers left. They cannot stop the approaching tide of destruction."

Crafter turned to look up at the massive beacon, the Source, and sighed.

"I guess there is nothing left to do other than fight and die," Crafter said as he drew his own blade.

Gameknight looked at the scene with an overwhelming sadness. If this is the future, does this mean I led everyone to this point, to failure? Is there really nothing left I can do? Why does my body, my entire being feel so . . . so . . . defeated? *He couldn't bear to witness the destruction of his friends . . . of Minecraft. He wanted to turn away, but he couldn't; he had no control over this body.*

I have to do something . . . I have to try to help them! *he thought.*

Gameknight could now hear the moaning of the monsters as they reached the foot of the stairway that led to the mountaintop. The clicking of spiders, wheezing of blazes, and wailing cries of the ghasts echoed across the strange landscape, making the defenders on the plateau all cringe.

"There is still something I must do," Gameknight said to all the NPCs.

NO! That's not me talking! *he yelled from within his mind, but his body would not answer.*

Moving on its own, his body put away his sword, then stepped up next to the beacon, the shaft of blazing light just inches from his face. He could feel the unbelievable heat from the beam, like all the heat in the Nether compressed into this glowing ray.

"Gameknight, what are you doing?" Crafter screamed.

What am I doing?! *Gameknight thought, panicking.*

Am I going to jump into that beam? Why aren't I trying to save everyone?

"*That's the coward's way,*" Hunter yelled. "*Don't give up, fight with us . . . with me.*" There was a peculiar sadness now to her voice, her eyes pleading for him to abandon this path.

"*No, this is something I must do,*" Gameknight's body said in a loud voice.

Looking at his friends, Gameknight saw disbelief on all their faces as they watched him move closer to the brilliant shaft of blazing death. Then, Mason stepped away from the other NPCs and stood next to Gameknight, a curious knowing smile on his face.

"*No, not you too!*" Hunter cried, disbelief in her voice.

"*You will come to understand in time,*" Mason replied.

Then, moving to the other side of the beacon, Mason raised his sword up high, grasping the hilt with both hands. With all his might, he brought the sword straight down, plunging it into the ground. It sounded like a crack of thunder when it pierced the bedrock, causing the whole landscape to shake. Grasping the hilt firmly with one hand, he extended his other blocky hand to the User-that-is-not-a-user, his green eyes locked onto Gameknight's.

"*For Minecraft,*" the big NPC said in a surprisingly soft and reassuring voice

"*For Minecraft,*" he heard his body repeat, then stepped into the blazing hot shaft of light.

Is this the end?! *Gameknight thought.* This can't be how it all ends. If this is the future, then is there any hope . . . can the future be changed? What about . . .

And suddenly, everything went brilliantly bright as pain erupted throughout his body, then everything started to fade. But just before everything

became completely black, he thought he could hear something . . . voices . . . hundreds of them, and one in particular that he hadn't heard for what seemed like forever. It was a familiar voice of a friend that he missed so deeply, and as the voice started to fill his mind, Gameknight999 almost started to smile. Then darkness claimed him.

CHAPTER 2

FOLLOWING THE TRAIL

Gameknight woke up abruptly, his mind swirling with confusion and his brain trying to comprehend what he'd just seen.

Was that just a dream, he thought, *or was it something else? It felt real, but different . . . like somehow he was looking into the future.*

He could still remember the look of resigned acceptance on all the NPC's faces as they stared down at the massive monster horde that was approaching. There was no way that small group of defenders could protect the Source from the invading army. They would surely lose and there was nothing that Gameknight999, the User-that-is-not-a-user, could do about it.

Shaking his head, he tried to push the images from his mind. But they just rattled around in his brain like little hammers, each one chipping away at his courage. Sighing, he sat up and glanced around the camp, looking or any evidence of that monster horde here. Fortunately, he only found NPCs; bakers, carpenters, farmers, tailors, diggers, builders . . .

every facet of Minecraft society now pressed into armor, weapons lying nearby. They were all here for him, because he'd guilted them into coming to the Source. They'd failed to stop Erebus and Malacoda on the last server and had followed the massive horde of monsters to this server, to the Source. But they were grossly outnumbered and didn't know where to go or what to do. So instead of making a plan and doing something useful, they were just following the blackened and charred path left behind by the monster horde in hopes of learning what the terrible creatures were planning.

Gameknight stood and stretched, reaching high up into the sky then arching his back, knots and cramps slowly releasing after sleeping on the hard lumpy ground. Looking up at the dark sky, he could see the square face of the moon starting to dip toward the tree line; it would be dawn soon. A faint red hue shone from the lunar body, something that they'd all noticed as soon as they'd come to this threatened land, something to do with all the monsters that had invaded, staining the very fabric of Minecraft with their violent hateful presence.

I wonder if the sun and moon will ever go back to their original color, Gameknight thought.

Scanning the camp, he saw soldiers stretched out anywhere that was flat, their army camped in a gentle valley on the edge of a pine forest. Small piles of armor-covered bodies here, blanket-covered NPCs there; they were spread out all throughout the bowl. He could see torches planted around the campsite, partially to keep monsters from spawning nearby, but also to put the NPCs at ease. Darkness seemed to make those from the Overworld nervous, for they had all learned a long time ago when they were but innocent children, that nighttime was monster time.

Stepping carefully around the sleeping bodies, Gameknight reached the edge of the campsite and came upon Mason, the actual leader of the army, walking along their perimeter.

"User-that-is-not-a-user," the big NPC said as he stopped and put his fist to his chest in salute, "you should be resting."

"I can't sleep," he replied, "so I thought I might check the perimeter."

"You are a wise leader," Mason said, "always being cautious."

Leader . . . right, what a joke, Gameknight thought to himself.

The army looked up to Gameknight999, the User-that-is-not-a-user, but he was not their general. That was Mason. He had a sense of command about him that made anyone listening to him *want* to do what he said. His concern for his soldiers was only matched by his concern for the safety of Minecraft. Mason was the real commander of this NPC army, and Gameknight knew it. Whether he liked it or not, the User-that-is-not-a-user felt like he was just a symbol, a figurehead that was supposed to somehow save the day and make everything better again. The problem was . . . he didn't know what to do or what to say.

"There has been no activity," Mason said as he turned and looked about their surroundings. "No monsters sighted anywhere."

"Doesn't that seem a bit strange?" Gameknight asked.

"Maybe Malacoda and Erebus are collecting those that they find and are taking them with them, making their army even bigger."

Gameknight grunted and nodded.

"That makes sense," Gameknight replied.

Of course it made sense, he thought bitterly.

Everything that Mason says makes sense!

"What are you doing up at this hour, Mason?"

"A good leader stands with his men and does what he asks his men to do," the big NPC replied, his green eyes sparkling in the moonlight. "If I did any less, then I'd just be an arrogant, spoiled general for whom the soldiers would not fight. They have to know that I will do anything they are asked to do."

"But what are you watching for?" Gameknight asked as he moved next to the big NPC. "Malacoda and his monsters are far away from here. They won't attack."

"Attack your enemy where he is unprepared and appear where you are not expected," Mason answered as if reciting something that he'd memorized.

That sounded familiar to Gameknight for some reason . . . curious.

"That's what I would do," the big NPC said, "so that's what I prepare for." He paused to scan the line of trees then continued. "Come, walk with me."

Gameknight walked next to him, trying to stand as tall as the big NPC, something that was difficult to do even if you were the same height as him. No matter how tall he was, Gameknight always felt small next to Mason.

As they walked, the pale crimson moon slowly dipped below the tree line, the eastern horizon starting to glow a deep red; it would be dawn soon. The camp was starting to awaken. Tired forms stood in the dim light of dawn, putting armor back on and picking up weapons. When they saw Gameknight the soldiers instantly cheered and snapped to attention, fist to chest.

"User-that-is-not-a-user will defeat the monsters," someone shouted.

"Gameknight999, the bravest Minecraft warrior

ever," said another.

More statements of praise came from the soldiers as they walked around the camp. This had been happening ever since they had come to this server . . . to the Source. For some reason, the warriors in their army had come to the conclusion that Gameknight999 was some kind of great hero, brave and courageous, and without fear. They all thought he would save them, defeat the monsters of Minecraft, and make everything all better.

What a joke, he thought. *They don't realize that I would run away right now if I had someplace to run to.*

Gameknight knew he wasn't as brave as everyone thought he was. He hated being afraid, but Minecraft had slowly worn down his courage and chipped away at his resolve. He cringed whenever they came across a lone monster or maybe a scouting party, and the thought of battling these creatures turned his blood to ice. He had learned much about facing his fears on the last server, but it was still difficult, still something that he wrestled with.

Mason was another matter. He *was* the first to go to battle. If someone yelled out for help, Mason was the first to be there. If monsters were spotted, then he was the first one to stand before them. In every case, Mason did not shy away from confrontation. In fact, he charged toward any threats to protect the warriors in the army as if they were his own children . . . curious.

Suddenly, an alarm sounded. Someone was banging on an iron chest plate with the flat side of a sword, screaming out loud.

"Spider jockey . . . spider jockey!" cried the voice.

Mason sprinted off toward the voice, Gameknight trailing hesitantly four steps behind. They ran to a sentry on the edge of the camp, his chest plate in his hand still ringing with the blows.

"What is it?" Mason asked.

"I saw a spider-jockey over there," the sentry said, pointing out onto the rolling, grass covered hills.

Spider-jockeys were skeletons riding on the backs of gigantic spiders. They were fast, could cover a lot of ground in a day if the skeleton wore a helmet, and could climb; they were fearsome opponents. Malacoda had probably sent out these monsters to find them and report back their position. Gameknight knew that they could not let this spider jockey report to its masters . . . that would be a disaster. But uncertainty gnawed at his confidence.

What should I do? Gameknight thought to himself. *Should I ride out and fight it . . . I've fought one before back when Minecraft was just a game. But now . . . I'm still not sure what will happen if I die. There are no more servers I could move up to; this is the highest in the pyramid of server planes . . . the Source. Will I respawn, or die for real this time?*

Uncertainty and fear flooded through his mind, drowning his ability to think. He looked down at the ground . . . afraid.

I don't want to fight a spider-jockey . . . not now. What do I do . . . what do I do?

Mason turned and looked at Gameknight, waiting for some command or sense of leadership, but he had learned to not wait very long. Looking up from the ground, Gameknight looked up into Mason's bright green eyes, his own filled with uncertainty and fear. But before Gameknight could speak, thankfully, Mason gave out the orders.

"You four, get on your horses and get that spider-jockey," Mason commanded to a group of warriors, is voice booming with confidence. "Make sure he doesn't report our position."

"Yes, sir," snapped the NPCs.

"Archers," Gameknight mumbled.

"What?" Mason asked.

"Archers . . . you'll want archers so that you don't have to get up close," the User-that-is-not-a-user said, his voice sounding uncertain.

Most skeletons carry a bow and arrow.

"Yes, of course," Mason boomed. "Take some archers with you as well. Surround them with the archers and only charge if you can't get them with arrows. No sense in taking any unnecessary risks. Now go!"

The soldiers ran through the camp, gathering weapons and armor. Within seconds, a squad of soldiers, some men, some women, were galloping out of the camp in the direction of the sighted monster.

"They'll get it," Mason said confidently.

Turning, he put his arm around another soldier and whispered something into the boxy ear. The soldier then took off in a hurry, gathering with him twenty other warriors, some of them putting away their swords and drawing a shovel from their inventory. Gameknight watched them run off away from the camp to a large hill that was nearby. On the top of the hill, they started placing blocks of dirt, one on top of the other, sculpting shapes that resembled people and horses. One of them placed a block of netherrack that had been brought from the Nether after the battle with Malacoda on the last server. Touching it with flint and steel, it instantly burst into flames, making the artificial figures on the hilltop easier to spot, especially at night.

"What are they doing over there?" Gameknight asked.

"They are setting up a little diversion," Mason answered.

He moved to stand next to Gameknight and admired